A Kiss of Fire

"In some cultures," he continued, "it is customary for someone to owe her life to the person who rescues her from danger."

"You rescued my hat, sir. It shall, one assumes, be indebted to you for eternity." She felt herself starting to grin. He held his finger to her lips. Its warmth acted like kindling on her body, which flamed in response.

"And now," he said, firmly, "it appears that hat is about to repay me my kindness."

The thought that at least no one could see them was replaced by the shock of his warm mouth on hers. She opened her lips to protest, but that was clearly a mistake.

Without thinking, she kissed him back. He groaned at her reaction, and his hand moved up the bodice of her riding habit to caress her. She leaned closer to him, and ran her hands up his chest as she had been dying to do since she had inadvertently touched him a few days before. It was hard and smooth, and she could feel the muscles lying just beneath the warmth of his skin. She felt them tighten underneath her touch, and he pulled her even closer. . . .

D0714448

REGENCY ROMANCE
COMING IN NOVEMBER 2005

A Christmas Kiss and *Winter Wonderland*
by Elizabeth Mansfield
Two yuletide romances in one volume by "one of the best-loved authors of Regency romance" (*Romance Reader*).

0-451-21700-4

Regency Christmas Wishes
by Sandra Heath, Emma Jensen, Carla Kelly
Edith Layton, and Barbara Metzger
An anthology of Christmas novellas to warm your heart—from your favorite Regency authors.

0-451-21044-1

My Lady Gamester
by Cara King
A bankrupt lady with a thirst for risk sets her sites on a new mark—the Earl of Stoke. Now she has to take him for all he's worth—without losing her heart.

0-451-21719-5

Lord Grafton's Promise
by Jenna Mindel
A young widow and the man who suspects her of murder find their future holds more danger, surprise, and passion than either could have dreamed.

0-451-21702-0

Available wherever books are sold or at penguin.com

A Singular Lady

Megan Frampton

A SIGNET BOOK

SIGNET
Published by New American Library, a division of
Penguin Group (USA) Inc., 375 Hudson Street,
New York, New York 10014, USA
Penguin Group (Canada), 90 Eglinton Avenue East, Suite 700, Toronto,
Ontario M4P 2Y3, Canada (a division of Pearson Penguin Canada Inc.)
Penguin Books Ltd., 80 Strand, London WC2R 0RL, England
Penguin Ireland, 25 St. Stephen's Green, Dublin 2,
Ireland (a division of Penguin Books Ltd.)
Penguin Group (Australia), 250 Camberwell Road, Camberwell, Victoria 3124,
Australia (a division of Pearson Australia Group Pty. Ltd.)
Penguin Books India Pvt. Ltd., 11 Community Centre, Panchsheel Park,
New Delhi - 110 017, India
Penguin Group (NZ), cnr Airborne and Rosedale Roads, Albany,
Auckland 1310, New Zealand (a division of Pearson New Zealand Ltd.)
Penguin Books (South Africa) (Pty.) Ltd., 24 Sturdee Avenue,
Rosebank, Johannesburg 2196, South Africa

Penguin Books Ltd., Registered Offices:
80 Strand, London WC2R 0RL, England

First published by Signet, an imprint of New American Library,
a division of Penguin Group (USA) Inc.

First Printing, October 2005
10 9 8 7 6 5 4 3 2 1

Copyright © Megan Frampton, 2005
All rights reserved

Ⓟ REGISTERED TRADEMARK—MARCA REGISTRADA

Printed in the United States of America

Without limiting the rights under copyright reserved above, no part of this publication may be reproduced, stored in or introduced into a retrieval system, or
transmitted, in any form, or by any means (electronic, mechanical, photocopying,
recording, or otherwise), without the prior written permission of both the copyright owner and the above publisher of this book.

PUBLISHER'S NOTE
This is a work of fiction. Names, characters, places, and incidents either are the
product of the author's imagination or are used fictitiously, and any resemblance
to actual persons, living or dead, business establishments, events, or locales is
entirely coincidental.

The publisher does not have any control over and does not assume any responsibility for author or third-party Web sites or their content.

If you purchased this book without a cover you should be aware that this book
is stolen property. It was reported as "unsold and destroyed" to the publisher
and neither the author nor the publisher has received any payment for this
"stripped book."

The scanning, uploading, and distribution of this book via the Internet or via any
other means without the permission of the publisher is illegal and punishable by
law. Please purchase only authorized electronic editions, and do not participate
in or encourage electronic piracy of copyrighted materials. Your support of the
author's rights is appreciated.

Thanks to Jessica Benson and Marianne Stillings, both of whom helped my writing immeasurably.

Thanks to my research partner, Jeff McLaughlin, who is also my dad, and the guy who first encouraged me to use my imagination.

And love and thanks to my husband, Scott, who believed I could do this from the moment I first mentioned it. Thank you, honey.

Dispatch from the Battlefront, March 1813

I am about to lay siege to the barbarians. Yes, I am embarking on my first Season, and my prize will not be a conquered land or the spoils of war, but something much less valuable: a husband!

I have come to the battlefield fitted out for war: armed to the teeth in sarcenet, velvet and silk, and a vast supply of simpering looks. I have already had my feet trod on three times in the course of dancing the quadrille, been told I look like an angel twice, and watched a young Buck split his breeches. It should prove to be an enjoyable time.

A Singular Lady

Chapter One

Titania slammed the door with a fierce display of energy. She squinted her eyes against the burst of sunlight, blinding in comparison to the dimly lit office from which she had just emerged.

"You would think," she fumed, "a person's demise would require they stop wreaking havoc with other people's lives."

A lump rose to her throat. "But not my father. His excesses live on, even if he does not." Titania dug blindly in her reticule for her handkerchief, careful not to let the papers, the wretched proof of her father's perfidy, slip from under her arm. She wiped her eyes, blaming her tears on the sun.

She looked around the London street where she stood, marking the subtle changes since she had been inside. The shadows were lengthening and the warmth of the spring day was beginning to ebb into evening, but that was as it should be. The world showed no signs of distress for her situation.

A rank of hackney coaches stood awaiting hire to her left and she turned towards them, her immediate instinct to head home and bury her head under the covers. Preferably for the next ten years. But London was not Ravensthorpe, and she had not taken three steps before she knew that she could not bear to return to her aunt's house in Russell Square straightaway. Her heart was at full gallop, her thoughts were in a jumble, and she had no wish to see her overbearing Aunt Bestley or her own talkative maid Sarah just yet.

What she needed was a long ride. Galloping until both she and her horse were breathless had helped her solve many problems in the country. But as a long ride was impossible—first of all, she smiled to herself, she had no horse—then she could most certainly walk a long while instead. She would return to her aunt's house on foot. An unaccompanied lady was certainly no more shocking than a father who had left all his money to his mistress.

Titania spun around abruptly, smashing her nose into a wall. She dropped her reticule, one of her gloves, and the papers as well, which scattered on the ground about her. As she regained her balance, she saw that it was not a wall she had struck, but a man, a broad-chested man, who was already stooping down to gather up her belongings.

"I beg your pardon, miss," he said in an amused voice. "I seem to have been masquerading as a door."

"Where did you come from, anyway?" Titania muttered as she crouched down in the dusty street. The man held her papers with a patient air as she crammed them into her reticule. A scent of musk and leather wafted towards her as he placed the last of them in her hand.

"America. Boston, where the ships leave from, to be specific," he replied, a hint of laughter edging into his voice. "Why, have we met?"

"Certainly not," she bristled. "You don't have an accent," she said in an accusing voice as she drew her now bedraggled glove onto her hand.

The man chuckled again. A soft, throaty laugh. She looked up at him, a commanding set-down on the tip of her tongue, of the sort that always worked when she was employing her Managing Ways, but when she looked into his eyes she felt dizzy and even more flustered.

His green eyes were tinged with gold, like a forest being lit by the sun. Tiny laugh lines branched from the corners. His lashes were long and full, their delicate beauty in contrast with his manly, rather stern, features. His dark complexion suggested he spent a lot of time in the wind and sun, and his tawny hair, cut shorter than fashionable, gave him an autocratic look.

Titania rose, ignoring the stranger as he offered his arm for support. "If you are done discomposing me, I must be on my way."

"And where might that be, miss?" said the tall man, his eyes still alight.

"I am sure it is of no concern of yours," she said with a sniff, and set off down the road. As she marched off, she was acutely aware of the man behind her, sure he was still watching her, still laughing with those extraordinary eyes.

Edwin Worthington, Earl of Oakley, was still smiling in the afterglow of his encounter with the flustered, rude, and impossibly striking young woman he had run into outside as he made his way into Mr. Hawthorne's offices. He lowered his long frame into a chair, still warm from its previous occupant, and studied his solicitor.

"Good evening, sir," said Edwin. "It is nice to finally meet the correspondent of my good news. May I first inquire if you know the identity of the distressed young woman—black hair, white skin, blue eyes—I bumped into on the street outside your office just now?"

"I do, sir," the man replied with a sigh. "She is the Honorable Titania Stanhope, daughter of the late Baron Ravensthorpe. She is to make her come-out this Season; it has been twice delayed on account of the deaths of her parents, her father's coming just last year. I fear the report I was compelled to give her was most unsettling.

"But," he said, drawing some papers towards the center of his desk, "now to your affairs, my lord, and a more welcome report, I am pleased to say."

Edwin nodded in assent, but his thoughts still lingered on the woman who had so briefly and tantalizingly placed her ungloved hand on his chest, whose deep blue eyes had stormed like an angry sea when she looked at him. So that was the daughter of the infamous Baron Ravensthorpe, he with the mind of a scholar but the heart of a rake.

"Do you know how she broke her nose?" he asked as Mr. Hawthorne assembled his papers on his vast desk.

"Pardon?" The older man looked puzzled.

"Miss Stanhope, that lady I just ran into . . . the one

with the black hair. And the crooked nose. Do you know how she broke it? Obviously it did not happen recently, but it is unusual to occur to someone who has not spent time in the boxing ring."

Why she would have mentioned such an accident to her solicitor in the first place was another excellent question, but Edwin ignored that irritatingly inquisitive voice in his head.

Mr. Hawthorne gave him as much of a glare as his courtliness would allow. "Really, my lord, I could not say. But if you will just turn your attention here . . ."

Edwin settled back in his chair, stretched his legs in front of him, and waved a hand towards the older gentleman.

"I beg your pardon, sir. Please proceed."

Mr. Hawthorne leaned forward in his eagerness to impart the news. "In sum, my lord, you have a handsome fortune. It is unfortunate you were not apprised of your inheritance for so long, but the boon is that the capital has accrued handsomely since your relative's demise. The house in Belgrave Square is awaiting your arrival, as is the manor house in Hampshire. Of course, there are a considerable amount of decisions to be made, but you can dispose of them within a few months," he concluded.

Mr. Hawthorne regarded Edwin with an expectant air, clearly waiting for a reaction. At last, Edwin spoke. He held Mr. Hawthorne's eyes so the solicitor would know he was required to comprehend every syllable.

"Thank you, Hawthorne. You have done well by me, sir, and by my unexpected good fortune. I trust you will continue to serve me as well now, for I shall ask you to hold this matter in total confidence. I do not wish it to be known in Society that I have inherited anything more than a few sheep and some dilapidated houses."

Edwin addressed the man's unspoken question, feeling his jaw clench as he spoke. "I have had some experience of what it is like to be viewed as nothing more than a fortune-per-annum, Hawthorne. I prefer to meet Society again on my own terms. I refuse to be looked upon as if I lined my hat with thousand-pound notes. Do I make myself clear?"

Mr. Hawthorne nodded vigorously, his startled eyes peering at Edwin from behind his spectacles. Edwin could not fault his surprise; they both knew it was not at all customary for gentlemen of the *ton* to be reticent about good fortune. And the message Mr. Hawthorne had given his client was extraordinary good fortune.

"You may rely upon me, Lord Worthington," said Mr. Hawthorne.

Edwin nodded and stood to take his leave. The solicitor rose also, and Edwin stretched his hand out across the desk. The shorter, slighter man extended his own; Edwin clasped it, careful not to squeeze too hard. He knew his grip was that of a boxer, not a gentleman of leisure.

"I am depending on you, Hawthorne," he said, moving to the door. "You are charged to remain silent on all aspects of my inheritance. If I should hear that someone has been talking, I shall come here first . . ." He smiled, but his meaning was clear.

"You have my word on it, my lord," Hawthorne replied.

"Damn him." Titania spoke softly at first, then repeated her words more loudly. Not that her father could hear her where he was now. She found a particular satisfaction in uttering the shocking phrase. And she was in no hurry to return home, even though a lady would never be caught outdoors without an escort. She swung her head up and slowed her stride to a deliberate pace.

Damn it, she was going to take her time. Always doing the right thing had certainly not gotten her anywhere: twenty-three, penniless, and unwed. Wonderful. If she just rushed, she could fling herself into the Thames and would not be missed until dinner.

Why did he do it? Did she and her younger brother disappoint him somehow? And how did she not realize what had happened? He had always left everything to her, and she had just assumed the will was the same as the one she had seen a few years earlier. Titania shook her head at her own carelessness. She should have guessed he might do something like this.

She paid no attention to the lengthening shadows as dusk fell or to the curious looks she received. The streets were rapidly thinning of pedestrians, but Titania remained oblivious, immersed in her own world. Her suddenly quite destitute world.

Titania had no real choice now. Not if she wanted Thibault, already giving indication of inheriting his father's feckless nature, to be able to raise his children on Ravensthorpe, and not in a debtors' prison. Thibault's future and her servants' livelihoods were in her hands.

She and Thibault had enough to live "very modestly," according to Mr. Hawthorne. To be sure, she had no doubt she could live very modestly until she gradually lowered herself into her grave.

Or she could beat fortune at its own game. She could prove herself truly her father's daughter and gamble it all. She would have the Season her mother had always desired for her, and capture the rich husband she must have because of her father's rashness.

Reducing the problem to an equation—one Titania plus one eligible and insanely wealthy bachelor equaled survival—made it a lot easier for her to stomach. Titania had always considered herself clever at problem solving, though she had to admit Euclid's geometry paled at this difficulty. If she could not find a way out of her dilemma by the end of the Season, all would be lost with Ravensthorpe and Thibault. Not to mention her own future.

She must choose the bold course, and she must succeed.

Having come to this resolve, Titania found she had also come near to the end of Southampton Row, where it emptied into Russell Square. The various mansions loomed with careless magnificence, and she forgot, for the moment at least, her own troubles as she drank in the opulent manifestation of London's elite. Her mouth gaped open at the sight of an obviously newly completed house. It was massive, with more windows than Titania could count, and she got dizzy peering up to where the building met the sky. Her eyes wandered to the other houses, marveling at their sumptuous facades.

Thus absorbed, she was doubly startled to hear a gruff voice almost in her ear. "See here, miss, it's not a go to stare, now innit?" said the voice. "Looks so you're needin' some manners—should I throw you over my knee or is there summat else you'd like me to do more?"

Titania whirled to look at the man who was addressing her in such a vulgar manner. He was apparently a common laborer, a muscular man who had obviously hauled a lot of bricks in his lifetime. He smelled as if he had more recently lifted a great many tankards of ale. He was so close to her she could see the individual coarse black hairs protruding from his nose. One of his beefy hands reached to snake about her waist, the other rested on his hip.

"I would like you, sir, to leave me alone," Titania said in what she hoped was her most commanding tone, although she was quaking inside. "What I am regarding is none of your concern, and I would be much obliged if you would let me pass."

"Oh no. You don't flit away like a pretty bird," the man said with a leer, the intent of which was clear even to a sheltered country miss such as Titania.

"See here," he continued, "you and me has a bargain to discuss, the same being what I could do to you and how many times."

Titania froze. A lot of use her self-assurance and ability to balance a ledger were. Her common sense would have been more useful now. Why did she have to decide just now, in London, a thriving metropolis with which she was utterly unfamiliar, to be so reckless? She was an idiot. She drew a deep breath to quell the onrushing panic and opened her mouth to speak when she was startled by another male voice.

"Sir," the deep voice spoke behind her, "do you have business with this lady? Because if not, I believe she asked you to let her by. Now."

Turning, Titania saw a man who was not as enormous as the brute who had accosted her, but one whose muscular build appeared lethal, not just massive. She felt—was it safe?—as the new arrival drew off his gloves with the air of a man who knew just what he was about. Then, just as methodically, he undid his cravat and tossed it to the ground in a negligently confident manner.

The ugly customer, who by now had his paw grasping her waist, barked a laugh. Titania felt his anger as he gripped her tighter, pinching her skin in a painful grasp. How would her rescuer prevail? That he would was not in doubt, even though she could not fathom how.

"It's none of yours, but I do have business with this wench," the man spat, "and if a gentry cove knew what was good for him, he'd be the one what was passing by so I could take care of it."

"Is that so?" her rescuer queried, drawing nearer. Titania recognized him as the man to whom she had been so snappish just a few minutes before outside Mr. Hawthorne's office. He wore sober, old-fashioned garb proclaiming a lack of acquaintance with a crack tailor, or even with current fashion. And his wardrobe was not just old-fashioned, but old: his coat was shiny at the elbows, as if he had spent long hours leaning on them. His boots were worn and dusty, the leather faded to a matte black.

He must be a clerk or tradesman of some sort, she thought, although she had never seen a tradesman with such an air of command. The man's face had lost all of the good cheer and humor it held when he was helping her to collect her papers, and the laughter that was in his voice then was now replaced with a steely edge.

"Let go of the lady," he repeated. A vile oath issued from the mouth of Titania's captor.

"Is that so?" the man replied, his tone hardening.

His green eyes suddenly glinted, the gold speckles in them lighting up with a fiery anger. With a movement so quick Titania had no time to flinch, he shot out a fist and landed a blow square on the ruffian's chin. The man let go of Titania and fell as if struck with a poleax.

The green-eyed man looked down at his prey—it hardly seemed right to call him an opponent—and seeing him insensate, drew closer to Titania. "You are not harmed, are you, miss?" he asked with a tone of concern.

"No, no, no," Titania jabbered. She drew a shallow breath and took a step backward, stumbling a little as she felt her legs tremble. He tucked her arm into his and moved her a few more feet away from the lummox lying prone on the ground. She concentrated on breathing normally, then tried to speak in her usual calm tone.

"I am not harmed. I apologize for putting you in such a scrape as this . . . although you did plant him quite a facer, did you not?" she said, lapsing into her brother's boxing cant as relief at her rescue turned her nearly giddy. She looked up at him as she finished babbling, and saw first he had not been shocked at her impropriety, but saw next that looking up at him was a different blunder.

His face loomed above hers, his green eyes focusing on her with an intensity that made her shiver. She lowered her eyes to his chest, but discovered that too was a mistake. The man's shirt was unbuttoned where he had removed his cravat, exposing an expanse of smooth, muscled skin that made Titania desperate to lean against him and be enfolded in the arms she now knew were solid and strong.

Her pulse thudded in her chest. She had never felt so weak-kneed, so helpless, so *girlish* in the presence of a man.

She forced her eyes back up to his, trying to regain control.

"Thank you, sir, for your assistance once again. I am quite all right. I must be on my way home. It is just there, so I will not encounter any more mishaps." She pointed with a shaky finger to a tall town house across the street. The man just continued looking at her, his green eyes beginning to warm.

Titania wished the ground would open up and swallow her. This man was merely being gentlemanly, but she did not deserve his kindness. Given the disastrous happenings of the day, all she wanted, all she *deserved*, was to be alone to stew in her own misery.

"As you wish, miss," said the stranger, inclining his head with a mocking air. "I have discomposed you once already today, and I should not wish to tempt you again. But first, before you go," he said, bringing his hand up to her face to push an escaped tendril of hair back into her bonnet, "first let me put you to rights." He tucked the stray tress into her bonnet, and then let his hand rest briefly on her cheek as if he could not stop himself from caressing her.

If merely looking into his eyes made her feel like a giddy girl, a state Titania couldn't recall ever experiencing, then she couldn't even name the feelings brought on by his touch. She quickly brushed his hand away from her face and tried hard to look anywhere but in his eyes. She felt as if all the breath had been knocked out of her, a slow, prickling sensation began creeping up the back of her legs toward the bottom of her spine, and she clutched her possessions tightly so she would not be tempted to reach out and touch him back.

"If you please, sir," she said with as much of her Managing Ways as she could muster, "I would not have you presume. I thank you once again."

Collecting what little pride she had left, she turned again

toward her aunt's house, her back as straight as her wobbly legs would allow.

She closed her eyes briefly as she realized her day's ordeals were not over. She had to look her father's sister in the eye and tell her the Stanhope name had been disgraced yet again. She shuddered at the prospect, and little more relished the vicious scold Sarah would give her, which she fully deserved, for going out about the town all alone.

Her Aunt Bestley was as comforting as ice down the back upon hearing the news. "No money at all, you say?" she queried Titania, disdain vying with disbelief for control of her tone.

"None." The syllable resonated in the sudden quiet of her aunt's sitting room. Titania stood facing her aunt. She refused to sit, as much because she might not be able to get up again as to show herself equal to her haughty relative.

Titania and her aunt had already come to an agreement about how much it would cost to sponsor her for the Season. Lady Bestley had seemed none too sanguine about her own daughter's chances for making a beneficial match, which would almost certainly lengthen with Titania on the scene. Her aunt had demanded a large sum for her trouble, which would assuage the pain if her daughter did not take.

"Well then, my girl," Lady Bestley said with a brisk air, "I see nothing for it but for you to return home at once. You will not be able to settle the bargain we made, and without a substantial dowry, there is little chance you would be able to attract anybody of note to marry you. Especially with that unfortunate nose.

"If you are lucky," she continued, as if it mattered not a whit to her whether Titania were lucky, "if you are *very* lucky, you can persuade one of the local gentry to marry you, although I do not know who would, given my brother's many disgraces. Who could have thought he would behave so reprehensibly, even from beyond the grave?"

"But, Aunt, going back to Ravensthorpe is precisely what I must *not* do. I must have my Season, in the present circumstance even more than before."

"Be that as it may," said her aunt, "I will not be a party to your behavior. If you are to cause a scandal, as your parents did with their marriage, then you will have to do it on your own. I will not stoop to help such a thing." She clamped her lips together as she finished, and Titania knew that was her aunt's last word on the subject.

"Very well, Aunt. If you really refuse to assist me, then may I remind you of our bargain?" Her aunt waved her hand in dismissal, but Titania held up her own hand in an authoritative gesture.

"Hear me out. I pledge you will have the money I promised you, and I will double that sum if I do succeed in getting married by the end of the Season. I still have my mother's jewelry, and I will sell the pieces to pay my debt to you, if necessary, so you can be assured you will get what is owed you, no matter what the outcome may be for me. Your only obligation is not to reveal the details of my father's will."

Lady Bestley's face revealed her unwilling interest at the proposal, and Titania continued. "I will handle my come-out myself, and just watch me snare the wealthiest man in England." Even if he's as bald as an egg with only one leg to hop about on, she finished to herself.

Her Aunt Bestley saw a bargain, but knew she could turn the screw a little tighter. The mole on her face quivered as she spoke. "You will not reside here." It was not a question. "I doubt you will succeed in finding a husband—but I will not have it said that I dishonored an obligation to family."

Titania nodded her head in agreement. Without speaking another word, she climbed up the stairs to the room she had barely known as her own, telling a surprised Sarah to pack again. They were going to look for a suitable house for the Season.

"At this time, Mrs. Baldwin," Titania said airily to her prospective landlady as she surveyed the cheerful, if slightly threadbare, house, "I do not have the authority to transfer funds from the family's account. But that is only a formality; you may be assured I will not live on tick forever."

Mrs. Baldwin seemed too engrossed in eyeing the elegant rose-colored gown in which Titania had arrived to pay overmuch attention to the detail of payment. After choking down the dry scones and watery tea her new landlady of-

fered, the lease was signed. Titania and Sarah spent the
rest of the day coughing on crumbs, unpacking the trunks,
and figuring out how to survive until more staff could be
brought down from Ravensthorpe to the modest house in
Little Chiswick Street.

When Sarah could be heard snoring in her room one
flight above, Titania allowed herself a full five minutes of
heartfelt sobbing in her bedroom. Then, wiping the tears
from her eyes, she pulled on her dressing gown, lit a candle-
stick, and found her way to the escritoire in the drawing
room. She drew a deep breath and dashed off a letter to
her governess, Miss Tynte, whom she hoped had not settled
too firmly into her retirement. The room was silent, except
for the scritching of her pen upon the paper.

My dear Elizabeth,

Please return to London at once. Don't be distressed, I am
well. I am not hurt nor in danger. But my future hangs in
the balance and it is vital that you come.
I send you my love,

Titania

P.S. Bring your best gowns.

She drew forth another sheet of paper and wrote a brief
note to Stillings at Ravensthorpe, commanding he bring
himself immediately to London, together with whomever
among the servants he thought would be essential to manage
a young lady's house in town. She made no explanation; the
servants had certainly been through enough havey-cavey business with her father to countenance whatever she might
present to them.

She laid down her pen, still unsure of the feasibility of
her plan. Would Miss Tynte take on the charade Titania
had fabricated?

Dispatch from the Battlefront, March 1813

It has been said the best offense is a good defense. If that is true, then why are so many of us so . . . offensive? We strike our suitors on the arms with our fans, fall into their arms in dead faints, demand liquid refreshment at every turn and persist in giggling.

Constantly.

I am no different; after all, I aspire to move from the ranks of the unwed (Private, Second Class, perhaps?) to a position befitting a wife (Brigadier General, with every vestige of authority the position holds).

I will fight my way to the front with every tactic in my power. I will strike, demand and giggle until the enemy falls to his knees.

A Singular Lady

Chapter Two

"Titania! I cannot impersonate your cousin! What if we are discovered?" Miss Tynte fluttered her hands in a gesture of dismay.

"If we are discovered, it will not be any worse than what will happen if I do not marry, and quickly."

Her governess leaned forward and gripped Titania's arm. Her face was ashen. "Titania, you do not mean . . ."

Titania gave an almost hysterical laugh. "No, you goose, I do not mean *that*."

Miss Tynte sat back, a look of relief on her face. "Then what?" she asked.

"I went and saw Mr. Hawthorne, Father's solicitor. He . . . he informed me that there has been another will found, negating the one we thought was valid. Father left all his money to a . . . to a . . . to some person."

"A person? You mean, a *woman*?"

Titania nodded, feeling her eyes fill with tears again. Who knew she was such a watering pot?

"Oh, you poor dear! That scoundrel. I know he was your father, Titania, but that was a terrible thing to do."

Titania's tone turned brisk again as she swept her hands across her cheeks, wiping away the moisture. "Yes, well, Father was not always so wise in his decisions, Elizabeth. Which is why I have to get married to a very, very wealthy man. And why you have to chaperone me; Aunt Bestley and I have already had a disagreement, so she will not help."

Miss Tynte repeated her question. "But what if we *are* discovered?"

Titania recalled Miss Tynte had always fretted over propriety. She assumed her most guileless face. "Oh, but we won't be; you are unexceptional in your manners, and as genteel as anyone in the *ton*; you exhibit those ladylike qualities you required me to learn, and that I still seem to have problems with."

Such as flouncing around London unescorted, but Titania brushed that memory away.

"Can't you see?" Titania presented the case again with an undisguised passion. "You must help me. Or else Stillings, and Cook, and Sarah, and the rest of them will be as destitute as Thibault and I are now."

Miss Tynte stopped her anxious fluttering and looked at Titania with a gimlet eye. "Destitute? That is a very strong word. Is there something you are not telling me? Has Thibault been up to mischief?" She narrowed her eyes in her best governess-y gaze.

Titania sat down on the sofa, pulling her friend down to sit with her. "Do you remember Tanner, the overseer?"

Her friend nodded. "He stole your father's favorite stallion when he left Ravensthorpe so suddenly. We all heard enough about the loss of that horse. There was certainly more outcry about that than when Thibault got himself stuck down that well for the whole afternoon."

"That was hardly the worst of it, although that was what made Father tear up to London. Tanner was a thorough blackguard." Titania ticked off each action on her fingers. "He raised the tenants' rents viciously—saying it was Father's order—and then embezzled the money. He depleted the breeding stock, lied about receipts from the cattle auctions, and pocketed the unreported profits. He left bills unpaid and kept the allocated funds for himself. He even stole from additional funds my father authorized when Tanner insisted on the need to buy new stock and make costly repairs—stock that was never purchased, repairs and improvements that were never made."

Her governess gave a grim smile. "One would think your

father would have checked references before hiring someone he met at one of his clubs."

"Anyone but Father would have done so. Father flew into a towering rage for the theft of the horse, but after that, he did not delve into the accounts themselves any deeper than ever he had before. It was only after Father died that Mr. Hawthorne and I discovered the true extent of the financial devastation. Ravensthorpe is barely beginning to recover. It will require years of prudent financial management. Thanks to Father's impetuous nature, Ravensthorpe does not have those years."

Her governess sat openmouthed as Titania related her subsequent efforts to ensure the credit of the family and the long-term husbandry of Ravensthorpe, not to mention the well-being of the many tenants the Stanhope farm had supported for generations. Titania had promised she would use virtually every shilling of their rent money for however long it took to restore the estate.

"My best guess," Titania said as she finished her litany of recovery efforts, "is that it will take at least five years. Five years during which I had expected to have other funds on which to live. Other funds that are now out of my hands." She turned to her friend, her hands held palm up in a gesture of supplication.

"So you see, there is no income. Not if Ravensthorpe is to survive. And we both know Thibault cannot help."

Titania had made a promise to Ravensthorpe's tenants and she kept her promises. She would not follow the lead of so many other landowners and impose brutal rack rents on the tenants in time of war or personal misfortune. She had deplored that greed in the newspaper columns she had written for the *Northamptonshire Gazette* under her pseudonym, "Agricola."

She would keep her promise to Thibault's holding and to Ravensthorpe's tenants, even if it forced her to sell herself. Her voice trembled as she spoke.

"I have no choice. I must have my Season, I must marry someone with so much money he can afford to save Ravensthorpe, despite my father's actions." Her face bore a fierce, determined look.

"I will do it, Titania," Miss Tynte said quietly, convinced at last.

"Thank you. Perhaps this will save us." Titania was thrilled she would be able to implement her scheme. Thrilled and appalled.

Titania tried to ignore the dampening reflection that success in the endeavor would yield a husband whose only important characteristic would be that he had buckets of money. Her governess's voice interrupted her depressing thoughts.

"Titania, I am so sorry. It would have been your father's fondest wish for you to find a suitable match, but I do not think that is what he had in mind when he wrote a new will."

"If he had given it a shred of his attention, he probably would have thought I could find a suitable match at home; why, I would have had the very cream of the crop from which to choose."

She felt her spirits lift a little as she rose to stand in front of her governess, hands placed demurely at her sides. She gave a wicked grin, then executed a flawless curtsey. Her friend nodded her head in response, an answering smile on her face.

"Why, there is Lord Atherton on only the next estate; of course, he is seventy if he is a day, and he does have a disconcerting habit of sniffing noisily as if there were an onion concealed somewhere on your person."

"Onions are a lovely vegetable, Titania, how can you be so cruel?" Miss Tynte gave a condescending sniff as she joined the game.

"And," Titania said, warming to her subject as she made another deep curtsey, "Squire Inchbald to the west quaffs brandy bingo at break of day and, they say, sleeps on the floor with his hounds. Lord Newbury to the north is of the opinion that 'Damme! Eh, what?' constitutes sparkling conversation. Not to mention Mr. Fripp, the vicar—"

"Or Lord Puddleby, who makes even Lord Delamore seem almost intelligent."

Titania rolled her eyes at her friend in agreement. "No, dearest *cousin*," she said with a wink, "I cannot believe I am so toplofty as to reject the myriad suitors found at home and must come to London to find someone with whom it would be worth spending the rest of my life." She stood up straighter, showing an enthusiasm that was only partially faked.

"I must plan the attack! I have new gowns, a chaperone, an almost fashionable London abode; Alexander the Great could not have been more prepared for his campaigns than I am." And with that declamation, Titania marched off to her room, brandishing her reticule like a sword.

Titania fired off the opening salvo of her campaign that afternoon by paying a call on an old friend who had won her own battle by marrying a viscount a few years earlier. Claire, Lady Wexford, of Wexford House in Mayfair, had been plain old Claire Smith when Titania had seen her last. Titania blinked as she saw the transformation from charming girl to fashionable Society wife.

"Oh, Ti," Claire sighed, her blond curls bobbing gently as she floated into the middle of the room, "how glad I am to see you again! You will never know how the London life wears one, and it will be good to have a dear friend with whom I can have a comfortable coze, not thinking about the next party or who has yet to call."

Titania wagged a chiding finger. "But, Claire, I am here on that very mission, to attend all the parties and receive all the calls. And you promised you would be my guide. Do not disappoint me by telling me you wish to be back in the country with the hens and the horses."

"For you, Titania, I will endure yet another Season, but I do so long for a simple life."

She struck a pose that Titania thought was intended to look mournful, but really only made her look dyspeptic. And if Claire ever planned to return to the simple life she had hated when they were young, she had best forget about wearing diamonds to receive her morning callers.

"Claire—" she began, then broke off as Claire's husband, Lord Wexford, entered. He was a barrel-chested man whose hearty voice filled up the room. "Miss Stanhope, Claire has been on pins and needles. Glad you're here. Hope you brought a full wardrobe. Claire's been planning outings and accepting invitations ever since she heard you were coming to town. So popular I have to make an appointment to see my own wife."

Lord Wexford stopped and beamed at Claire, who ducked her head in an attitude of shyness. "Now, Wex," she demurred, "you know I am only doing all this so Titania may enjoy London to the utmost. I have already had my Season. She must now be the belle of the ball. And," she finished coyly, "if it should happen that she become engaged to some eligible *parti* in the course of her time here in town, well then that's only for the best."

"I hardly think—" Titania began to say, smiling, when a loud, insistent knock at the door below interrupted her. Claire and Lord Wexford's eyes showed matching panic, and after a moment, Claire crept to the window.

"Wex, it's them again," she said, obviously agitated. "Make them go away."

"Yes, yes, dear," Lord Wexford answered, and, ignoring the bellpull, scurried out of the room. Titania heard him give an angry shout down the hall.

Titania was too polite to ask, but her face must have shown her curiosity. Claire plopped down on the sofa, a disgruntled look on her lovely face.

"These cent per centers! Tired of waiting for Wex's father to stick his spoon in the wall. Can I help it if he persists in continuing his wretched existence? They simply don't understand that there are so many things one needs, and when one needs them, then one does not put off getting them until the next quarter's dividend day. I just had to have a new opera gown, and my morning gowns were in tatters. As for Wex, he is widely admired for his ability to judge horseflesh; he can not very well go tooling about in the new phaeton with no-goers."

Titania murmured some sort of sympathetic response, not that she understood much of Claire's London slang. She considered confiding in her friend about her own financial state of affairs when something made her pause. Claire's affect had changed since last they were together; there was a brittle brightness about her now. Perhaps she wouldn't understand after all.

"So, my dear," Claire began afresh. "Would you like to go shopping? I saw the most clever little bonnet the other day that would just suit you."

Only if the clever little bonnet came with a tiny little price; it would be fun, though, to pretend to be a normal, carefree debutante for just a few hours.

"Certainly, but should you not be at home during your at-home hours? That is the point of them, is it not?" Titania laughed as she spoke, but her friend did not seem to find Titania's gentle ribbing amusing.

Claire's lips twisted into a pout. "At home to those nasty bill collectors. No, I would rather go out."

Titania waited while Claire gathered her things, idly wondering if her friend was going to find even more diamonds to put on, and if so, just where she would find to put them. She looked down at her own deep blue gown, contrasting it with the embellished, embroidered and altogether extraordinary confection her friend was wearing.

Titania's gown had not seemed plain in Northamptonshire; it had precisely one bow, no frills and no embroidery. Compared with Claire, Titania appeared almost austere.

At least it was not white; Titania had put her foot down when the local dressmaker insisted all debutantes wore white. White, she knew, made her look like a particularly vapid flake of snow.

"Are you ready, Titania?" Claire stood at the door, a fetching little hat placed just so on her curls. Titania envied those curls as much as she had ten years ago, when the girls were thirteen, inseparable, and beginning to notice boys. Titania's own hair would not curl at all, even if threatened with a pair of scissors. It seemed her hair was as stubborn as she was.

"You know, Claire, I would barely recognize you, you have become so fashionable as to be intimidating." Not to mention so festooned in jewelry any other light was almost redundant.

Claire gave a simpering smile. "Yes, well, Wex likes me to look my best. He is such a dear man. I have a reputation as a leader of fashion to uphold, and he is very proud of that." As they walked outside, Claire assured Titania it was not a long ride to Bond Street.

It was the longest carriage ride in Titania's memory. There was indeed much to learn in London, she thought, such as the amount of time one woman could talk about herself and her clothes. She was contemplating ripping one of the many bows from Claire's gown and stuffing it into her own ears when she felt the horses slowing.

Thank goodness, she thought. Another few minutes and she would have flung herself out onto the road. And she still had more hours in Claire's company. Was this to be her future? A Society lady filling up her hours with idle pastimes and an even idler existence?

Dispatch from the Battlefront, March 1813

In battle, one must trust one's companions in arms implicitly. Winning the war requires tactical maneuvering, a clever, multifaceted battle plan and above all, a solid, united front.

So ladies, remember that as you march into Almack's.

The enemy—otherwise known as the eligible bachelor—will notice if there is dissension in the ranks, and will despise where he once admired. If his opponent can be so shrewish to her comrade, he wonders, how will she be when her castle is stormed by him?

Pettiness, jealousy, malicious gossip; all treason, and subject to the worst of punishments: spinsterhood.

A Singular Lady

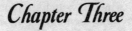

Chapter Three

Renewing her acquaintance with Claire made Titania wish she had any other path than the one she needed to follow. It was with an implacable air, therefore, that she responded to Miss Tynte's continued agitation about playing the part of a chaperone. She looked her in the eye and assumed a stern tone she had learned from the very woman now staring at her in panic.

"All you have to do is sit in the corner with the dowagers and nod approvingly every time I look over at you. I can manage the rest on my own." She softened her voice. "Tell me, do you prefer the peach or the green gown?" she asked, as much to distract her friend as to garner her opinion.

Her friend finally soothed, Titania escaped upstairs to dress, only to find Sarah had already made the choice of evening wear for her—"the blue will match your eyes, miss"—and would allow for no disagreement.

The money I paid for this single gown, Titania thought as Sarah buttoned her, would have paid the staff's salaries for at least a quarter of the year. I hope it will earn its keep.

Titania scrutinized the gown as if it were an opponent, narrowing her eyes as she examined its ability to display every attribute while also maintaining her modesty. Its overskirt of white gauze gave her the illusion of being a fresh-faced debutante, while the dark blue ribbons at the waistline drew discreet attention to her breasts, possessions that until now she considered more of an embarrassment than an attribute.

Sarah expertly twined a matching blue ribbon into Titania's hair, all the while bemoaning its inability to take a curl. Titania, glad to be distracted from her thoughts, pulled the curling iron from her maid's hands.

"Sarah, you know whenever you use the curling iron, I just end up looking like a slightly mad sheep." Still grumbling, Sarah smoothed her skirts down, poked an errant ribbon into position and stood back.

"I guess as 'ow you look well, miss," Sarah allowed. That was as effusive as Sarah ever got. Titania hugged her maid quickly, kissed her cheek, and bounded down the stairs, pieces of hair already flying from the careful arrangement. She stopped and twirled in front of Miss Tynte, who had already descended and was fussing with her wrap. The two ladies surveyed themselves in the glass. Both seemed satisfied by what they saw: one debutante, one chaperone, both entirely respectable.

"You'd hardly think," Titania whispered, "that neither of us is what we seem. I am a pauper and you are a governess." Miss Tynte shuddered at the deception, but when the two walked outside, the chill air firmed their resolve.

Lord and Lady Hagan's sumptuous new town house on Lisle Street in the West End was ablaze in lights for the party, candles melting in chandeliers suspended every five feet, giving off an almost overpowering odor. Titania tried not to wince as she inhaled the suffocating smell.

"Look," Titania said, holding her nose discreetly as she pointed to a cluster of people in the far corner of the room, "there is my friend Claire, now Lady Wexford. I will introduce you. Thank goodness none of my friends' parents ever allowed them to visit me so you are unknown to them. It will make this lie much easier." Miss Tynte winced at Titania's words.

Claire spotted Titania and waved gaily, then led a procession to greet her, several languid dandies in tow. Titania introduced Miss Tynte to Claire, who began speaking in a high-pitched breathy voice that made her sound like a wheezing nine-year-old.

"Oh my dearest, dearest friend, let me present Lord

Quimby, Lord Chatham and Mr. Alexander Harris. Wex is deep in cards, and I have to fend for myself, so these gentlemen have kindly offered to keep me amused. Of course, now you have arrived, I shall no doubt be obliged to join Miss Tynte in the chaperones' chairs. I should resign myself," she finished with mock woe, "to sitting out the dances. I am an old married woman, after all."

"Lady Wexford," one of the three immediately declaimed, "every moment spent with you is a delicate flower in the bouquet of my heart." Titania noticed his head moved in a slight twitch as he spoke, perhaps to encourage a particularly fetching curl to fall over one eye. The other two, apparently dumbstruck by their comrade's eloquence, merely nodded their agreement. Claire giggled.

"You gentlemen are too delightful. Now which one of you wishes to lead me out for a dance?" Claire blinked expectantly, apparently anticipating their eagerness to partner her.

After a duel of overly effusive compliments, Claire and her chosen swain trotted out to the dance floor, Claire's guinea-gold hair glinting in the candlelight. The two losers sighed after them. After a brief moment of mourning, they turned towards Titania, their faces almost ludicrously downcast.

Lord Chatham, or at least that is who Titania thought it was, asked Titania to dance. If she were under any illusion that he was actually interested in her, his first question made his interest crystal clear. "I envy your role as Lady Wexford's dearest friend," he said with a sigh. "She is a goddess among women, a rose among the thorns, a—"

"Queen bee among the drones?" Titania finished brightly. The lord's mouth gaped open, then shut. Then opened, then shut again.

At least he was remembering to breathe. Just what was it about her that made people get that confused look in their eyes when she spoke? Lord Chatham was completely silent, which she supposed she should be grateful for.

At last, the music ended and the lord, still mute, escorted her to her chair. He made a deep bow, then scurried off to where Claire had already begun assembling another entourage.

Over the next hour, Titania met an array of men she

presumed were eligible—tall, short, young, old—but their conversation was not nearly so varied.

"Is this your first Season?"

"How are you enjoying London?"

"Is the weather not exceptional? I wonder what it will be like tomorrow?"

"What kind of name is Titania? Is it . . . foreign?"

"And you say this is your first Season?"

"London is very different from Northamptonshire."

"What weather, what?"

By the time the orchestra stopped for a brief interlude, Titania was ready to scream. "I swear," she hissed to Miss Tynte as they found chairs, "if one more man talks about the weather, or makes another condescending remark about the country, I will box his ears. Or mine, just for a distraction."

Miss Tynte gave her an amused look. "What, did you expect you would find a scholar amidst this crowd? One or two might be here, Titania, but they will not reveal themselves so soon. Even a rustic such as I knows disclosing that one actually paid attention to one's tutors is not the thing. You must be patient, my dear, getting to know new people takes time."

Titania's reply was short. "I do not have time." Miss Tynte's look of amusement quickly turned glum.

"No, you do not, my dear. I would like to box your father's ears, if anyone's ears are to be boxed. Of all the irresponsible—"

"Predictable things for him to do," Titania corrected. She patted her friend's hand. "He got us into this mess, but I am going to get us out of it. I just have to remind myself to stop being such a martyr about it. Now, where is that footman? I am sure you are parched." Titania rose to beckon a footman over, and remained standing to survey the festivities.

In her Northamptonshire daydreams, Titania had nursed a secret hope she would meet someone on her first night on the town who would prove to be the embodiment of her requirements: intelligent, witty and handsome. Now he only had to be loaded with so much gilt he would not notice the encumbrance of a much-beleaguered estate, a spend-thrift brother and a host of faithful retainers.

She sighed, thinking what a foolish girl she was proving to be, when she was startled by a large, very male, presence next to her.

"Lost in reverie again, Miss Stanhope?" a voice spoke softly. "In the short time we've been acquainted, those wool gatherings have always resulted in something—or someone—hitting the ground." Titania turned to see who was speaking and was shocked to see her hero from the day before, this time attired like a perfect gentleman: no scuffs, shine, or outdated fashion. The broadest shoulders she had ever seen were encased in a sober, but perfectly respectable, black coat. His black pantaloons sheathed his long legs, his muscles evident through the thin fabric. She briefly regretted the necessity of his wearing a cravat as her mouth went dry. "I am sorry, sir, but we have not been introduced," she said, pressing her lips together in a prim line, "although I must admit I am surprised to see you here. Judging by your attire yesterday, I would not have guessed you were accustomed to going out in Society."

"Are you implying that you believed me less than a gentleman because of the way I was dressed? I had thought better of you." He grinned down at her, his green eyes dancing.

Titania felt a slight blush come to her cheeks. Something about this man seemed to draw out her shrewish qualities. "No . . . Well . . . What I mean to say is that with your . . . unusual garb and the fact that you were entering Mr. Hawthorne's offices . . . well, I had assumed you were just recently arrived here, and so would not have acquaintance so soon. I am not in the habit of judging people by the way they dress, sir, if that is what you are asking," she added hastily.

"No, Miss Stanhope, I had assumed you were in the habit of judging people by feel."

It took Titania a moment to grasp his meaning, and when she did, she felt herself flush with embarrassment. "Sir, you have the advantage of me. You know my name, but I do not know yours. And given our . . . history," she conceded, "it would be best if you relieved my situation rather than requiring me to wait for some mutual friend to make the introductions."

"I am Edwin Worthington at your service, Miss Stanhope. Earl of Oakley, for formality's sake." He clasped her hand tightly, enclosing Titania's delicate fingers in his strong grasp. "Are you named after Shakespeare's queen of the fairies, or perhaps your parents were astronomically inspired? You share your name with a planetary moon, correct?" He furrowed his brow as if in search of an elusive thought.

Titania found herself unable to answer because his hand was still holding hers. Even through their gloves, the warmth of his palm clasping her fingers was igniting a similar warmth in places she had not thought much of before.

"Yes, well, it was very pleasant to meet you. And if you will excuse me, I must locate my cousin, she will be wondering where I am." Titania hoped he did not know to whom she was referring; Miss Tynte was directly in their line of vision, as plain as day, and was even now peering at them interestedly.

Titania pulled her hand away from his, gave him a brief curtsey, and moved quickly towards her friend, trying hard to compose herself in the short distance between the two points.

Edwin watched her retreat. She moved as if she were certain everyone would shift out of her way. He chuckled as his thoughts were confirmed by a slight, pimply aristocrat scooting out of her path. His eyes remained riveted on her until she was swallowed by the crush of people.

It was only then he became aware of a buzzing in his ear. The buzzing gradually became actual words, and he stared as a man spoke directly in his face, punctuating each word with a finger-poke to his chest.

"You would think seeing your best friend after such a long time would be worth waking up for. Hello, Worthy, nice to see you. Glad you could rouse yourself for the occasion."

Edwin gazed at the man in shock for a moment, then gathered him up in his arms and delivered a hug so strong it seemed he might extinguish the man's very breath. Although the man was taller than Edwin by a few inches, his breadth was not nearly so imposing. His long, lean face was canvassed by deep lines, lines that seemed to indicate weariness, pain or both. His skin was even darker than his friend's, bearing the marks of long days in the sun.

"Alistair, what a surprise. In your last letter, you said you would be on the Continent until the army threw you out."

His friend's toneless reply conveyed more than any histrionics. "They did. Some shrapnel caught me in the leg at Salamanca. They insisted I return home."

"I am glad you are here. I need a friend badly."

"I would say you do," Alistair replied. A familiar sardonic look appeared on his face. "Tell me, does everyone on the other side of the ocean dress as plainly as you, or is that your own particular aberration?" He flicked an invisible speck of dust from his bloodred waistcoat, a garment even Edwin knew was of the first stare of fashion. Edwin surveyed his friend, noting the impeccable grooming, faultless linen and perfectly cut hair.

His friend had aged—there were strands of silver amongst the black, and the crow's feet branching out from his dark eyes were more pronounced than five years ago—but his bearing and physique revealed he was still in prime condition.

"You," Edwin said accusingly, "have become a dandy."

Alistair sighed. "Ever the astute scholar. So, Worthy, what did it take to lure you back to these shores? I thought your father had washed his hands of you."

"As it happens, Alistair," Edwin said frostily, "it was an old and revered cousin, one of my mother's relatives, who passed on." He drew a long breath, and grinned. "I will miss him sorely, if only because his being dead means I can't kill him for leaving me his dilapidated holdings in the country and an enormous mess involving practices of animal husbandry and accounting that must have involved the phases of the moon, since they make sense no other way."

"Ah, still the math-minded practical man I once knew," Alistair said. "Math makes my head spin. The only cure for that is to sit down and have a drink. Shall we?" He bowed elegantly, gesturing towards the refreshment table. Edwin shrugged, took a couple of glasses from a nearby footman's tray, and handed one to Alistair, who downed it in one gulp.

Alistair smiled at him from over the rim. "That is just to last until I make it over to that corner of the room. Look, I see a chair still warm from some dowager's ar—"

"Alistair, let us go before your mouth gets us into trouble . . . again."

Dispatch from the Battlefront, March 1813

Is it possible to mount an attack without the enemy knowing you are actually engaged in battle? Some of the foes seem to be unaware of what is happening at the front, and it is really quite aggravating.

There is the mushroom, who is only concerned about the people who are not speaking to him, the Corinthian who is far too superior to condescend to admit that there is even anybody else in the room, the ninny who is too busy aping the Corinthian to indulge in conversation (besides saying "What ho!" and "Gammon!" every few minutes) and the newly titled enemy who is so frightened by the prospect of marriage—er, battle—that he hides in the gaming room, emerging only when his estates are in jeopardy.

What a lot!

And yet, these are the opponents I am forced to contend with. I will find a worthy foe somewhere in the throngs, and pursue him until he has surrendered. After all, with the arsenal of weapons I have in my cache—playing the pianoforte, dabbing at watercolors, talking knowledgeably about the weather—how could any man refuse?

A Singular Lady

Chapter Four

"Ah, Titania, you have returned." Miss Tynte darted a quick glance at her, then spoke to the man sitting next to her. "Mr. Benson, would you trot off to find us some more refreshments? And maybe some more of those cookies with the stars?" The man bowed in reply and marched off to the refreshments table, orders in hand.

Leave it to her wise governess to know something was distressing her. Titania placed her hands on her cheeks, noting the contrast between her icy palms and her hot face. She probably looked as flushed if she had run around the block. Or found herself incredibly attracted to a completely ineligible man.

Mr. Benson returned, handing her a glass. She gulped the lemonade, relishing the tangy wetness as it slid down her throat. Then her eye caught sight of a broad pair of shoulders. A spark of energy zinged down her spine, and she knew she was not feeling the lemonade's effects. Her fingers still tingled where he had touched her.

It was a good thing, she reminded herself, she was a sensible person not given to mad crushes. Otherwise she would have to wonder just what she was feeling towards the Earl of Oakley. What she needed to do, she told herself sternly, was go home and get a good night's sleep. This campaign was scarcely begun, and her troops—her spirit and her Managing Ways—were exhausted.

Sleep eluded her, however, when she had finally donned

her nightgown and snuggled into bed. Instead, her obsessive brain reviewed every scrap of information it knew about Edwin Worthington. Her father had mentioned the Marquess of Taunton's son had been unceremoniously shipped off to America. He said the banishment was related to the scandal caused by a jilted engagement. Titania wished she had paid more attention at the time, but she did vaguely recall some of the details: the groom-to-be had simply not shown up at the church, leaving his betrothed mortified and with a barrage of gossip to face. Obviously the earl was the rogue son, and he had just recently returned from abroad. That would explain his provincial style of dress.

He was like her, she thought in amusement, both of them having a come-out, although his was evidently a second go-round. No matter what—or how much—she thought of Lord Worthington, however, the fact remained that no renegade son, no matter how lofty his title or how well he looked in evening clothes, was going to be the answer to her problems.

"So you just . . . didn't show up?" Alistair's voice was incredulous. They were sitting at a back table in a tavern, Edwin having lost interest in the party when he observed Titania's departure. Alistair was just happy to be able to drink something stronger than champagne.

Edwin felt the five-year-old guilt sting him anew. "No. I never told her I overheard her that day. I delayed breaking it off until I knew she was waiting for me at the altar. Then I sent a note, telling her I would not appear, and that she—and her lover—knew why."

"That was rather harsh, wasn't it?" Alistair placed a pinch of snuff on his hand and inhaled, then shot Edwin a penetrating glance. "But you were terribly hurt, I suppose, to find she only wanted you for your father's money. You were rather infatuated with her. I remember one time you found she loved daffodils, and you placed them all over your—"

"Enough." Edwin spoke in a harsh tone that would have dissuaded a lesser man. Alistair was not a lesser man.

"How *did* you get the daffodils to stick to your skin like

that?" he mused. "I would have thought it would cause a damnable rash."

Edwin's lips twitched in spite of himself. "It did, actually. I holed up in my room for four days until the worst of it was over."

"One thing I've always wondered: why didn't your father just buy you colors and be done with it? He would've been rid of you, and your disgrace, and you could have redeemed yourself in battle."

"When I suggested that, he said, 'And have my heir die on me in a glorious death? You will not be allowed to assuage your honor in some heroic action. You will not be around to torment me in my lifetime, but I will be damned if you torment me with your death.' I did not think so at the time, but it was an excellent speech."

"So he sent you to North America. I read the occasional letter you sent, but of course my brain does not retain such information. What exactly were you doing over there?"

"I ended up in Boston, where I served as the confidential envoy for a merchant trader in negotiations with Halifax shipowners."

"As I suspected," Alistair said, shaking his head, "I am still confused."

"That position was only after I had a few satisfying months exorcising my rage in the boxing ring. I worked on the docks, advanced my employment, rediscovered my academic interests and began publishing papers in some of the news journals there. Ironically enough, my specialty is battle history. And you, what are you doing now the army has no use for you?"

"They are using me, just not on the battlefield. That is all I can say." Alistair gave an exaggerated wink. "But enough about me. Have you communicated with your father at all?"

"No."

The two men fell silent for a moment.

"Do you know what happened to your fiancée? What was her name again?"

"Leticia Merriwether. Alistair, you would forget your boots if they were not held on to your feet."

Alistair straightened up with a flourish worthy of a peacock. "I could never forget these boots, you fashion misfit."

"And I will never forget the lesson Leticia taught me when I heard her making plans to deceive me on our wedding night: marriage is a deadly trap, and I will never be caught in it."

"You have renounced women entirely, then? No wonder you dress like that."

"On the contrary. I have enjoyed, and will continue to enjoy, the company of women. I just know that when it comes to marriage, the female mind is more interested in the state of my bankbook than in my heart. Temporary companionship is one thing. A permanently shackled state is another."

"A born cynic," Alistair said, shaking his head.

"Not born, my friend. Made."

Titania woke the next day with a determination not to let anything—quick fists or an even quicker wit—get in the way of her campaign. She and Miss Tynte sat together in the small sitting room and reviewed the likely bachelors, or combat missions, as Titania insisted on referring to them.

"Let me see. Mr. Clark was that young man—barely older than Thibault—who kept trying to look down my gown. Definitely scratch him off the list. Lord Davis was very nice, did you meet him?"

"Was he the one with the nice wife?"

"Oh. Scratch him off the list, too. There was a Mr. Alistair Farrell. He was dressed more beautifully than I. That would bother me, I think. Then there was that Viscount Rotten—"

"I believe his name is Rotherham. Are we scratching him as well?"

"Yes." Titania wrinkled her nose. "He smelled. There was that very pleasant fellow, you know, the one with the—" She gestured towards her ears, but was interrupted by Sarah.

"Miss?" Sarah's face was unusually solemn.

"Yes?" Titania was grateful for the interruption. This self-sacrifice thing was no fun. It was even harder when you were unable to forget that a very long future loomed once the banns had been read.

"A Mr. Stanhope is 'ere. Says 'e is your father's brother. Should I show 'im in?"

Titania sprang to her feet. Had her long-lost uncle somehow heard of her plight? Was there a chance of rescuing

Ravensthorpe? She beckoned to Sarah, hopping in her excitement.

"Yes, yes, show him in." She looked at Miss Tynte. "Would you . . . ?"

Miss Tynte smiled as if she could read her mind. "No, of course not. It would certainly be a surprise to find out one had a relative one had never heard of before." She slipped out of the room while Titania ran to the mirror. Even her hair seemed to recognize this visit was important, since it remained uncharacteristically neat. She smoothed her suddenly damp palms on her gown and turned towards the door expectantly.

"Niece." He was broad, his large frame leaning heavily on a cane. He hobbled into the room and glared into the corners as if searching for something. Titania rushed to pull a chair towards him, and he sank down into it, uttering a tremendous groan. She wondered how much it chafed him to be so immobile. Since he was related to her father, chances were good forced inactivity made him act like a sore bear.

She regarded him from under her lashes as he settled himself, grunting and muttering. The comparison to a bear was apt in more than just personality: his shaggy brown hair grazed his collar, and his almost as shaggy eyebrows looked like two caterpillars perched above his eyes. She couldn't see their color, but they were deep-set, with heavy lines creased under them. He was about as opposite his dandified, languidly elegant brother as possible.

"Uncle?"

He scrutinized her from head to toe. She could almost swear he stiffened as he gazed at her face.

"Yes. I am Uncle Norbert. I don't suppose your parents ever spoke of me, hm?" He glowered at her from under his eyebrows.

"Oh, yes, they did," Titania replied in surprise. "As has Aunt Bestley, your sister. Father always wished we could meet you, but . . . "

"But I am a cripple, is that what he said?" the man rumbled, glowering at her with an even fiercer gaze.

Titania recoiled a bit at his venomous tone. So much for finding solace in meeting a long-lost relative.

"No, that your responsibilities would not allow you to be

away from the country for so long, that is all. But tell me," she said, sitting on the carpet near his chair, "what brings you here now?" She looked up at him with a smile, not to be dissuaded by his bearishness.

Her uncle's eyes, as blue as her father's, glittered with an icy cast. "We get word of things. My sister writes me your father did you a bad turn. And I've spoken to Mr. Hawthorne. He mentioned the new will." He turned his eyes to the floor, twirling the cane idly as he spoke.

"Yes . . ." Titania replied slowly. "Father was . . . well, you would know better than I, but Father could be a bit . . ." Her voice faltered.

"Thoughtless?" The rage in his voice was unmistakable.

Titania scurried back on the carpet a few inches, alarmed by his almost palpable anger. She began to wonder at the real reason she had never met him before.

"Father was reckless, and of course he did an exceedingly reprehensible thing, but it is no more than I would expect of him. He loved too well, and too often. Mother kept him in check, but when she died—"

"I have no doubt he led your mother a fine dance," her uncle growled. For a moment, his eyes seemed to soften. Then he narrowed them, staring at Titania so hard she felt as if he were trying to see into her soul.

"But I am not here about your parents. I am here about Ravensthorpe."

Titania exhaled, tracing a pattern on the carpet with her finger as she spoke. "If Mr. Hawthorne explained about Father's will, you know the situation is bad. Making it worse is that Ravensthorpe needs a substantial outlay of funds in order even to maintain itself."

"And how do you propose you find the money?" he demanded.

Titania did not want to reveal any of her plans. Thus far he had growled, derided and mocked herself and her parents. She had no wish to give him any more artillery.

"Thibault is working on it. Thibault is brilliant at numbers and accounting," she lied, hoping his country home was far enough away for him not to have heard Thibault was more likely to balance a spoon on his nose than a column of numbers.

"And if he fails?"

"If he fails, Ravensthorpe is lost," she replied simply.

He sat for a minute, twirling his cane faster. In the silence, she heard his breath laboring, a hoarse wheeze punctuating each exhale. Then he slid his eyes toward her and smiled. A smile completely devoid of any friendly emotion.

"Then Ravensthorpe will be lost to me. Thank you for the good news, niece, I am certain you will be helpful when I regain my rightful place. Haven't been there for twenty-five years, and now your father's blithe spirit is handing it to me on a silver platter. Oh, this is rich." He leaned his head back and laughed.

Titania stood, shaking in anger. How dare he come here and threaten her? "You will not have Ravensthorpe," she said in a low, steady voice. "Thibault and I will figure something out, and the taxes are not due for several months. Ravensthorpe belongs to Thibault, Uncle."

"How?" He waved her away with his beefy hand. "No, don't bother telling me. I have an offer for you and your brother, the *baron*." He said the word with an ugly sneer. "If you cede Ravensthorpe to me now, I might just let you live there. Of course, you will have to earn your keep, none of your fancy lady ways will be tolerated at my home."

Titania grimaced to herself as she reviewed her "fancy lady" ways at Ravensthorpe: managing the servants, dealing with the tenants and the creditors, keeping her father from reaching the gaming tables too often, making sure Thibault fell in the well only once a season.

What her uncle offered would be unpleasant, no doubt, but not difficult. Should she talk to Thibault and take his offer? She would not have to auction herself off in marriage for the privilege of keeping Ravensthorpe. She and Thibault would always have a home. But what kind of home would it be?

"I've been friendly, niece, as befits our relationship. But let me warn you, I won't be so friendly if you make me wait for your decision." He considered *that* friendly? That settled it. No husband could possibly be as nasty as her uncle. She would take her chances, and hope he would not be able to call her bluff until she held all the cards. She rose, briskly rubbing her hands.

"No, thank you, Uncle, I have every confidence Thibault and I will manage to hold on to Ravensthorpe."

He gave a short bark of laughter. "Ha. I'll just wait. And when you cannot pay, I will buy up the notes. There's not much for an old bachelor to do in the country except make money. And I've got plenty. And then you can find yourself another home, because I will be master of Ravensthorpe."

He rose, using his cane as a crutch for support. Titania felt a wicked desire to kick it out from under him, but she sensed it would please him for her to behave as spitefully as he. And besides, she could not really be that spiteful.

"No need to show me out, niece. I know my way." He stumped out the door, leaving a furious Titania in his wake.

She stood as stunned and silent as a jilted lover. Her knees buckled, and her foot caught on something on the carpet. She bent down to retrieve it with the automatic impulse of a conscientious manager.

She picked up a large, wooden splinter, its jagged edges as threatening as the man who had just left. It must have fallen off his cane as he thumped it on the floor. She clenched it in her hand, gasping as its sharp edges pricked her palm. The pain she felt would be nothing compared to what would happen if she failed and her uncle was able to buy up the notes. Her stomach roiled as she pondered the possibility there were more debts outstanding. Her uncle was certainly confident she and Thibault would not survive.

What could she do? She held the splinter even tighter, shutting her eyes as she felt the wood pierce her skin enough to make it throb.

She could renege on her promise to the tenants and keep Ravensthorpe at the price of being a cruel landholder, even the thought of which made her cringe. But how much could she squeeze from them, even if she were bent on being ruthless? And what would happen when they left, or her crops were bad?

She could present Thibault with the truth. But what could he do? Sadly, spoon-balancing and well-falling were about all the skills he had. If she could not rescue them from their situation, he certainly couldn't. And the truth would devastate him. He still thought their father the most wonderful, charming man on earth. Which Titania had to admit he was, only she would also have to add fickle, insensitive and occasionally devious.

She could plead with her uncle to lend them the money

with the promise of return on his investment. And while she was at it, she could beg for twenty-five hours in a day and a week's worth of London sun, for all the good it would do her.

No, the only solution she could see was to marry money.

She barely had time to stomp around the floor about a thousand times before Sarah appeared again.

"Miss?" she said in surprise. "Did your uncle leave? You look a fright. What have you been doing?"

Titania's eyes flew to the mirror. She saw a banshee, hair in wild tangles about her head, her face deathly white with matching patches of flushed red on either cheek. She willed herself to stop pacing and began to run her fingers through her hair.

"Doing? Oh, trying to solve problems. Nothing a good set of dueling pistols wouldn't fix."

Sarah rolled her eyes. "Oh, is that all. Well, I'm here to tell you your friend Lady Wexford is here to see you."

Before she even stopped speaking, Claire bustled into the room, pulling her hat off, and dropped into the nearest chair with a loud exhale.

Titania quickly put the splinter in her pocket and held her aching hand in her other, hoping Claire would fail to observe the telltale red marks. She should not have worried; Claire's only observations were for herself.

"Titania! Was the Hagans' rout not a mad crush? Much better than the theater, which I attended the night before. Very dull, and whoever told that playwright he could tell a story must have been a doting aunt, there is no other explanation. Such nonsense."

"What play was it?"

"*A Midsummer Night's Dream*. But tell me, did you enjoy meeting my cicisbei?"

"Ch—what?"

"My admirers." Claire rolled her eyes at her friend's naïveté. "All the fashionable married ladies have them."

"Ah . . . yes, of course. Thank you for allowing them to dance with me."

Claire waved a beringed hand. "It is the least I can do until you get admirers of your own. I did see a tall man speaking with you; who was that?" Her blue eyes sparkled with salacious interest.

Oh, the one with the chest, and the shoulders, and those eyes? That man?

"Uh, I am not sure which one you mean. I met so many gentlemen last night."

Claire gave a satisfied smirk. "Of course, you don't know anybody yet. Well, I know a few gentlemen—actually, one gentleman in particular—who would be delighted to meet you. I will have to find out *that* man's name, though," she mused, tapping her fingernail against her teeth. "He had quite an air about him. I am surprised you don't recall which one I mean."

"Claire," Titania said, feeling awkward as she tried to steer the conversation to something—anything—else, "what are you wearing this evening?" An almost inanely simple topic. Would Claire see through her obvious subterfuge?

Claire's eyes lit up. Apparently her diversionary tactic was successful. "An absolutely lovely gown, Ti, you really should see it. Of course, you will tonight. It is cream colored with pink ribbons. It sets off the Wexford diamonds beautifully. And you?"

"My gown is dark green, it reminds me of the trees at Ravensthorpe." As well as matching a certain man's eyes, but of course that had nothing to do with her decision to wear it.

"What a lovely gown, Miss Stanhope. It reminds me of leaves reaching their peak, just about to fall."

Just like me, Titania thought, nodding at the gentleman with a smile. She had so far stood up for every one of the dances, and her popularity seemed to be gaining as the night wore on. Titania was not so vain as to think it had much to do with her gown, however lovely, nor much to do with anything of her appearance.

It had everything to do with advance reconnoitering. And thanks to her uncle's visit, her position was that much more desperate. Sarah had divulged details of her mistress's vast fortune (and her equally vast desire to be wed quickly) to some of the servants she had met at the various shops to which she had accompanied Titania and Miss Tynte.

Titania was just finishing a dance with some young man who thought Ptolemy was a new tailor on Bond Street when she spotted Claire, accompanied by a tall man with exceedingly proud bearing. Her friend flitted up and began speaking all at once.

"Titania, Lord Gratwick has been pestering me all evening to be presented to you. Miss Titania Stanhope, may I present Lieutenant Colonel Lord John Gratwick of the Royal Fusiliers. He has just arrived from the Continent. He has not had any feminine conversation for some time, so do indulge him, dear, for my sake," she said, patting Titania's sleeve with a condescending air.

"Miss Stanhope," Lord Gratwick began with a bow, "it is true I have been away, but I have not been quite so cut off from Society as Lady Wexford envisions. In fact, I was acquainted with several respectable citizens, all of whom could speak in complete sentences and drink tea from a cup."

Claire, apparently having discharged herself of her duty, drifted away towards another cluster of people. Most of them male, Titania noticed. She turned her attention to Lord Gratwick.

"It is lovely to meet you, sir. Tell me, is there any news that has not yet appeared in our newspapers?"

"I am surprised to hear you peruse the newspapers for news. I did not think it customary for ladies to read the actual news items." The man's eyes crinkled in a grin.

Titania gave him a conspiratorial smile in return. "You would be surprised, my lord, how many ladies tell the males of their household they just want the newspaper for the gossip or the fashion, and then secretly read the sections deemed too sensitive for our eyes. It is our husbands and brothers at the battlefront as well."

The man gave an approving nod. "It is ladies such as yourself, Miss Stanhope, who give the men at the front a reason for fighting."

Titania wondered just how Claire knew this gentleman. He was not one of her lovesick swains, and he did not appear the type who would be one of Lord Wexford's cronies. As he nodded at an acquaintance, she took the opportunity to examine him more closely. He was taller than most of the men in the room, and was whip-thin. He was dressed in the subdued manner championed by the Prince Regent's arbiter of style, Beau Brummell, and had followed Brummell's severely elegant example precisely. He had a full head of blond hair that curled slightly at his collar, but before she could complete her review, she was startled to see his light, watery blue eyes gazing intently at her.

"Lady Wexford told me you were an intelligent woman. She—"

"I can guess just how she said it, too," Titania interrupted. "Were the words 'blue' and 'stocking' thrown about? Perhaps the phrase 'far too inquisitive?' "

The man coughed a discreet chuckle into his hand. "Yes, well, Lady Wexford does not hold learning in as much regard as it appears you and I do. Tell me, have you found anyone in Society with whom to discuss matters of import? Because," he said, leaning closer towards her so as to speak softly into her ear, "I have been back for about a week, and so far have found at least twenty young ladies who know that we are at war, but not exactly why. I would enjoy finding someone to discuss matters beyond last week's weather and next week's rout."

Titania felt the thrill of meeting a kindred spirit. "Oh, my lord, I would enjoy that as well." Claire reappeared just as Titania was speaking.

"Enjoy what?" Claire's eyes glittered with mischief. "Lord Gratwick, are you actually trying to tempt my upright friend into enjoying something?"

"Claire, I enjoy many things—"

Her friend interrupted again. "Yes, books, books and more books. It is a good thing you left the country, Titania, else you might never have seen the world. You cannot experience everything through books, you know." Lord Gratwick shot a reproving look at Claire, then just as suddenly turned it into a sweet smile.

"Lady Wexford, are you accompanying me to my uncle's house? You said you would review his furnishings, and tell me what you think would suit my bachelor housing."

Claire sighed. "Yes, since you insist, but I must demand some recompense. Oh," she said, tapping his arm with her fan, "I have a splendid idea! I believe you mentioned your uncle also had a vast library?"

"Yes, but—"

"If Titania will accompany us, I will look at chairs and moldy rugs until my eyes fall out. I think she could spend some time in your uncle's library? Perhaps advise you as to what should be saved?" Two pairs of blue eyes turned towards Titania's face, waiting for her reply.

"How could I decline? It sounds lovely." Titania did not trust the look in Claire's eyes, but she could not refuse without appearing incredibly rude. She wondered just why it seemed so important for Claire to arrange such a visit, when just a moment before she had expressed disdain for Titania's love of books.

Claire's coterie soon claimed her once again, leaving Titania and Lord Gratwick at the edge of the ballroom together.

"Should we find your chaperone, Miss Stanhope? Although, to be honest, I would prefer to converse with you a bit longer." His mouth curved in what Titania guessed was supposed to be a charming smile. She darted a glance at Miss Tynte, who was engaged in quiet conversation with an older man with twinkling eyes. She did not want to intrude.

"In just a moment, Lord Gratwick. Now, if you would, tell me some of your battlefront experiences."

As Lord Gratwick began speaking, Titania stopped listening as she caught sight of the earl—that troublemaker, she thought crossly—bending to give a young red-haired beauty a flute of champagne. She felt a stab of possessive jealousy spear through her, and tried to nod when Lord Gratwick's conversation paused, her thoughts racing.

How could that girl wear that canary yellow gown with that hair, did she not know it made her look like a rooster? And what was she thinking now, leaning in so close to Lord Worthington? As she was working herself into a state of outrage, Edwin turned and caught her eye. He smiled, one eyebrow raised as his gaze raked her as thoroughly as she had him. He murmured a few words to his companion, who pouted prettily at his departure, and made his way over to Titania.

"Miss Stanhope, what a pleasure it is to see you again." Her stomach fluttered as he bent over her hand.

"My lord," she replied in a voice that even to her sounded breathy. "Lord Gratwick, may I present Lord Worthington, the Earl of Oakley? Lord Gratwick has recently returned from the Continent. And Lord Worthington from the New World. I have just arrived from the very dull country of Northamptonshire." The two men bowed, Lord Gratwick narrowing his eyes in concentration.

"Are you the Marquess of Taunton's son? Lord Edwin Worthington? The author of some battle strategy papers?"

"I am, yes; I am honored you would know my work." Titania wrinkled her brow in thought.

"Lord Worthington, I had not made the connection," she exclaimed. "Of course, you are the author E. G. Worthington."

Oh, dear, now I really am in trouble, she thought. He is a writer, too, which means we have more than our witty repartee in common. And she knew firsthand the meager pittance offered by obscure news journals. An estranged son, those dusty boots, probably an excellent collection of obscure reference books; his finances were probably even worse than hers.

She had put her uncle's splinter into the pocket of her gown to remind her of what she needed to do. She grabbed it and squeezed hard.

Lord Gratwick gave a frosty smile. "I recall some tent-bound general exhorting us to read your theses. He assured us your insights would assist in our battle preparations. In my experience, there is no substitute for actual wartime experience."

Edwin stiffened at the insult, but replied in a mild tone. "You may well be correct, my lord, nothing compares with firsthand experience." Titania hastened to speak to try to stop the impending storm.

"I have read some of your papers, sir, they really are quite insightful." She turned toward Lord Gratwick. "You see, my lord, I have not had the advantage of being at the front, either. I rely on expertise such as Lord Worthington's to give me the information I desire."

"Thank you, Miss Stanhope," Edwin said, sketching her a bow. "It is always a pleasure to be defended by a soldier as fierce in her defense as you."

His eyes crinkled in the corners as he smiled warmly at her, and she felt herself respond with a smile that emerged from the depths of her chest. How nice it would be to have someone smile like that at her every day.

Titania pushed that traitorous thought away, and tried to pay attention to what Lord Gratwick was saying. He was discussing the current state of the war, a conversation that would normally have been fascinating to Titania, who, preoccupied, had to force herself to follow along. Her natural curiosity finally won out, however, and she soon found herself asking questions with as much pesky inquisitiveness as if she were a lively schoolboy, and not a young lady of fashion. The three were arguing over a fine tactical point when Claire returned and interrupted, her eyes as hard as the diamonds clasped around her throat.

"Titania, my dear," she cooed, "you are monopolizing the most interesting men in the room! Everyone is abuzz to know what you are talking about so interestedly. I have not been introduced yet"—she smiled at Lord Worthington—"but as this gentleman is acquainted with Miss Stanhope and Lord Gratwick, I see no reason to bother with formalities." She held out her hand to Edwin. "I am Lady Wexford, Titania's dearest old friend."

Claire peeked up at Edwin through her lashes and Lord Gratwick gave a bleak smile. "Yes, Lady Wexford, allow me to introduce Lord Worthington, who is an author of war analysis, just returned from—I'm sorry, just where is it you have been sequestered of late, my lord?"

"America," Edwin said curtly. "It is an interesting place, where being a gentleman means more than having a title."

Lord Gratwick paused, his politeness warring with his anger, then his courtesy won and he threw his head back and laughed. "Touché, my man, touché."

"Well, no matter," Claire said, a bit peevishly. "I am perishing for a glass of something, and one of you gentlemen must go fetch it for me . . . Lord Worthington, perhaps you will be so kind?" Her voice trailed off expectantly. Edwin bowed in assent, glanced quickly at Titania, and then strode off for the refreshment table. Titania's eyes would not allow her to stop watching him, so she surrendered, enjoying the sight of those broad shoulders as he walked to the other side of the room.

As she watched him, Claire leaned into her ear and began to whisper eagerly, "That is the man! I found out all about him. He is striking, isn't he? Too bad he has no money, at least not until his father dies. And perhaps not even then. His father banished him, you know, and has still not forgiven him. And his father is in very good health."

"Then why did he return?"

"His uncle left him some property, I believe, but there is no money there, either. The beautiful Lord Worthington is going to have to sell himself to the highest bidder, but with those looks, he should be able to secure quite a dowry. Much uglier men have, and he is his father's heir, after all, even if it takes him twenty more years to become a marquess."

Why, he's in the same situation I am, Titania thought. Neither of us can marry for love, or even good companionship. Titania frowned, thinking about what she had to offer a prospective husband: a sharp brain, a broken nose, black hair that would not curl, and an impish brother. She was going to have to work on her charm.

The earl returned, holding glasses for each of the ladies. "Lord Worthington," Claire said, touching him softly on the arm as she accepted her drink, "if you are any indication, I think all our gentlemen should go overseas for a while to allow their . . . manners to mature."

Manners, my foot, Titania thought to herself. Claire's eyes were narrowed in what even Titania could recognize as a sensual glance, and Titania saw her draw a deep breath, her chest rising but not seeming to fall again.

It would be only for practice, Titania told herself, when she impulsively decided to work her own charm on Lord Worthington. Certainly it was not because Claire looked in danger of suffocation, nor was it because Lord Worthington's hair was ruffled where he had run his hand through it, giving him a boyish look that tugged at Titania's heart. She pushed her hair back, straightened her shoulders and smiled directly into his eyes.

"Lord Worthington, when you write, do you have an idea in your head as to the eventual outcome or do you just write as you go and figure out where you are going as you make your journey?"

That was possibly the least flirtatious thing she could have said, and she wished she could retract her words even as she spoke.

"You mean, Miss Stanhope, do I work towards the climax or feel my way through the body of work?" He met her eyes with a smoldering glance. Apparently she was onto something.

She tried again. "I mean, do you strive for perfection the first time, or do you have to grind through several drafts until you are satisfied with the result?"

"Oh, the first time it is hard to find perfection, but it has occasionally happened, at least that is what I have been told. But grinding through each draft, as you say, is also pleasurable."

Titania frowned, confused. "I write also, and I would not say the act of writing is pleasurable, exactly. It is pleasing to have finished it, but perhaps I am missing something."

"Yes, I think you might be, Miss Stanhope. Perhaps I can give you some practical assistance in the near future."

"Yes, that would be . . . educational." She looked at him for just a moment longer, long enough to register that his eyes were regarding her with a gaze she could only describe as predatory. He seemed to realize what he was doing and his face relaxed, his eyes losing some of their greenish glow. Her breathing returned to normal.

"May I request the honor of a dance, Miss Stanhope, if your card is not already filled?"

Titania nodded, her imagination already soaring as she thought about what it would feel like to spend a few moments in his arms. It would probably surpass the joy she felt when she brought the ledger books into balance, and it most certainly would be more fun than watching Claire's bosom heave.

Seeing that Edwin was claiming a dance, Lord Gratwick too advanced towards Titania. "Miss Stanhope, you must do me the honor as well. As someone who has only recently returned from the perils of war, I have not been able to enjoy the fine art of dancing in some time. My lord, here," he said, gesturing negligently to Edwin, "has not that excuse to claim, but he has probably had his head in so many dusty libraries that he has had no chance to enjoy the company of the ladies." He paused very briefly. "It is only natural that he would want to partner the most stunning dark-haired beauty in the room," he continued, nodding in acknowledgment to the blond Claire.

Edwin bowed towards Lord Gratwick. "My lord, since you have been gone longer than I, please take the first dance. Miss Stanhope," he said softly, "I will have to delay my gratification for a few moments. I am noted for my restraint. I believe our dance will be that much sweeter when it finally arrives." Titania held her arm out to Lord Gratwick, who escorted her onto the floor.

Lord Gratwick's grasp, already firm, tightened as he spoke. "Miss Stanhope, I am completely undone by meeting you this evening. You are intelligent, lovely and clearly not a foolish young girl. Is this your *first* Season?"

"Yes, it is. How do you find being home after such a long time?"

"Civilians cannot comprehend just how enervating it is to be at war. I have longed to be home, where the most exhausting thing I could do all day is dance with a charming woman. Oh, and cajole an old friend to introduce me to her old friend. *That* was truly exhausting. I would not want to have faced someone with Lady Wexford's ferocity on the battlefield."

Titania looked over to where Claire was holding court, her trilling laughter audible even over the din of conversation.

"Yes, she has . . . changed since we last saw each other. But then I believe most of us have. I know I am not the same serious girl I used to be; that girl would have disdained an evening such as this as not being sober enough."

"Well, we should get this girl some champagne, then." He grinned, dancing her over to where two glasses were being held out by a yawning footman. He raised his glass to her, saying, "A toast to new acquaintances, may they become old ones soon." The bubbles tickled her nose, and she giggled. Lord Gratwick raised his eyebrows in surprise.

"I did not think goddesses were allowed to giggle."

"Only if the occasion warrants, my lord. We goddesses do not giggle lightly."

"I am pleased you chose to honor me with this special occasion, then. I hope we can find other opportunities for you to unbend from Mount Olympus in the future." His pale blue eyes caught hers in an intense gaze. She almost gasped in relief as she saw Lord Worthington approach to claim her for the next dance.

It felt right to be in his arms, to inhale his intoxicating, musky male scent. She wished he would hold her a bit closer, but she quickly stifled that thought for fear she might blurt her desire out loud. Unfortunately, stifling what was on the tip of her tongue also stifled her ability to make any sort of conversation. The long moments of silence between them made it apparent that he, too, was speechless.

When he did eventually speak, it was not with his usual smooth, low tone. His voice was husky and labored.

"You are lovely, you know." A tiny part of her rigid control relaxed as she exhaled softly. "It's not just your face; it's you yourself. And," he said as he smiled into her eyes, "I must also count your tendency to run, sometimes rather forcefully, into things and people that are of interest: the war, Russell Square . . . me."

Titania laughed, glad he had given her an opportunity to lighten the mood. "Yes, it is one of the more annoying aspects of my personality . . . rushing headlong into things. The war, my family's financial affairs, dancing, poetry, Russell Square."

"And me?" She caught her breath at the intensity of his tone.

"My lord," Titania said, feeling the weight of her uncle's threats lodged in her pocket, "I am always glad to meet someone with whom I can have excellent conversation. I have found such conversation somewhat lacking in London. And I just do not know enough about the weather to keep my company suitably interested." She felt the pull of his gaze on hers, and drew her eyes back up to his face. "I am hoping that you are not alone in your species, Lord Worthington."

She was hoping so more than she was allowed to say. If she could find a man of means who had just half the wit Edwin Worthington so obviously possessed, she would not feel as if she were being dealt a bad hand.

The chances of that, she thought, looking up at the staggeringly handsome man now leading her back to her chair, were slim. She plopped down in her chair, giving herself a good scold regarding impoverished authors as he sauntered away. Miss Tynte returned to sit also, a look of understanding on her face. Titania suddenly felt bone-tired.

"Would it be acceptable to leave now, Elizabeth, rather than later? I am completely worn out."

"You poor dear. The life of a debutante is rather fatiguing, is it not? All those compliments, dances, fancy foods . . ." Miss Tynte wore a slightly mocking smile as she spoke.

"Yes, actually. Have you ever discussed every single permutation of the weather for fifteen minutes straight?"

"Not to mention trying to ferret out which men in this room are worth how much. I can sympathize, truly, I was just making fun of you. You are always so in control, I have to have fun on the rare occasion you are flustered." Miss Tynte patted her hand, smiling at Titania as she did so. "Yes, we can go. I am tired, too. Schooling you and your brother was not nearly as tiring as trying to comprehend what all those turban-headed dragon ladies are saying."

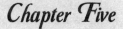

Chapter Five

The next morning, Titania woke before dawn with a headache that matched the dull ache in her heart. Since she had long ago decided that in her own case, misery loved an empty stomach, she headed downstairs in search of something to eat.

Despite the early hour, Miss Tynte was already at the table. "Elizabeth," Titania murmured, reaching for the bread basket, "please tell me that this morning's toast, unlike any of last night's suitors, has some substance to it."

Elizabeth looked up from her book and raised a brow. "And good morning to you too, Titania. You don't think, do you, that perhaps you might be slightly quick to judge? After all, how many of us could hope to pass muster on such brief acquaintance? Even yesterday morning's toast could not hope to live up to such a quick appraisal."

But Titania, set on her course of complaint, ignored her friend. Now possessed of the toast—which even she had to admit was of admirable substance—she said, "How can I even think of selling myself off to the highest bidder, when they are all so shallow, so silly, so tedious, so . . . stupid!"

"Perhaps. But considering the circumstances you might do better to worry about whether they can afford you as well as their stupidity. And, of course, one hates to mention it, but whether they will decide to . . . *bid* at all."

Titania laughed. "Oh, Elizabeth, I am so glad you are here. But tell me, am I unreasonable in my standards? Is it not more acceptable to look for more in a husband than one does in toast? My requirements are not so many, after all, but I *would* prefer to be able to venture off the topics of weather, gossip and fashion once or twice in my wedded life."

"I only meant, Titania," Elizabeth said, equably, "you are rather quick to judgment. You met only a few people last night, and each only briefly at that. Why, by my admittedly less exacting accounting, there were at least four gentlemen present who spoke with intelligence."

Titania took a second piece of toast and pointed it accusingly at her friend. "Then I can only suppose you were hiding them from me, as the only two gentlemen I spoke with last night who could even remotely fit that description were Lord Gratwick and Lord Worthington and I did not observe you in conversation with either of them."

"And nor did I see you speak with Mr. Chaucery or Viscount Arnold, both of whom also match the description. But tell me, was Lord Gratwick the sleek-looking, blond man? And Lord Worthington, he is the one who had all the gossips' tongues wagging, is he not? It is too bad his scandalous past is such fuel for the loose lipped, he is a most handsome man, to be sure."

"And very quick-witted, too."

"Yes," her friend replied dryly, "I am sure it was his *wit* that first caught your attention."

"Well," Titania said, hearing a defensive tone creep into her voice, "*he* knew for whom I was named, and did not ask me, as they generally do, if my parents were *foreign*."

And he *was* quick-witted, she thought to herself, chagrined her friend might think she was being shallow as well as judgmental. Elizabeth had pointedly returned to her book, leaving her uncomfortably alone with her thoughts.

But if she was honest, it *wasn't* Edwin Worthington's intellect that initially attracted her, and kept her thinking about him even as she was steeling herself to accept a loveless marriage.

My mission, she reminded herself, is to find a man of substantial means and property, not someone who makes me all warm and prickly. Prickly does not pay the bills. And alas, as of this moment, neither did anything else.

This morning was not for musing, though; it was fit for

only one thing: a good head-clearing, spirit-raising ride. She knew she was little more than a mediocre horsewoman, but in this case she did not care she was less than excellent. It was almost a relief.

A short time later, she and Sarah set off for the stable. At least, Titania told herself, the imminent danger to life and limb was likely lessened by the fact that most of fashionable London was still safely ensconced in bed for the next few hours. That is, provided they could sleep through Sarah's voluble stream of chatter.

"And then I told Molly, that's Lady Lorimer's maid, that yer family had so much money yer pa used'ta use 'is pound notes to wipe 'is boots after riding. Lady Lorimer has one son, a spiffy gent by the name of 'Arold."

"Arold? Oh! Harold!" Titania corrected absentmindedly.

"That's what I said," her maid replied indignantly. "Anyhows, this 'Arold 'as got 'imself a tidy fortune 'cuz of 'is grandmother, 'oo left 'im everything. Apparently, she was none too fond of 'er own child, so skipped 'im over."

"I met Harold last night. I do not think I would care to meet his father if the gentleman's own mother judged the son the preferable of the two."

Sarah sniffed. "Well, miss, you know you can be a bit picky."

"So I've already been told this morning," Titania replied, pleased they had arrived at the stables so she had an excuse for declining to participate further in this unhelpful conversation.

"He be Whiskers, m'lady," said the sleepy-eyed young groom as he brought round a Cleveland bay gelding who stood a full fourteen hands. "Mind, he be fickle, but nowt but lively under a good hand."

"He is certainly large," Titania said cheerily, hoping a brisk tone would assuage the skeptical look she had seen the boy give her—not to mention the one she suspected the horse might be directing at her behind her back. "I hope you may accompany me, my maid is a bit frightened of horses." She gestured to Sarah, who was muttering threats to a docile little filly eating hay in a nearby stall. The boy nodded, helping her mount the stallion, then led the way out of the yard.

She leaned forward and spoke in the horse's ear. "You

are a stunning specimen, my lord. Show me what you can do." And, since, to her surprise, Whiskers did not appear inclined to get up to anything beyond her abilities, she gave him his head and let him glide into a canter along the sandy track of Rotten Row in Hyde Park. The boy was right behind her, no doubt mumbling comments to himself about her riding she was glad she could not entirely hear.

She was just beginning to relax when a mongrel hound suddenly burst onto the track, barking angrily.

"Damn and blast." Titania felt her world tilt crazily as Whiskers proved her illusions of being in harmony with the beast were just that. Surely no horse could move this fast? She had to steel herself not to close her eyes against the sickening blur that had been the familiar ground beneath them just moments ago.

Not the trees, she almost chanted to herself as she pulled back the reins, willing herself not to terrify the horse further. Please, not the trees. They were her greatest danger.

She could hear the hoofbeats of the stable boy's horse approaching behind her, and tried desperately to cling on to her horse's side. If she could just hang on and keep the horse away from the trees until he could reach her, she knew Whiskers would respond to the young man's greater strength and sure touch. She had never wished more fervently to be a better horsewoman.

Finally, he was there. He grabbed the reins, yanking gently but firmly on them until the horse, responding to the authority in his touch, slowed, and Titania was able to dismount.

"Oh, thank you," she gasped, clutching at her throat. "I do not—Oh!" she squeaked as her hat, already loosened by the wild ride, got caught by a sudden gust of wind and flew off towards the bedeviled trees where it sailed to ground about a hundred feet away. She stared at it forlornly, noting its jaunty little feather was now a lot less jaunty.

"Miss, if y'could just get back up on Whiskers we could go rescue yer bonnet," the boy said. "Yer maid'd have my 'ead if I let ye go wiv'out me. She said she would, so I know." Titania looked at the horse, then at the hat. Then back at the horse. The last thing she wanted to do was get back on that damn horse, but she could not bear to lose her hat.

"I will wait here. You will go fetch the hat," she said in a voice that had caused men twice as old to quake in their boots.

"No, that I will not," the lad said. He gave her a defiant stare, and she knew she would have to choose between losing her hat or losing her dignity. Again. She stared blankly at the horse, now calmly cropping grass, as she weighed her options.

"Is this yours?" a deep voice asked. Titania looked up to see her hat, its feather drooping, but otherwise none the worse, in the grip of a large, ungloved hand. Lord Worthington's horse was even bigger than Whiskers, although he seemed entirely comfortable on it and looked very masculine, Titania thought, wondering at herself for thinking such an unexpected and irrelevant thought.

"Yes, it is. Thank you, my lord." She extended her hand to grab the hat, only to have him hold it out of her reach, just above her head. It was unclear to her how much of her shallow breathing and thundering heart could be attributed to her near-death adventure courtesy of Whiskers, and how much to the sudden appearance of the earl. Perhaps I am having a delayed reaction to almost dying, she told herself optimistically.

He dropped to the ground easily, smiling at her with a knowing smirk, and she knew it was no delayed reaction. The thundering and pounding was nearly all due to him. And he had seen it. Likely the entire humiliating incident. "Could I have my hat, please?"

He sauntered towards her, holding the hat with only his little finger. "And to think, I had thought the Stanhopes renowned for their ability to ride a horse? Ah, Miss Stanhope, you have thrown cold water on the fires of my fantasy." He clutched his chest, rolling his eyes towards the sky.

Titania stared at him, wishing she did not long quite so much to clutch his chest as well. She cleared her throat, nodding slightly to the stable boy, who was gaping at them.

"Lord Worthington, *my* fantasy is that you return my hat. Please do so." She held her hand out expectantly, the other planted on her hip as she summoned every Managing Way she had. He smiled at her, showing white, even teeth and a very unexpected dimple.

"Look here, Lord Worthington, what do I have to—" She stopped short, noticing a little edge of white parchment peeping out of the satchel slung across his back. Without thought, she walked a few short steps, grabbed a small sheaf of papers from his bag and threw them into the air. His face changed from teasing humor to outraged annoyance in a second.

"Why did you do that?"

"I do not know," Titania admitted. She bent down, aghast at herself now that the impulse of the moment had passed, and started to pick up the few scraps that remained close by. Edwin's callused hand reached out and grabbed her by the wrist.

When he spoke, the annoyance was gone, and it was again with an amused tone in his voice. "Tell me, Miss Stanhope, is that the first impulsive action you have ever taken? I am exceedingly honored to be the recipient of your temper. Here," he said, speaking to the stable boy, "go hunt down those papers. I will keep the lady company." The boy obeyed the commanding tone in his voice, scurrying here and there as he chased random sheets that were still being blown by the wind.

"I am sorry." Titania looked down, scarcely daring to believe she had done something so idiotic. "Those were your writings?" She could not imagine ever being able to meet his gaze again.

"Yes, they were mine. I believe you mentioned admiring them last night? What would you have done if you actually disliked them? But do not feel too bad. Here, are you really so remorseful?"

Titania nodded, still looking down. Her right foot was drawing circles in the dust.

His long, thick fingers reached to grasp her chin and raise her face to his, the other hand still holding her hat.

"Don't be. I deserved that for teasing you." Titania caught her breath at how he was looking at her, as if she were a particularly delicious saucer of milk and he were a hungry cat.

"In some cultures," he continued, "it is customary for

someone to owe their lives to the person who rescues them from danger."

"You rescued my *hat*, sir. It shall, one assumes, be indebted to you for eternity." She felt herself starting to grin. He held his finger to her lips. Its warmth acted like kindling on her body, which flamed in response.

"Not just any hat, Miss Stanhope, a very fetching hat." He held it away from his body, as if to examine it more closely. "And it encases your head, which is one of your better features." He cast his eyes slowly down her body and she felt a corresponding quiver in each body part. "I would not wish to judge one feature better than another, I have so many favorites. Which would it be? Your eyes, your lips, your neck, your br . . ."

"Sir!"

"Brains," he finished with a smirk, bringing his eyes up to meet hers.

Titania drew a deep breath. "My hat."

"No, your hat is not a feature."

"No, I meant, you overstep your bounds, sir. Can you please return my hat?"

"Of course—" He held it out, then withdrew it to his side. "But—perhaps it is too soon to entrust you with the hat that now owes its very existence to me. Perhaps you are still in shock? Most ladies would be swooning with gratitude—or terror—after such an experience. Tell me," he asked with a hopeful gleam in his eye, "would you not care to swoon right here?" He held his arms out to her.

Before she could squeak out a reply, he placed his hands around her waist, pulling her to him. She looked over his shoulder, noting the horses were forming a sort of equine sight barrier. Whiskers, in fact, apparently suffering no remorse at having almost killed her, appeared to be dozing on his feet.

Worthington lifted her dratted hat in front of them to, she presumed, further obscure them from view. "And now," he said, firmly, "it appears the hat is about to repay me my kindness."

The thought that at least she could not be seen was replaced by the shock of his warm mouth on hers. She opened her lips to protest, but that was clearly a mistake. No Northamptonshire boy's kisses had prepared her for the use of tongues. His moved into her mouth, causing her spine to melt and her body to feel as if it were being set ablaze with a thousand matches.

Without thinking, she kissed him back, moving her tongue in his mouth as he had in hers. He groaned at her reaction, and his hand moved up the bodice of her riding habit to caress her breast. She leaned closer to him, and ran her hands up his chest as she had been dying to do since she had inadvertently touched him a few days before. It was hard and smooth, and she could feel the muscles lying just beneath the warmth of his skin. She felt them tighten underneath her touch, and he pulled her even closer, stroking her breast with one hand and moving down her waist towards her hips with the other.

Titania heard, rather than saw, the stable boy's approach and pushed Edwin away. "I got all but a few of 'em, my lord," the boy said with glee. "Miss, d'ye feel as if you can ride?"

"Yes, Miss Stanhope, do you feel as if you can ride?" His meaning was so clear it was a single entendre. One which she, of course, should not have had the least hope of understanding. She snuck a glance at his face, which was both amused and lustful. Probably the way he would look if he were having a good time in b—. Titania clamped down on her thoughts before they ran away with her. Like the horse did.

"Yes," she said as primly as possible, "I feel once again fully able to control my horse, Lord Worthington. Thank you for asking. And once again, for rescuing my hat." He handed it to her, and she jammed it onto her head, turning to the stable boy as she did so. "Thank *you* for rescuing the papers. Can you assist me, please?"

"I will help the lady." Edwin's hands moved back around her waist, and he had hoisted her up onto the saddle before she could utter a word of protest. He leaned against the stirrup, looking up at her with the same devilish look of mischief that had been dancing in his eyes before he kissed her. "Miss Stanhope, take good care of that hat. It is now indebted to me for life, after all. I should be a poor protector indeed, if I were to allow you to treat it with further carelessness."

"Good day, Lord Worthington," Titania said, very firmly,

as she and her companion set off, the boy making sure they were going so slowly there was no chance for mishap.

It was later than Titania had anticipated when she and Sarah returned home. She was bone-tired and wanted to sit and unravel her tangled thoughts. But Miss Tynte met her at the door, an alarmed expression on her face. Now what, Titania wondered. Has there been yet another will discovered? Does my recent behavior show on my face? Or was there some emergency at the lending library? She gestured to the sitting room, following her governess with a weary step.

"Thibault is here!" Miss Tynte announced.

"Here?" Titania queried. "But he is supposed to be at school. He's not due out for a few months now."

"He's been sent off to rusticate for the remainder of the term," said Miss Tynte. "Disgraceful behavior! He is not at all suited for the academic life. Apparently there was some mischief with a honey pot and a master's hair pomade . . . You will want to discuss it with him yourself, to be sure. But now we must decide what we are to do with him. Should we tell him what we are about?"

"No!" Titania commanded. "That is all we need. I should not want him to concoct one of his grand schemes and end up with all of us in the soup!"

"Are you in the soup, too, Titania?" an enthusiastic voice sang out. Thibault followed his question by popping his head into the door of the drawing room. He shared his sister's coloring, the dark hair and blue eyes, but in him the shades were more subdued, and his complexion was ruddier than her swan white. His most attractive feature was his sunny, disarming smile—which he employed to winning effect much too often, Titania thought severely.

"No, Thibault, I am not in the soup," Titania said haughtily, ignoring the voice in her head reminding her of her morning encounter. "But apparently you are. Would you care to explain?"

"Oh, don't get all missish with me, Ti," Thibault said with the assurance of an inveterate scamp. "I'll just stay with you until Mr. Tupper calms down. I'll be back at Eton soon enough. But what it means is that if you need someone to stand up with you at those fashionable parties, I'm

your man. I know it must be very hard for you to find
gentlemen willing to put up with your bluestocking ways."
He gave her a saucy wink.

"Thibault, here you are, in probably the worst scrape of
your life, and you have the audacity to change the topic
and throw my superior knowledge in my face."

"Not the worst scrape—" Thibault frowned in delibera-
tion. "There was the time with those chickens and Mama's
dressing gown, and when I stole Mr. Fripp's sermon and
replaced it with—"

"Yes, dear, I did not mean to imply this was your absolute worst scrape. I am certain you will find a way to outdo
yourself. Just please, do not do so while you are here."

"Speaking of being here, I am confused. I thought you
were to stay at our Aunt Beastly's . . . I mean Aunt Bestley's," he corrected quickly at Titania's disapproving look.
"But when I went there, that flounder-faced butler of hers
told me I would find you here. What's going on, Ti?"

"Oh, a slight misunderstanding," Titania said, waving a
hand in dismissal. "It is nothing to signify . . . and it is
much cozier here, don't you think? Stillings and some of
the other servants are on their way, and we shall all be a
little family again."

Thibault seemed to accept her explanation without need
for further query, and Titania heaved a sigh of relief. She
had never kept anything from her brother before, and she
felt like the lowest kind of sister to be hiding things from
him now.

Titania's sanguinity was quickly overturned when the siblings were alone together in his upstairs room.

"So what is really going on, sister? Why are you set up
here rather than with our aunt? Did you have a dustup?"

"I should have known you would not be so easily
fooled." She moved to his bag and removed his shirts,
hanging them in the wardrobe slowly to buy some time
for herself.

"Ti, I know you better than that. I know you would not
upset your plans if there were not something untoward.
You are the most excruciatingly detailed, well-organized,
least spontaneous person I know, and of course I mean that
in the nicest way."

Titania only nodded in agreement, her hands smoothing

out a wrinkle; it was a comment he had made many times before. He lounged back on the bed watching her continue to unpack. Apparently it did not cross his mind to help.

"Take your column, for example," he continued. "You wrote about, of all incredibly dry things, how the Peninsular War and the American blockades at sea affected the price of corn and the fortunes of farming. Those were your main concerns, right?"

Titania nodded again.

"And you were excited by just how boring it was! Imagine if you had been writing a local gossip column, or poetry, or something that was at least interesting to the general population. You probably would have suffered a seizure."

"If you think I would have been overset, just think about how upset my readers would be to find out just who 'Agricola' really was. It would be bad enough a person who was supposed to have nothing better to do than sit in their enormous house counting their ducats was scribbling away like a Grub Street hack. It was hard to relinquish the column to Mr. Powell."

Titania turned and looked sternly at her brother, pointing at him accusingly with the sleeve of one of his shirts. "And are there not enough gossip columns out there anyway? Who needs to know who is courting whom, and always with those annoying initials, so you feel stupid if you do not know to whom they are referring. I would prefer a Society column that reveals not salacious gossip, but a person's feelings or opinions on a variety of subjects."

"That would at least be better than corn prices, although still probably as dull as Mr. Tupper's endless lessons. Say, Ti, do you think that waistcoat would look suitably dashing with that jacket?"

"Thibault, I do not think that waistcoat looks good at all. It is a travesty against cloth."

"Ti, what do you know about fashion anyway? That waistcoat is in the first stare."

"Staring is all I can do at it."

"Very funny. And what party are we attending tonight?" He gave her his most engaging smile as he spoke. Even if he was in the way, at least he would be amusing. Rather like his waistcoat, actually.

*　　*　　*

"As dull as Mr. Tupper's lessons" rang in Titania's ears as she reviewed the correspondence from Ravensthorpe her aunt had forwarded to her. Already she was encountering some unexpected expenses, not least of which would be supporting a burgeoning dandy in his newfound town ways. *Was* she so dull and predictable?

She had taken on the task of managing Ravensthorpe as soon as she realized how haphazardly her parents treated the responsibility, and had embarked on the *Northamptonshire Gazette* column as an outlet for her creative and analytical skills, which were simply not satisfied by deciding whether to purchase a five- or ten-pound roast. Just then, a glimmer of an idea hit her, and she rang the bell for her maid, exercising her newfound impulsiveness before she could regret her action.

Titania was donning her pelisse as Sarah poked her head around the corner. "Sarah," she said with a calm she did not feel, "you will accompany me on an errand, one which we need not mention to anyone else in the household." With a final word to Thibault to stay inside (but out of the way of sweet condiments—Miss Tynte's hair pomade was not to be tampered with), she and Sarah hailed a hackney before Sarah could ask exactly where Miss was planning on going.

The two women rode to the old City of London, to Newgate Street in the shadow of St. Paul's Cathedral. Behind the magnificent church was Paternoster Row, whose shops and signboards proclaimed it the center of London's printing and bookselling trades. Titania searched the addresses until she found a narrow building with a sign that proclaimed the offices of *Town Talk*, one of the more literate—though still scandalous—London magazines of social satire. A crowd was gathered outside the street-level window, eyeing the latest prints-for-sale that the proprietor had pinned up.

Titania left Sarah to join in the badinage outside and entered the premises. She purposely spoke in her haughtiest tone. "The editor is available, I presume, to see me. I wish to be taken to him immediately." Her temerity was rewarded by being immediately escorted to an inner sanctum, where she was seated at a comfortable chair in front of a large desk.

After a short time, the editor appeared, holding a fresh letterpress proof sheet, which was rapidly staining his hand. The slight widening of his eyes was the only indication that a lady in his office was an unusual occurrence. He dropped the proof on his desk. "Good day, Madam. I am Samuel Bell Harris. My assistant said you wished to see me? How may I oblige you?" He took his seat, nervously straightening the various papers strewn carelessly across the desktop.

"I'll come directly to the point, Mr. Harris," Titania said, leaning forward in her chair. "I have a proposition for a column for your newspaper. I have had some modest success writing for our newspaper in Northamptonshire and would like to continue my writing while I am in town for the Season. I have a few samples of my work, if you would be interested to review it. Of course," she continued hurriedly as he held his hand out for the yellowing pages of newspaper, "the column I am proposing for your publication is not at all the same sort that I have been accustomed to doing. But I wish to assure you at the outset that I have some acquaintance with English prose."

Harris began to read her column, glancing up with a look of frank surprise as he finished the first. After reading partway through a second and glancing quickly at another, he dropped the papers on his desk and leaned back in his chair.

"It is not usual, you understand, for ladies of quality to come into my offices at all, and if they do, it's usually accompanied by tears and threats," he said, scraping his thinning blond hair back from his forehead. "Your work is, as you must know, well written; such analysis is hardly what we require, but your abilities and your bona fides are established to my satisfaction. What would you like to do for *Town Talk*?"

"Thank you, sir. I like to think I can write. As for *Town Talk*, well—" Titania began slowly, unconsciously pulling her hair out of its chignon.

"I am interested in informing the public about all sorts of things, whether it be the war in Europe or more intimate details of life. I am about to embark on my first Season, with the purpose of capturing a husband, and I would like to chronicle my progress in a series of columns. I think your readers would be delighted to have the opportunity to have a glimpse into the mind of a Society lady, written, I would hope, with wit and with an informed mind, of course," she said.

Harris regarded her silently for a moment or two, then leapt up so suddenly Titania was startled into dropping her reticule onto the floor.

"Excellent!" he exclaimed. "Exceedingly good! Not the dubious memoirs of some ancient belle, some Mrs. Bellamy or Sally Poole, with principals as old and forgotten as my mother's aunt . . . No! This is fresh stuff, direct from Almack's and St. James's, and only available with *Town Talk*. Capital, m'lady, capital!"

He rubbed his hands together, practically bouncing out of his seat as he spoke. "We'll set Cruikshank to work on caricatures, perhaps hire old Gillray as well if we can find him in a sane moment. And when we reveal—subtly of course—who you are after you've landed your fish, why we'll have trounced the competition yet again and *Town Talk* will be the talk of the town until next Season. And then we shall put out the columns as a book, illustrated of course . . ."

Titania attempted to interrupt, but his eyes were closed and he continued to spin out the future. "Perhaps," he continued enthusiastically, another idea seeming to take shape in his mind, "we could make it into an annual column, and find another young lady to detail her progress next year . . ."

He abruptly gave over his woolgathering and looked directly at her. "After all," he said matter-of-factly, "there's certainly no shortage of young ladies attempting to secure a bit of the ready through marriage, is there?" He blinked a few times, cracked his knuckles, and then seemed ready to drift off to his dream state again when Titania interrupted.

"Now, Mr. Harris, sir, if you please!" Titania said, rather more loudly than she had intended. She was nervous now but determined to make sure he understood what she was proposing. She ticked off her demands on her fingers as she spoke.

"I very much appreciate your enthusiasm, but you must grant me a few concessions before we proceed. We must have a suitable sum paid for my work, with the stipulation that if this venture is a success you will employ me to write for you in the future, although obviously not on the same topic. And you must guarantee my anonymity in perpetuity, so there will be no unmasking.

"Yes, Mr. Harris," Titania said, holding up her hand as he opened his mouth to object. "I will not humiliate my future husband before I've even met him. Nor will I hold my family up to ridicule. As you should well comprehend, it is one thing to marry for money; it's another thing entirely to document the farce for all the world to read. My identity shall remain a mystery."

Harris sighed, then sat back down in his chair, shaking his head. "The column in which your identity is revealed would be our best selling edition. You don't suppose your husband and family would agree if asked, do you?" he queried, a hopeful gleam in his eye.

"No, sir, I do not. That is my proposal, considered and final. If you do not agree to my terms, I should be most happy to approach the editors at *The Satirist* or *The Scourge* . . ." she said, letting the sentence trail off and hoping he would not call her bluff. It had taken all of her nerve to bring herself here, and if he declined, she doubted she would have the nerves necessary to propose her idea a second time.

Titania saw a shudder pass through Harris, most likely at the thought of one of his paper's fierce rivals having the opportunity to print a column he had as much as said he thought would be the *on dit* of the social world.

"Very well, then," he acquiesced. "I agree to your terms."

After Mr. Harris settled down a bit, he and Titania discussed the specifics of their agreement. She would deliver her first column in a week, with publication set for the week following. The first week's grace would give Titania enough time to survey the likely candidates to ensnare, and figure as well who her potential competitors in the Marriage Mart were. The second week would allow Harris to build anticipation in the public. Although the pay would be inadequate to keep most ladies in shoes for a dancing season, it would suffice for now. Harris, perhaps already fending off potential bids for her column by jealous competitors, hinted at a raise should her writing prove as successful as he supposed.

The beauty of her plan was that it depended on Society's notoriously salacious nature to make her column a success, and perhaps establish her as an author, which would enable her to eke out enough of a living so she and her dependents wouldn't starve. That eventuality, of course, would be absolutely necessary only if she were unable to attract anyone with enough of the ready that she could overlook the fact she didn't love him. She swallowed hard when she thought about how she had come to define success.

Dispatch From the Battlefront, March 1813

Choice. Freedom. Love.

Three simple words, but how many ladies have actually experienced even one of these firsthand?

And no, being in love with one's newest gown or making the choice between sherry and ratafia do not count. And please don't even mention being free in the afternoon to pay a visit to one's closest friend.

How many of us can actually choose our future? How many of us will ever get to be in love, the kind of love that makes the poets (notice almost all of them male) embark on prose so rapturous as to make a debutante blush?

That is the life of a soldier, I am sad to say. We are not free to choose our battles, merely to fight them. We are not free to love where we choose. We can only follow orders.

We can only hope the foe is worthy of our efforts, and make the best of things when the smoke has cleared and the white flag has waved.

A Singular Lady

Chapter Six

"What the?—" Titania heard the commotion even before she reached the front door. So much for getting a chance to relax; she'd be lucky if she could even hear herself think.

As she turned the doorknob, the noise grew even louder, if possible. The coach had arrived from Ravensthorpe, apparently accompanied by a full marching band. The entrance hall was filled with the sounds of joyful greetings, exclamations on the length of the journey, and lively phrases commenting on how wonderfully grand but exceedingly sooty the city was.

Titania paused at the doorway, smiling; the familiar voices allowed her to imagine for a moment that she was back in the country, but the warm thought flitted away as she suddenly remembered where she was truly, and why her retainers—most of whom had never before left Northamptonshire—had all descended on the house in Little Chiswick Street.

Titania walked into the middle of the fray and held out her arms. "Welcome, all of you, to London. I am so glad you have arrived; there is much work to be done. Not least of all—Miss Tynte, what have you got?"

Usually coolly elegant, always the picture of decorum, her old friend rose from where she had been sitting on the floor, chuckling with laughter as she clutched two decidedly dead chickens in her hands. "It seems Cook was not certain she could trust the London mongers to know a proper hen." She gestured towards the many baskets littering the floor. "What she will do when this fine collection of country foodstuffs is depleted is probably a question best posed another day."

Thibault bounded down the stairs, his face alight with pleasure. "Ti, for once it is not me causing the ruckus. Look at 'em all, and look how much stuff they have brought. Say, Stillings, did you bring Satan?"

Titania rolled her eyes. Sometimes she forgot he was so young. "Thibault, seeing as how you were not supposed to be here, how could Stillings have known to bring your horse?"

After much fussing and unpacking (Ravensthorpe's housekeeper had sent almost everything in the house except for herself), Titania was able to get Cook in the kitchen with her arsenal of foodstuffs, the younger servants disengaged from each other and settled down, and Stillings properly set up in his bedroom, situated discreetly on the first floor not because of his rheumatism—of *course* not—but because he would have to be on call to open the door for Titania when she and Miss Tynte returned home from their evening's pursuits.

At long last, the hubbub subsided. Titania climbed the staircase back to her own room with a weary tread. She was sure she had experienced quite enough of Society—both high and low—for one day, and now just wanted to sit. Alone. At last.

"Ti!" Thibault yelped, jumping onto her bed and bouncing like an overlarge puppy. Titania clenched her teeth and forced herself not to tear his head off. Verbally, of course; Thibault had already outgrown her height-wise a few years ago.

"Thibault, how many times have I told you that you have to knock before popping into my room like a rowdy brawler? I am resting. Unlike you, I actually had a lot of work to do today. That is, I assume mischief is only a preoccupation, and not an occupation in itself."

Thibault tilted his head up to look at his sister, then nodded in agreement. "You do look a little peaked, crosspatch! You have to remember, sister," he said, dropping his voice to a confidential murmur, "you are not as young as you used to be. You might—" he continued, but before he could finish, Titania picked up a book of Ovid's poems and flung it at his head. Luckily for his artfully disordered hair, it glanced harmlessly off the wall and fell with a soft thud to the floor, the pages splayed open, as disarrayed as Titania's thoughts.

"I am not nearly as old as people would have me be," she grumbled as she picked the book up and carefully smoothed the pages. "And I will ask you to stop reminding me! You are as bad as Electra constantly reminding Orestes to avenge the death of his father!"

Thibault looked blankly at Titania for just a moment, then fell back onto the bed, laughing hysterically. "You, my dear sister, have to have the bluest stockings in the land. You have the ability to turn any conversation into an occasion for study!"

"And so should I, my dear brother," said Titania, fixing an overly sweet smile on her face. "You above all should find more occasions to study. There has to be one Stanhope capable of getting a degree . . . even if it's the wrong one . . . Oh, I wish I had been born a man!"

Thibault looked at her seriously. "No, you don't," he answered. "When you are not pursing your mouth up and pretending to be a thousand years old, you are a good writer, a dab hand at accounts, and you happen to be a lovely lady as well. The only thing you are terrible at is horse riding. You remind me of our mother, and you know more than anyone she was the most wonderfullest creature alive. It is not your fault that it is bad *ton* to be anything more than ornamental."

Could it be Thibault was actually growing up?

She reached out to him and ruffled his hair until he wriggled out of her arms and ran to the glass on the wall.

"Now you've done it," he complained. "Dash it all, Titania! I spent half an hour on this, and now look! I look like the worst kind of cully." She could hear him still grumbling as he marched down the hall.

At least you don't yet look like a boy whose home has been stolen away from him. At least not yet, Titania corrected to herself as she sat back in her chair. She felt a tiny bud of optimism try to blossom in her chest as she started thinking about her column.

That night, when Thibault had been safely sent off in another ludicrously loud waistcoat and Miss Tynte had retired early to bed, furtively clutching a lurid romance novel, Titania settled down to work.

She pulled out some paper and started to make a list of the husbandly essentials, only to pause when she realized her list consisted of "intelligence," "humor," "green eyes" and "broad shoulders." Frowning, she scratched out all the words, replacing them with "wealth," "an agreeable mama" and "some education." This list did not look nearly as exciting as the first.

She let her mind wander to the morning's kiss—her first real one—and how Lord Worthington's arms had felt around her. She had never dreamt that a kiss could be that exhilarating, and that she would be left wanting . . . what? She wasn't sure just what it was she wanted, but she was both dreading and anticipating seeing Lord Worthington's handsome face again. Not to mention the opportunity to converse with him, too, she quickly added to herself.

It was someone she did not want to see who paid Titania her first morning call.

"Titania!" Claire exclaimed, peering at Titania's face. "You must not be used to town life, you look positively done up!"

Muttering "dusty library" and "too many costermongers," Titania showed Claire into the drawing room.

After tea had been poured, and general comments on the entertainment the other evening had been exchanged (yes, the ballroom was far too hot; yes, the musicians could have used more practice; no, the Ponsonby girl did not look well), Claire leaned forward in her seat and gave Titania an intense look.

Oh no, Titania thought. She's going to ask me why I'm here and not with my aunt. What should I say? Quickly, she ran through the possibilities—whooping cough, redecorating, a morbid fear of facial moles—when she realized Claire was not asking anything of the sort.

"What did you think of Lord Gratwick, Ti? He was much smitten with you, unless I am very much mistaken. He has just sold out his army commission; it seems he had to return to handle his uncle's estate. From what I hear, he is exceedingly plump in the pocket, and ever so attractive, too, don't you think? Wex remarks it's a good thing he offered a better title—the silly thing—because otherwise I would have married Lord Gratwick. At the time, of course, there was no thought of Gratwick inheriting his uncle's estate, I believe there were at least three people in line before him. But my loss is your gain, Ti!" she finished gaily.

Titania's hackles were raised instantly. She had found Lord Gratwick intriguing, yes, but something in Claire's tone made her want to dampen her friend's enthusiasm. A shared interest in books and one conversation was hardly enough on which to judge a person. A shared interest in books and the best kiss ever experienced, well, that was another thing entirely.

"Claire, I have only just met the gentleman. I do not think he could have been 'smitten,' as you say, in one evening's encounter. Nor should you suppose that I could ever feel so." She continued, deliberately using her "lecturing to Thibault" tone.

"Lord Gratwick appears a distinguished, learned man and I am looking forward to reviewing his uncle's library," she finished. She quickly cast fresh bait to change the subject. "You must know, Claire; I understand that there is a new modiste who is responsible for creating some of the gorgeous concoctions I have seen the ladies wearing. Perhaps she is dressing you? I understand her name is Madame Felicité."

Claire could not resist. She seized at the new conversational gambit as a trout to a fly, a hound on a fox, a magpie after a shiny coin. "Yes," Claire said, looking with great pleasure down at her own gown, "she made this little trifle for me—you do like it? Perhaps, Ti, I can persuade her to take you on? It appears," she continued, gesturing towards Titania's simple frock, "you are in need of her assistance. It wouldn't do for you to look fresh out of the country, not with so many other ladies making their debut. And I wouldn't say this but to a good friend, but it's not as if you are in your first blush of youth."

There it was again. Could she really look that old at twenty-three? Her eyes drifted towards the mirror over the fireplace. She was relieved to discover that her hair was still black, her face was unlined, and she hadn't suddenly developed a hump. She might have a chance yet. She chuckled to herself, then turned to Claire.

"Thank you, Claire, that is awfully sweet of you, but I would not be able to carry off Madame's gowns nearly as well as you. I will stick with my plainer fare. I can only hope I will have something to wear as I escort those apes to hell."

Claire laughed, a trilling giggle. Titania wondered if she practiced it daily. "Titania, I did not mean to imply you were an ape leader! Be assured, some gentlemen prefer a lady to be more mature than the chits from the schoolroom. Lord Gratwick, in fact . . ." she continued, returning to her theme and restoring Titania's dismay. "Lord Gratwick has remarked the young ladies this year are all so insipid, and cannot discuss anything of import."

Before Titania could reply, Claire glanced at the clock on the mantel, then shuddered in mock horror. "My word, Titania, I did not realize it was so late! I must make some more calls and go home to get ready to return here later with Lord Gratwick. You may not credit this but it takes me positively ages to get ready. Wex tells me it only proves the best things are worth waiting for. Isn't he the dearest man?" she concluded with a simper.

Titania murmured agreement, thinking he must also have the patience of a saint. After Claire's departure, Titania heaved a gusty sigh and retreated to her bedroom before anybody could coerce her into lying again. There would be plenty more opportunity for that later on.

"Where are they?" Titania was dancing with impatience in the drawing room, waiting for Claire and Lord Gratwick to arrive. She was not accustomed to the city way of waiting for events to happen; at Ravensthorpe, she had always been on the move. And since she had long since read every book in her father's collection, she was looking forward to discovering new ones, even if it was in slightly shady company.

"Miss, Lady Wexford and Lord Gratwick are here. May I show them in?"

Claire pushed past Stillings, glaring at him as she headed towards Titania. "As if I were not your oldest friend."

Lord Gratwick's silky voice spoke from behind Stillings. "Do you not mean *dearest* friend?" Claire turned her glower on him, as well. "Ignore him, Ti, he has been a grumpy bear all day."

"If you did not insist on changing your hat not once, but three times, I would not be nearly as grumpy."

Titania laughed, placing her hat on her head as she

spoke. "Never mind that, you two, you are here and we should be on our way. I am so looking forward to viewing your late uncle's collection."

Claire sighed in bored torment, and glided towards the mirror to review her reflection.

"And I have been eager to see you again, Miss Stanhope," Lord Gratwick said, "the best treasure in my uncle's library may not have arrived yet." He waggled his eyebrows significantly at her, and she hastily turned towards Claire.

"Claire, your hat is well worth the delay." Titania did not see what made it different from any other hat she had seen Claire wear, but discussing it made her a lot less uncomfortable than hearing Lord Gratwick pay her such open compliments.

Her uneasy feeling ebbed as soon as she set foot in Lord Gratwick's uncle's library. Titania found books on classical subjects, but also natural philosophy, political economy, history, and a substantial collection of modern works. Perhaps, Titania thought wryly, she should return each morning to reread Coleridge's "Fears in Solitude" to better reflect her present state of mind.

Claire, having absolutely no interest in books—after all, Byron seemed to prefer brunettes, so what was the point?—had by now wandered off in search of more interesting sights—another mirror, no doubt, Titania thought.

As Titania explored, Lord Gratwick seemed content to spend his time observing her, commenting on the various items she found, but without the zest of a true book lover. His present demeanor was a marked contrast to the other evening. Now and then Titania happened to glance over at him in the course of inspecting yet another dusty treasure, and her feelings of alarm returned.

He was looking at her—but no, she saw, rather, he was seeming to look through her, his hands methodically tearing a piece of paper in half and half again until nothing remained but tiny pieces. His face wore an expression Titania could only describe as foreboding, making her grateful her taste in books did not run to Gothic novels, as she would have been shrieking in terror by now. He noticed her scrutiny, and reassembled his genial countenance. Titania noticed his smile did not reach his eyes—indeed, she reflected, it had not once since they had met.

"Titania"—Claire's voice penetrated her thoughts—"is it not time to go? It is not quite ladylike to be hunched over musty books when one could be doing civilized things such as shopping or leaving cards at friends' houses."

"Yes, of course, Claire, Lord Gratwick, I am sorry to get so engrossed. But Lord Gratwick, your uncle's library is stupendous, and I very much appreciate the chance to view it."

"Hmph," Claire snorted. "The question is, Titania, will Lord Gratwick be able to make any money from this pile?" The three stood and surveyed the small stack of books Titania had sorted through. Many more still rested on the shelves.

"No, I think not immediately," Titania replied. "The newer books are not yet in short supply, whereas the older books have obviously been read many times, so a collector would not be interested."

Lord Gratwick moved to assist Titania with her pelisse, a deliberate, measured tone in his voice as he spoke. "A collector, Miss Stanhope, is interested in all sorts of things, especially if they are older."

My goodness, Titania thought, if that is his idea of a compliment, I would not like to hear an insult. She giggled to herself as she pondered what other backhanded compliments he might offer: "Miss Stanhope, your hair is as disheveled as my emotions;" "Miss Stanhope, if all the candles in the world went out, I could still read by the pale light cast by your skin;" or, more to the point, "Miss Stanhope, you are old, with terribly white skin, messy hair and a crooked nose. But by some miracle, I still admire you."

"Titania?" Claire spoke in a querulous voice. "We should leave, if we are to have enough time to prepare to go out. You gentlemen, Lord Gratwick," Claire said archly, patting his arm, "do not need to do nearly as much as we ladies do."

"Ah, but the results are well worth it, Lady Wexford. Especially if the result promises to dance with me this evening. Miss Stanhope, I hope I may have that honor?" Titania smiled weakly, nodding, and began to brace herself for the evening to come.

Chapter Seven

And after he licked her neck, he was going to slide his tongue across her collarbone, gently loosening her gown. He would slide his fingers below the neckline, feeling the fullness of her breasts before he saw them. Then, slowly, slowly, he would pull her gown off her shoulders, exposing her bosom to his gaze. He wondered if her nipples were pale pink, or more of a dusky rose. Then—a sharp tug on his neck startled him out of his daydream.

"Edwin, you must stand still. You are fidgeting so much I cannot get this knot right. I know *you* do not care, but I have a little pride in your appearance." Henri stood in front of him, a white cravat lying limply in his hand. Edwin planted his feet and threw his head back in a stance of ostentatious compliance.

"Is that better? I do not want anyone to mock you because your master looks like a ragamuffin."

"Or a recently returned exile who has spent five years taking tea with bears. There is no excuse for poor grooming, Edwin."

Edwin grimaced. "You sound like my father, and that is one person of whom I do not wish to be reminded."

"So you have not seen him yet? I know you thought you might; have you been hiding out deliberately, or do you think he does not know you are here?"

"Oh, he knows I am here, all right. My Uncle Joseph

made sure of that. Apparently Father is still in the country, but comes to town soon."

"Will he make an effort to see you?"

Edwin's face became tight and drawn. "He has not made any attempt to contact me since he saw me off on that boat."

Henri was uncharacteristically discreet, remaining silent as he finished getting Edwin ready. After it seemed he was satisfied, he stood back, wiping his hands together and looking Edwin up and down.

"Well, will I do?" Edwin stepped back, holding his arms out.

"I wish you would let me purchase some new items, but yes, you will do." Henri smoothed a slight wrinkle and let out a sigh.

"Henri, old friend, I cannot allow that until I am certain I will not be caught by some avaricious maiden on a husband hunt. If I look as if I am in need of funds, no lady will even give me a second glance. If anyone even thought I could possibly be eligible, I would be in as much trouble as when I left here the first time, and that situation will not happen again."

"Not every female is like the Leticia trollop."

"No," Edwin smiled, thinking of Titania and her forthright tongue, "not every female." He slid his finger under his neckcloth, wiggling it in frustration. "Damn, Henri, but these cravats make my neck itch."

"Without a cravat, *my lord*, you would not be fit company for any lady, at least not any you did not have to pay for the pleasure."

"And some of them actually want to be paid with a wedding band, which is why it is best if I look like a pauper." He picked up his handkerchief, stuffed it in his breast pocket, and set out, in search of his bluestocking enchantress.

Just then, his enchantress was nose deep in one of her favorite books, Julius Caesar's commentaries on his military campaigns, and was not thinking of broad-shouldered men fussing with their neckwear. But she did find her thoughts straying from Gaul. Surveying the enemy—in her case, all the eligible bachelors on the scene—with an eye to attracting their interest meant that she had to speak their language, attack them on their own field of battle, so to speak.

The only weapon she needed, Miss Tynte had always told her, was confidence.

"I am confident. Confident I will be attracted only to the most penniless man, confident I will say something that will give some bachelor a disgust of me, confident I will make a face and show exactly what I think," Titania declaimed to herself as she waited to dress for yet another party. It was to be at the Clifton's (the earl and his countess, whom Titania had heard were a somewhat ill-suited couple whose passions were cards and cuckoldry, respectively), and Miss Tynte had promised to introduce her to the son of one of the dowagers who had bent her ear a few nights earlier.

Just before she left her room, she grabbed the fragment from her uncle's cane and placed it in the pocket of her gown. She felt it brush against her leg as she moved towards the mirror. If nothing else, it served as a palpable reminder of everything she had to lose.

As Miss Tynte and she drove up to the house in their carriage that night, neither one of the ladies could suppress a gasp of surprise.

"This house is three times the size of Ravensthorpe!" Miss Tynte narrowed her eyes as they entered. "With one-quarter of the taste."

The house, Titania had to agree, was beyond opulence, with gilt and scagliola and paintings and a chandelier big enough for her, Thibault and Miss Tynte to swing from. Not, she assured herself hastily, that she had any plans to do anything so shocking. She could not speak for Thibault.

As she and Miss Tynte made their way into the crowded ballroom, Titania smelled the tang of ladies' perfumes mixing with the aromas of food being toted around by footmen in red jackets and smart cream-colored waistcoats, who looked almost as regal as the guests. Underlying those pleasant aromas was the unmistakable odor of rank sweat, the sweat of people who were nervous, drunk or just not all that fond of bathing. The colors, smells and blazing lights, along with the thrum and chatter of hundreds of people gossiping and flirting, were overwhelming. Titania tried to move towards the corner of the room to gather herself, but was stopped by a brightly colored clump of men.

"Titania," one of the clumps yelped, "look who I found!"

When Titania could focus without feeling faint, she saw her brother surrounded by three young men. Each of their waistcoats was as loud as the last, a profusion of swirls, color and, Titania could almost swear, a few animals and a fanciful depiction of the solar system.

"How lovely to see you, Mr. Smith." Percival Smith was Claire's younger brother, and Titania had not seen him since he was in short pants. "And these two?"

"Ti, that is, Miss Stanhope, let me introduce you to Charles and Colin Chubb."

"So very pleased to meet you," the twins said in unnerving unison.

Mr. Smith swept Titania a deep bow and said, his voice cracking, "How do you do, Miss Stanhope? You are looking divine this evening."

"Ti, you won't believe it!" Thibault interrupted. "Percy, Charles and Colin have all been sent to rusticate too!"

"Strangely enough, I would believe it. So, what kind of scrapes are you up to now?" She smiled at them warmly.

"Oh, no, Miss Stanhope, think no ill of us now," said one of the twins—Colin?—affecting a sober mien. "We're gentlemen now, and those days of childhood are behind us." He accompanied his comment by gazing off into the distance with what he apparently hoped was a devastating Byronic sigh.

"Is that so? And just what do gentlemen do with themselves, since they're not quite out of school?" She was hardpressed not to giggle, but knew Thibault would never forgive her if she did.

"Oh, you know," Percival said, staring at a point above her head. "Dressing in the latest stare of fashion, eyeing the horseflesh at Tattersall's, composing verses to the fairest of Belles . . . that kind of thing." Thibault started hopping up and down in his excitement.

"Oh, Titania, it's going to be wonderful! We're resolved to be young men of passion and deepest melancholy, and we shall sigh a lot. And of course," he mused, "as Lord

Byron did, I might find time to go to Gentleman Jackson's for a few lessons."

"You could use that kind of instruction," Titania replied, sliding her finger along her nose. "Next time you practice boxing, though, could you let me know so I can beg another engagement? I have no wish to end up with another disfigurement."

"It is no disfigurement, Miss Stanhope."

She caught a glimpse of amused green eyes and that devastating dimple before she remembered what had transpired between them the other morning. She found herself suddenly fascinated by her shoes.

"Good evening, Lord Worthington."

"Miss Stanhope, would you introduce me to your young friends? As you have already informed me, my clothing is of an unseemly provincial cut, and it looks as if these gentlemen might well be able to assist me in my plight."

The four boys straightened, fingering their finery with pride.

"Lord Worthington, I am pleased to introduce you to these young men. This is my brother, Lord Ravensthorpe, and his friends, Mr. Percival Smith and Mr. Charles and Mr. Colin Chubb. I believe you were introduced to Percival's sister, Lady Wexford, the other evening. This is the Earl of Oakley."

"The pleasure is mine, gentlemen. I would be glad to find some new friends in London; those I have made have proved to be most enjoyable." He shot a conspiratorial glance at Titania, who rushed to speak before she had a chance to blush again.

"Lord Worthington has just returned from some years abroad in Nova Scotia and New England, Thibault."

"Thibault?" Edwin asked. "And Titania? It would seem your parents were rather fanciful sorts. Do you have any other siblings lurking about, perhaps Ophelia or Romeo or something? Hopefully not a Malvolio . . ."

"America!" Thibault interrupted. "What an adventure! Are there really forests there as big as Wales? Is it true that men can make their fortune overnight, even if they're not gentlemen? Did you meet the noble savages?"

"Enough questions, Thibault," Titania said, trying to look stern, but unable to suppress a smile. Turning to

Edwin, she said, "My lord, I must apologize for this scamp. He has not learned yet to hold his tongue."

"Neither have you, Miss Stanhope," Edwin whispered as he bowed deeply towards her. Before she figured out what he had meant, he spoke again, this time for everyone's ears.

For once, Titania blessed Thibault's penchant for interruption. "My lord, you must tell us more about America. And Smith here was just saying he heard you were a boxer?"

"Being handy with your fists has its advantages. It can extricate all sorts of people from unpleasant situations. Especially if they are the impulsive sort." He looked at Titania as he spoke, and, spurred by her new impulsive self, she winked at him. He gave a surprised laugh, then winked back.

Thibault's face showed his confusion. "Impulsive? Do you mean if someone is acting dangerously?"

Edwin's face wore a knowing smile. "Acting dangerously is exactly what I meant." Titania felt herself blush scarlet. "But, gentlemen," Edwin continued, "have you seen any matches worth reporting since you arrived in town?"

Lord Worthington and the boys were soon in deep discussion of the Fancy, and were loudly describing boxing matches none had ever seen as Titania excused herself to find Miss Tynte. The younger men were too engrossed in conversation to notice her departure, but Edwin gave her a look that made her insides churn.

She could not lie to herself. She wanted him to slide his tongue into her mouth as he had done that morning. Oh, and if his hands happened to touch her breasts, that would be nice, too. She tried very hard to look completely bland as she arrived at Miss Tynte's side.

"Titania! My dear, please allow me to present my cousin to you, Your Grace—Miss Titania Stanhope. Titania, this is the Duchess of Bellingham. Her son, Lord George Ward, has just arrived in town, and the duchess is joining him for the Season."

Titania made a curtsey. She had never met a duchess before, and was surprised when the noble lady, so far from looking down her nose, actually beamed at her.

"Miss Stanhope, your reputation precedes you, and I find mere descriptions do not do justice to your celestial charms.

Ah, here is my son now!" the duchess said animatedly, waving towards a stout man who was just then escorting a dance partner back to her chair.

"George! Please approach us; there is someone you must meet." She spoke confidingly to the two ladies. "He is my third son, you understand, after William and Henry. We thought he would go into the church, but so far," she sighed, "he has shown no aptitude. Not that he is not— Ah, my love, here you are. Miss Stanhope, may I present my son, Lord George Ward? George, this is Baron Ravensthorpe's daughter, Miss Stanhope." The man looked confused. "Miss Stanhope of Ravensthorpe, George," his mother said with a meaningful look.

"Oh, Miss Stanhope," George said eagerly, "I have heard of your beauty, but I must say the rumors do not nearly do you justice. Your beauty would make an angel blush." He looked quite pleased with himself at this utterance.

It was her second, no third, divine compliment that evening, and just as foolish as the rest. "Thank you, my lord. It is not often one puts one of Heaven's caretakers to the blush. I am honored." He gave her an extremely contented smile, then drew a deep breath, glanced at his mother, and spoke in a ponderous tone.

"Miss Stanhope, I have heard of your reputation for loving books, and I would like to invite you to join me at Mrs. White's literary gathering this week . . . It is a small weekly salon, frequented by people of taste and culture."

"I would be delighted; I always enjoy meeting new people." Maybe someone there would be able to explain the *ton's* passion for angels. She looked up at him, realizing he was having some difficulty glancing down at her. His cravat was nestled uncomfortably high on his neck, while his coat seemed to be cut just a little too tightly, or perhaps he had just eaten too many cakes since arriving in town. He cleared his throat, setting his heavy jowls into a merry jiggle.

"Miss Stanhope, would you allow me the honor of this dance?" Titania caught an encouraging look from Miss Tynte, then nodded, placing her hand in his.

Dancing with Lord George left Titania plenty of time to look for a pair of broad shoulders. Already, she missed the agonizing feeling of excitement she had in the pit of her stomach when he was near. Not to mention that tongue thing—but if she kept thinking *that* way, soon she would be as sweaty as Lord George, whose gloved hand had somehow managed to seep some unpleasant moisture onto hers.

More partners, more of the same questions, the same feelings of hopelessness. As Titania waltzed and quadrilled and performed any number of other fancy dances, she tallied her debts, reviewed her prospects, and lifted her chin. Her father might have left her bereft of any kind of reasonable future, but he had bequeathed her his indomitable spirit, his gambler's heart, his reckless fealty to those whom he loved. She could not deny his legacy. It was up to her to deny what her uncle thought was his.

Dispatch From the Battlefront, March 1813

The rabbit runs to his warren, pursued hotly by the foxes . . . the pheasant strolls about in his field, happily unaware that a predator is lurking nearby.

Unlike these hapless animals, the male must be lulled into quiescence, then captured before he realizes he's been taken.

The other hunters in the field are formidable opponents, too: there is the devious fox, a red-haired charmer who beguiles with her seemingly innocent gestures, only to coerce the prey into a compromising situation; the gray-eyed wolf who bares her teeth and snarls at all but her chosen mate, whom she attacks with all the energy that orgeat and sweetmeats can provide; the hunter who has felled her chosen mate, but continues to prowl the field, bedecked in diamonds and roses, and armed with knowledge of the quarry that no single lady has the advantage of; the old hound dog, who is not hunting for herself, but for her young dog of a son, who is already too fat and too lazy to even let himself be captured.

The next offensive line: to narrow the field to the most likely targets, and assess their strengths and weaknesses. Until next time, I remain

A Singular Lady

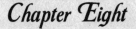

Chapter Eight

After a brief, nerve-wracking silence, Mr. Harris hooted in delight as he read the first three columns Titania presented to him. "This is astounding! Terrific! Devilish good! Miss Stanhope, if I may be so bold, I never suspected your gender held such, er, interesting opinions. It is refreshing, to say the least, and sure to titillate our readers, both those moving in your circles and the rest of us, noses pressed against the glass."

Titania gave a self-conscious smile, trying to get accustomed to her new editor's enthusiasm. Her previous assignment, dealing as it did with such mundane matters as crop prices and the availability of decent brandy and fine silk, had never provoked such a reaction from the *Northamptonshire Gazette*'s editor. Mr. Harris tugged his hand through his hair—a gesture that was going to cost him the few blond strands he had left if he made a habit of it— and regarded the pages of close writing more intently. The cadence of his voice seemed to increase in proportion to his zeal.

"Miss Stanhope, the illustrator who provides the images for your words is going to do a bang-up job. I rather like the idea of a battleground covered with ladies and gentlemen engaging in combat. Yes, I think we might even rival Mr. Ackermann's pretty papers if we do it right. I think," he mused, pulling out a particularly long strand and wrapping it around his little finger, "we shall put your column

on the cover, in a neat box. That'll draw attention to it!"
He gave her a triumphant grin, as if daring her to think of
something better.

Titania was stunned to silence by what he was proposing;
her only point of comparison was her prior column, and
that was buried between the local financial transactions and
the positions-wanted section. To have her work on the front
cover of a London newspaper was more than she had
ever imagined.

"And of course," Mr. Harris continued, "we will sign
you to an exclusive agreement, and if it proves, as I am
guessing it will, to be popular, *Town Talk* will gladly take
only a small percentage of any book sales."

Book sales! Titania looked in disbelief at her familiar
writing covering the pages Mr. Harris held in his hands,
and began to understand what the "power of the written
word" might mean to her in her current circumstances. If
she was to get published, and the book was a success, she
might not face the looming financial disaster at all. In fact,
she might never have to get married. Somehow, the idea
did not fill her with glee.

Mentally dismissing the image of growing old by herself
with only a group of even more elderly caretakers to keep
her company, she listened as Mr. Harris gave her the sum
she could expect upon signing her contract for the column.
It was much more than they had originally discussed, and
she was relieved to realize that she could comfortably meet
her expenses for the Season, although she still did not have
enough to sustain Ravensthorpe for as long.

Mr. Harris, meanwhile, had finally unearthed a writer's
contract from under the massive pile of papers on his desk
and was holding it out to her, his face alight in excitement.
"Miss Stanhope, please take your time reviewing this
agreement—but not too long, mind!—and I will begin to
query which of our caricaturists would be most adept at
bringing your words to life. Ah!" he said, rubbing his hands
together. "I feel like a boy in short pants. This is the dawn-
ing of a new era!"

Titania, still overwhelmed by her editor's flights of
enthusiasm—and turns of phrase—accepted the sheaf of intimidating looking papers and stuffed them into her reticule, its sides bulging out preposterously.

"Mr. Harris, I must thank you for the faith you appear to have in me. You have afforded me the courtesy of treating me like a writer, not a female who writes, and I am beyond grateful. You cannot know how difficult it is to pretend to be something you are not." Titania halted her words, a tremendous lump in her throat threatening to engulf her in tears. Really! Of all the moments to cry! What must Mr. Harris think of her?

Her editor quietly withdrew a large handkerchief from his pocket and was even now holding it out for her, a gleam of understanding lurking in his eyes. She took it quickly, blowing her nose and wiping the errant tears away from her cheeks.

"I must apologize, sir," she said when she could speak again. "I do not usually get in a pucker like this. I will return this to you later," she said, gesturing to the by now sodden handkerchief.

"Keep it," he said, waving his hands towards her. "Consider it a bonus." She laughed, then rose and pushed a strand of hair behind her ear.

"I will review these papers. Once I am certain everything is in order, and I am sure it will be, we will strike a bargain." She gathered her shawl and reticule and left the office, her thoughts in a jumble as she collected Sarah, who was waiting outside.

She walked along Paternoster Row, thinking to herself, as Sarah chattered on. To be free of the constraints under which she had placed herself. Perhaps to be able to choose her own future.

Half an hour ago, it was easy to slip into the role she, and everyone around her, had created for herself: caretaker, advisor, the sturdy Titania. But if she were able to create a new future, a new Titania, what did that mean? She was dismayed to realize that what she had hoped for—freedom from her responsibilities—was also what scared her. Maybe, she thought disgustedly to herself, my wildest hopes will be realized and my writing won't be successful and I won't get published and I won't be able to support my family and I will have to marry some random lord with enough money and tolerance to keep my family going. Is that what you want?

As Titania was chiding herself, Sarah stopped her own

monologue and started plucking at Titania's sleeve urgently. Titania looked up to see Lord Gratwick, his blond hair no more than ruffled in the breeze, his walking coat immaculately clean despite the dirty city streets. *Why did the image of scuffed boots and a disarranged cravat seem so much more appealing?*

"Miss Stanhope," he said, sweeping her a deep bow. "I see you are alone. Might I foist my presence on you? I have been anxious to see you in the hope you will agree to visit my uncle's library and find me a treasure. Not that I can hope to find a treasure as lovely as you." He placed her hand firmly on his arm, and they started to walk, Sarah a few paces behind.

Titania's tone would have quelled a less determined man.

"Of course there are better treasures in books read and cherished than in a person's beauty merely admired, my lord. With proper care, books last many lifetimes, while beauty fades over time. I would enjoy perusing your collection again; I am actually in search of some items from my own library I did not think I would require while in town."

"Require?" Lord Gratwick queried, his light eyebrows shooting up into his forehead. "I did not realize ladies required anything more than a new gown and a ball to show it off at. At least that is what our mutual friend Lady Wexford has told me repeatedly after I have tried to engage her interest in the opera."

Titania gestured towards a shop door. "I am going here, Lord Gratwick; you need not accompany me."

"Oh, but I want to, Miss Stanhope," he said, swinging the door open for her. He waited patiently while she made her purchases: a sober waistcoat for Thibault (something Titania's sense of style, if not Thibault's, was desperately in need of), a new pair of gloves for Stillings, whose old ones had been destroyed in a chicken's fruitless dash·from Cook, and some ointment for Miss Tynte's feet, which were not accustomed to the vast amount of dancing to which she was subjecting them.

Her purchases paid for, Titania allowed Lord Gratwick to gather her bundles and walk her outside. The sun was beginning to set, and she glanced at the sky, hoping she could make it home in time to do some writing before she went out for the evening. Lord Gratwick inclined his head to hers and began to speak.

"Miss Stanhope, it has been a delight and a saving grace to meet a beauty like you in this city that is so filled with dirt and ugliness. At times London almost rivals the ugliness of the battlefront, but I would not shock you with stories from my time there." Titania blinked up at him, astonished to discover how many things he had just said to make her get into a pucker.

First of all, there was no way he could possibly admire her as he said he did; although Titania was enjoying her first Season, she was no green miss to be taken in by a suave gentleman. He hadn't displayed any of the signs of appreciation Titania had started seeing on her admirers' faces and which she was able to recognize even as a naïve girl of sixteen. And he spoke with none of the passion she knew was essential to the process of falling in love—not that she had experienced any of that firsthand, of course. Secondly, she was passionately interested in what was happening at the front, and continually frustrated that so many well-meaning men refused to tell her. She had thought Lord Gratwick was different. When she replied, her tone was sharp.

"Lord Gratwick, I am not a silly girl who is only concerned with new gowns, the price of tea and vouchers to Almack's." She picked up her stride a bit, hoping to make it home faster. He kept pace with her easily, but she could hear Sarah start to puff behind her. She slowed again.

"I did not think you were, Miss Stanhope. I was being selfish, since I do not want to recall that horror when I am here enjoying your company. Forgive me. Tell me, do you plan on attending Almack's tonight?"

"No, I am engaged to attend a literary society with Lord George Ward. And I have not yet received vouchers to Almack's anyway," Titania replied, feeling chagrined she had gotten so angry.

"Then I shall not attend either, Miss Stanhope. I would rather stay at home than ponder the evening without a chance of seeing your fair face."

"Oh, please, Lord Gratwick, there are plenty of young ladies who are just as lovely to look at—many more so—

than I. Thank you for the pretty words, but I cannot believe you."

He raised his eyes heavenward. "You wound me, Miss Stanhope. May I wish that you find the night just a little duller without me? Ah, if that were only true, I could die a happy man, slain on the battlefield of love."

He could not think he would impress her with that ridiculous speech, could he? And if he did, he certainly did not know her very well. She was Titania of the Practical, Managing Ways, not someone who swooned if some man spoke pretty words at her.

"Ahh, Lord Gratwick, your duty is discharged. That is my house over there. Thank you very much for your assistance. Sarah can take the packages from you." She held her hand out to him, hoping he would not say anything else to embarrass her.

"Good-bye then, Miss Stanhope. A pleasure to run into you today."

"Good-bye, Lord Gratwick." She scurried into the house after Sarah, leaning back against the door with relief. She raced upstairs, pulled out her writing materials, and started scribbling frantically. At least Lord Gratwick's presence was inspiring, even if it was not the kind of inspiration he had been hoping for.

"There. Finished." Titania looked at the words she had just written, a contented smile on her face. Her self-satisfaction was interrupted, however, by a knock on the door. Goodness! Was it really that late? She heard Lord George's voice downstairs as she heard Sarah's footsteps heading towards her door. She hid the papers and ran to the door, opening it just as her maid was about to enter.

"We are certainly running late, are we not?" She gave Sarah what she hoped was a charming smile.

"Mmph. I was thinking the green tonight, miss, and you can stop trying to win me over." Sarah strode over to the wardrobe, pulling out the gown. Although Titania had seen it when she had purchased it, she could not help but gasp when she saw the gown again. Sarah must have correctly interpreted her response.

"It *is* lovely, miss. You will look a right treat in it, too. Now, mind, 'urry up, you do not want to keep that lord 'oo's downstairs waiting. 'E looks like 'e needs 'is feed reg'lar."

Titania let out a giggle from underneath the fabric. She emerged from its folds and stood, patiently, while Sarah adjusted it. She batted Sarah's hands away when they reached for her hair.

"Never mind that now, Sarah. Just twist it up. You know it all falls down anyway."

"It wouldna if y'could keep your 'ands out of it. I swear—"

"I know, I know. Just make it neat, will you please?"

Straightened, smoothed and neatly coiffed, Titania descended the stairs to where Lord George waited.

"Thank you, my lord, for your patience. Should we go?"

"Yes, indeed, Miss Stanhope, we should. Your cousin, she is coming as well?"

"Yes, of course I am, my lord." Miss Tynte appeared from the drawing room, nodding at him.

"Good, good. Ladies, shall we?" He led the way out to the carriage, which was emblazoned with his father's crest. He gave a little satisfied sigh, then helped the ladies up. The carriage lurched as he entered, and he settled himself in the backwards seat facing the ladies.

Lord George had an expectant look about him, and he kept rubbing his stomach as if he were a Buddha attempting to grant his own wish. That there were likely to be some erudite discussions at the evening's salon did not seem to make him uneasy; from his comments, Titania gathered that he was looking forward to amusing himself at the refreshments table rather than indulging in any literary fancy. He wandered off topic as blithely as she spouted ancient aphorisms.

". . . I was just saying to my friend Quigley, right after he had the audacity to question if a tangerine waistcoat was appropriate with mulberry pantaloons. I mean, they are both types of fruit, are they not? Quigley would have it that only that light brownish color would work. I ask you, is there such a fruit as 'light brownish?' I think not." He nodded his head in satisfaction. He poked himself in the nose, thrust his head out the window, and began to yell instructions to his coachman.

Titania leaned over to Miss Tynte, keeping her voice very

quiet. "Apparently the lord is not familiar with the pear. I think he is a good soul, but watching him think is like seeing a cat try to nudge a milk bottle open; they both know they want to do it, but they just are not sure how."

Mrs. White's house was ablaze with candles. There was a general hubbub of activity that foretold a lively evening. Once inside, their hostess emerged from the vast array of lights to greet them.

"My lord, how honored I am to have you join our little gathering. I was not sure you were going to return after the dull talk we lapsed into at your last visit. You would think, my dear," she said, turning to Titania, "that we were all prosing on in Greek for all that Lord George paid attention. But we have not met," she declared, holding out her hand, "I am Mrs. White, the friend to all these dullards."

Titania shook her hostess's hand as Lord George quickly made the introductions. Mrs. White appeared to be about forty, although Titania thought she might be a bit older. Her face was marked by laugh lines, and her dark eyes seemed to dart about as if looking for the next bit of fun. She reeked of confidence, the confidence of an older woman who was aware she was still attractive. She put a hand on Lord George and Titania's backs and pushed them forward.

"Please come meet everyone. We gather once a week on Wednesdays when all those other people are traipsing over to Almack's. I do not like to deny entrance to anyone, so I thought it would be a fine thing to open my house when so many people are pining to go somewhere, if only to forget they are not allowed at that dungeon of dragon ladies. And as Lord George can attest, my table is just a bit finer than that stodgy old place."

Titania let herself be swept up in the tide that was Mrs. White, landing in a large room filled with people. One of the gentlemen stepped forward, directly in Mrs. White's path.

"Honoria, I beg you, do not let them discuss Byron one more minute! I am sick to death of him!"

"That is only because he has found fame with the same kind of scribbling you do, Julian," Mrs. White replied. "If you would just find your own voice and follow it, you would be as well-known as he is."

The man who had approached her was young; Titania guessed he was probably around her age. His dark blond hair hung loosely around his face, bits of it dangling romantically in his eyes. His face was a striking contrast between strength and beauty—straight, dark eyebrows on top of the most gorgeous brown eyes Titania had ever seen. He paused dramatically in the course of his recitation, and his eyes paused on Titania, moving on after just a moment. Titania discovered she was quite piqued to be so nonchalantly regarded.

She grabbed a glass of champagne—after all, her father had taught her some courage came from the bottom of a glass—and took a sip, its bubbles tickling her lips. She snorted as one flew up her nose, and it was then the poetic angel took notice of her.

"Egad, Honoria, your champagne is wounding your guests!" he exclaimed. "Ah, if only we had the nectar of the gods to drink, for then even the most . . . sturdy ladies would be able to imbibe."

Titania was livid. True, she was not a fragile waif, but she was not an ox. In defiance, she drained the rest of her glass. Mrs. White, rather than being embarrassed at the man's untoward behavior, gurgled in amusement and chucked him under the chin.

"Julian, my sweet, you are a bit too blunt. And in this case, you are wrong. Miss Stanhope, may I present my ill-mannered son, Julian Fell?"

Titania extended her hand to Mr. Fell, a smile that showed very little teeth and even less good will plastered on her face.

"Miss Stanhope, I beg your pardon for my indiscretion. It is not often one meets a goddess from Mount Olympus, and I did not mean to cause offense. As my mother will no doubt tell you, I have been accustomed since I first put A to Z to speaking in more elegiac phrasings than most other mortals. But you, Miss Stanhope, are a star in the firmament, a timeless melody that wafts on the wind like a feather, a . . ."

Titania threw her hand up in surrender.

"Stop. In the space of one minute, sir, you have likened me to a divine being, a stellar object and a song. You must stop before my head swells like a balloon, and I cannot fit through the doorway of your mother's lovely house." Titania was not expecting the charming, slightly boyish grin he gave her.

"Miss Stanhope, forgive me. But there are so many buffoons and charlatans and hangers-on who frequent my mother's salon I have become callous. I am not suited to be a knight errant," he said, gesturing down at his slight frame, which seemed built to hang clothes on, "and I fight my battles as I can."

"Understood, Mr. Fell," Titania responded. "I myself was used to shielding my parents from harm; it is hard, is it not, when the ones who sired you are in need of some gentle protection?"

Julian moved towards Titania, gesturing towards a sofa in the corner of the room that was almost obscured by the cluster of people thronged in front of it.

"Would you care to sit and tell me what brings you to my mother's gathering? Surely it cannot be the possibility of discussing learned tomes!"

They walked together to the sofa, an elaborate striped concoction with claw feet and exceedingly uncomfortable-looking bolsters perched at either end. Titania perched in one corner, while Julian settled deep into the sofa as much as its uncompromising fabric would allow.

"Now I know you are not the usual idiot who comes here," he continued, "I need to know more about you. You are not in your first Season, are you? You look a little older than the usual debutante. But I have never seen you before, and despite appearances to the contrary"—he coughed discreetly—"I am interested in beautiful women, and would have noticed you if you had been here before."

Titania blanched, both at his mentioning her age and his direct response to a question she had not asked.

"No, this is indeed my first Season, Mr. Fell, despite the fact that I am a wizened old crone. My father has only recently passed away, and before that . . . well, before that there were things to be done, and somehow I was the one to do them. All of them, from managing servants to planning menus. Otherwise we would have starved and wandered about naked."

"Your parents sound worse than my mother. She, at

least, always ate properly. But you do not seem at all the type of person to emerge from such chaos."

Titania smiled ruefully. "I have been told I am a bit controlling, but I do not think I had much of a choice. I did have a brief, very brief, period of rebellion, but my parents applauded me for that. They worried I was too serious." Julian leaned forward, his eyes lit with a curious glow.

"What kind of rebellion?"

"I went horse mad, and refused to wear anything but my favorite black habit, even to breakfast and whatever social gatherings I was allowed to attend."

Mr. Fell chortled. "Oh, you would not believe some of the atrocious choices I have made! There was a period of about six months when I would only wear white, all white all the time. I looked even more angelic than I do now."

"Do you often get compared to angels, then? I, too, have been so compared to celestial beings I am surprised that no one asks to see my wings."

"That settles it," Julian said. "You and I are destined to become friends. And your companion, the lord rather alarmingly stuffed into his waistcoat? Is he your friend too?"

"Not yet, but I believe he has a good heart. He takes such a wonderful enjoyment in things. I envy that."

"Especially food," Mr. Fell added.

"Especially food," Titania agreed. "And of course he likened me to an angel when we first met. I have found some, if not most, of the gentlemen I have met here to be either skittish of young ladies or determinedly in pursuit of them. It seems as if there is no middle ground."

"Is there anyone in particular you are thinking of, Miss Stanhope? Someone who has offered you something not quite acceptable to a young lady? Or some gentleman who has taken liberties?"

Titania tried not to think of the liberty she had allowed Lord Worthington, lest she blush yet again. Yes, he had taken the liberty, but she did not slap his face and glide away in icy condemnation, as most other young ladies would have done. No, she had to babble at him incoherently and make yet another ignominious departure. Engrossed in her thoughts, she completely forgot Mr. Fell was still waiting for the answer to his question.

Was London causing this streak of unladylike daydreaming? This . . . *impulsiveness*? Or was it something that was being slowly unlocked by a pair of broad shoulders and a quick, intelligent mind?

"Oh, no, no one has done anything improper. It is just the general feeling of being appraised when you venture forth, all on display in your best frock, where some men shy away as if you're about to pounce on them like some sort of voracious animal, and others eye you up and down as if you were that same animal on exhibit at the zoo."

"I see," Mr. Fell said, chuckling. "You are tired of being the—hm, what animal do you most resemble?—the penguin, and you would like a more domesticated animal, say the chicken or a sheep or something, is that it?"

Titania howled in laughter, attracting attention from all corners of the room, including both Julian's mother and Lord George, who was still steadfastly trying to clear a footman's plate of tidbits.

Mrs. White was the first to move towards them—Lord George was hampered by his busy jaws and his not so swift reactions—and she bore down on them, a pleased smile on her face.

"Julian! You are neither sighing nor reaching for your snuffbox. I am so pleased. Could it be you have found someone who does not wish to discuss your hair, trade gossip or pronounce judgment on your wayward mother?" She plopped down on the sofa between them, apparently able to find some comfort in its unforgiving depths.

"Mother, the lady and I were having a lovely conversation . . . that is, until you settled in. Do go away, would you?" His words were said with so much affection as to remove any ill humor from them, and the two beamed at each other.

"He is such a rogue," Mrs. White stage-whispered to Titania. "How he came to be born to Mr. Fell, a lovely man but certainly not the most exciting individual, and myself, a Cit's daughter, I will never know. Why, just look at him, he reeks of gentility and higher thoughts and all those things. I am just lucky to be able to float beside his celestial cloud."

Both Titania and Julian burst out in giggles at yet another heavenly reference, and Mrs. White beamed on, blithely unconcerned she was not in on the joke. When their laughter had subsided, she turned to Titania.

"When did you arrive in town, Miss Stanhope? I believe it is your first Season? Are you enjoying it? And why aren't you at Almack's as debutantes usually are, and why aren't you wearing white, not that it would suit you, dear girl, you'd look like a sheet of paper," she added in an aside.

"Mother!" Julian expostulated. "She cannot possibly answer all of those questions at once."

"I do not wear white, Mrs. White, because I would indeed look like a sheet of paper . . . I am not at Aimack's because I have not yet received vouchers, I have just arrived in town for my first Season, but I am, as your son has already commented, a little long in the tooth for such an event."

She ticked the replies off her fingers one by one, and when she finished, the mother and son—clearly partners in baiting unsuspecting bystanders—smiled in glee. Julian rose, turning to assist his mother from the couch.

"It is time, Mother, to get to the point of the evening. Miss Stanhope will think our wits have gone begging, and we are nothing more than a forest of mushrooms encroaching on polite Society with our fancy talk about literature, poetry and art."

"Yes, well, do hush now, Julian," his mother admonished. "We will get to the discussion in due time. Meanwhile, would you read to us?"

Julian quickly dove into his pockets, retrieving a slightly grubby piece of paper. He cleared his throat as his mother silenced the gathered crowd.

> *Alas! A lass!*
> *She came through the weeping willow*
> *Weeping! Will you?*
> *And I could not but mourn*
> *The passing season as she wept, passing me.*

Was it the worst poetry she had ever heard? Titania was not certain, but she knew it ranked amongst the top three. She clapped her hands with the rest of the applauding crowd and peered up at Mr. Fell. It was as she feared: he was wearing a beatific smile that could only mean he thought it was really and truly good.

Her worst fears were realized when he came bustling back to her, opening his mouth in the question she dreaded. She was scrambling for words in her head when a familiar voice spoke.

"Mr. Fell, we have not yet been introduced, but I must say something after that most unique and unusual poetry. You have a way with words other authors do not. Truly memorable."

Julian grinned in delight, then shook Edwin's hand with vigor. "My dear sir, you cannot know what your words mean to me. I am honored. And you are?"

"Edwin Worthingon, Earl of Oakley. I am also an author, although my métier is scholarly, not reaching the heights of language you scale."

Titania stifled her chortle at Edwin's use of words; he wasn't being mean, his tone was even and sincere, but she knew with as much certainty as if he had told her that he was just as appalled as she was at Julian's awful poetry. He was using his ready mouth—no, scratch that, she corrected hastily, enticing images beginning to dance in her head—rather, using his facility with language to put Julian at ease without exactly lying. She was impressed by his consideration, and admired his quick handling of the situation.

"Miss Stanhope, I did not realize you would be here," Edwin said as he sat down beside her.

Really, the sofa ought to be more comfortable by now, Titania grumbled to herself, what with all these people hopping on its springs.

"I had assumed that like all the other young ladies of my acquaintance you would be at Almack's dancing on the slanted floor and gamely trying to swallow what passes for refreshments there. The company is certainly lovelier, more *impulsive* here." He turned towards Titania, his green eyes fastened on her with a passionate stare.

He was so gorgeous. And smart, and witty, and . . . Titania realized she'd better say something before she leaned over and kissed him.

"Lord Worthington, how does London seem to you after such an absence? You were gone several years, yes?"

"Five," he replied. "I left rather precipitously, as someone has no doubt already informed you." A self-conscious smile played about his lips. "I was lucky to end up where I did. It was not my choice; the idea of dying gloriously in battle was a fleeting fancy of mine, but that was not an option offered to me. For a long while, I did not care if I lived or died." He looked down, but not before Titania glimpsed his face, which held a pained expression.

"Wh—what happened?"

He gripped his hands together tightly in his lap. "I jilted my betrothed at the altar. I knew I could not marry her, but I should not have behaved that recklessly. I broke my father's heart. And damaged mine in the process, too."

"Have you and your father spoken at all since?"

"No. He made it very clear that he wished to have nothing more to do with me. I have obeyed him in that demand, at least."

Her voice softened. "Is there a chance of reconciliation?"

"What I did was too wrong, at least in his eyes, ever to be forgiven. He is a man of honor above all things and my actions were not honorable."

"Surely," Titania ventured, "after such a long time—it is clear you deeply regret causing your father pain. If he only knew, maybe he would forgive you?"

"You are not acquainted with my father if you think he would relent. No, he made that quite clear at our last meeting that we would never willingly see each other again. Now that I have returned to London, it is inevitable we will meet, perhaps sooner than either of us would wish. I think I spotted his carriage earlier today, so that day is coming. But even then, we will be no more than civil."

He heaved a great sigh, his massive shoulders dropping in resignation. They sat in silence for a few comfortable minutes, then Edwin glanced over at Titania with a grin on his face.

"Now that I have revealed my most dishonorable deeds, my fair Titania, what dark secrets do you have hidden? That your brother has been sent to rusticate, or that your stickler aunt of yours dislikes you intensely? I saw her cut you at the Cliftons' ball—what could you possibly have done to arouse her ire?"

Titania chuckled, thinking if she were to tell him her

dishonorable deed—that she was dangling for a fortune and documenting it in a vulgar publication, no less—he would not be nearly as lighthearted in his questioning.

"My aunt has taken exception to me, and I am equally appalled by her decorating. Do you know," she continued in mock horror, "she has placed her rococo pieces in a drawing room decorated in the Greek period? I vow, I am shocked, *shocked* at her daring. I should be the one disapproving of *her*, what with her trampling over all notions of design so much that it makes me positively faint."

Edwin tugged on his cravat. "I must say I am the last person to offer any kind of design and fashion advice. I would as lief wear one of those ridiculously ornate waistcoats your brother and his companions were wearing than one of these silly things. They wrap around my neck like a noose. I can scarcely breathe. The only reason I continue to endure the suffering, Miss Stanhope, is that without one I would not be deemed as fit company for you." She chuckled, but did not respond to him.

"Have I actually found another way to quell your ready tongue? I am not at all sure I like this way better than the first. I cannot tell you how many times I have relived our meeting at the park the other day." He stared into her eyes, and she felt a sizzle of something she feared naming flare through her chest.

"My lord, it would be best if we did not dwell on that particular incident. I myself have forgotten it entirely," Titania responded in an overly bright tone.

"Have you, Titania?" He gave her a skeptical look, his right eyebrow shooting up. Then he smiled at her, his green eyes seeming to see within her soul. Titania quickly turned her eyes to the ground, occupying herself with looking at his feet, which were shod, once again, in somewhat worn boots. It was too bad Lord Worthington was not as rich in money as he was in charm.

Sighing, she looked up again, and realized that Lord Worthington had just asked her a question.

"Pardon, my lord?"

"Yes, it appears you were in a brown study. Is there anything I can help you with, Miss Stanhope? You observed that I seemed troubled, and I have to return the comment. And I hardly think your distress at your aunt's taste warrants such reaction."

No, nothing as serious as that. Only worrying about the rest of my life.

"You know," he continued, "I've been laughing since I returned to London. I never thought I would be in good humor again. You must be a good influence on me. That, or I am becoming aware that not all beautiful women are conniving; sometimes they are compassionate and intelligent, if not very good horsewomen."

Titania, who had been holding her breath as he spoke, exhaled in a gasp of outrage. "My lord! If I were riding one of my own horses, I would easily best you in a race."

If his horse had three legs and hers had wings. Maybe.

"Care to wager on it, Titania?" Edwin asked. "I am not sure you could afford the stakes, though."

Titania was taken aback for a moment, thinking he had ferreted out the fact that she was penniless. Then she realized he was hinting at something else entirely, and her body began to heat up in an increasingly familiar way. He inched a fraction closer to her on the sofa until they almost touched. She was achingly aware of his shoulder, his arm, his thigh, his calf; she wondered what would happen if she did what she most wanted to do, and rest her hand on his leg. She blushed even harder.

"Miss Stanhope, when you color up like that, you are the most stunning creature I have ever seen. Thank goodness we are in a public spot, or I would be using my mouth for something other than speech." Titania knew she had to put a stop to this dangerous relationship, even as the thought of it made her stomach churn. She wished she had remembered to pocket her uncle's splinter this evening so she could concentrate on the pain it caused rather than the pain in her heart.

"My lord," she said stiffly, placing her hands primly on her lap, "it is not appropriate to speak to me in that manner. I would beg you to go away."

Go away, go away, and do not say a word, she begged him silently. If he spoke, she was going to lose her will and confess everything: her father's betrayal, her own need for funds, her greater need for him. She watched his legs out of the corner of her eye as he rose slowly from the sofa, as painfully silent as her future.

She felt him staring down at her for what seemed an eternity, then walk away. It was all she could do to keep staring straight ahead. Only when he had turned his back did she allow herself to look. A big crying gulp welled up inside her throat. She looked around the room desperate for a distraction. Where had Miss Tynte gone to? And why did her heart feel as if it were breaking? Just as her eyes began to scour the crowd for two broad shoulders she spied Claire in the center of the room accompanied by Lord Gratwick.

Lord Gratwick's presence made sense, but why was Claire here? She was about as literary-minded as Lord George. Maybe Almack's posed too much in the way of competition, since most of the ladies there were dewy seventeen-year-olds and neither Claire, nor herself (as had been pointed out far more times than Titania cared to count) were in their first flush of youth. Better to cast lures in smaller ponds where the bait was less . . . fresh, so to speak.

Maybe she would have to do something in her column on day-old fish. Cook would appreciate it, even if none of her other readers would.

"Claire. And Lord Gratwick," Titania called, striding towards them. "My brother has arrived and most of my staff has descended on me, too, and I have not had a chance to breathe."

"Titania!" Claire exclaimed. "I should have known you would be here." She sniffed in obvious disdain. "Lord Gratwick," she said, patting his arm in a proprietary gesture, "could you fetch some refreshments? I'd like a moment with Titania."

Titania guided Claire over to that still remarkably uncomfortable couch. Claire settled herself daintily on the edge, looking as contented as if she were lying on a cloud. How does she manage that? Titania thought, feeling a random spring poke her in an unpleasant spot.

Claire's words made her squirm even more. "Lord Gratwick has confided in me, Titania, and I must say you have made quite a conquest. Since he's returned home, he's been the object of every debutante's attention, and he has told

me he is seriously considering asking you, well, you know."
She simpered and smoothed her hands down her skirts.

The news was not as welcome as Claire seemed to assume it would be. "Well. That is interesting."

Claire's lips tightened into a thin line. "Interesting? I tell you about a probable proposal and you say it is . . . interesting?"

"Yes, Claire, *interesting*." Titania tried to keep the sharpness from her voice, but Claire's high-handed machinations were both obvious and beginning to get on her nerves. Why was favoring Lord Gratwick so important to Claire?

"Oh," Claire observed in a caustic tone, "the penniless peer is here."

Titania looked up to see Edwin stalking back, his emerald eyes flashing. He nodded at Claire, then stood in front of Titania extending a hand to her with a look that promised he would make a scene if she did not take it.

Titania rose, one hand held tightly in his, the other giving Claire an 'it's all right' gesture. Her gloves did nothing to disguise the warmth and strength of his grasp, and she felt a tiny bit of the tightness in her chest recede as he drew her to a small anteroom that opened off the main room. Once alone with him, she tried to make her voice as disdainful as her aunt's.

"My lord, I thought I made myself clear when we spoke. I do not wish to engage in the sort of conversation you think I am interested in. Now if you want to talk about the fine weather we are having or the books we are purportedly here to discuss or . . . ohh!" She squeaked in surprise as Edwin's mouth came crashing down on hers.

It was an angry kiss, one borne of frustration and loneliness. She could only hold her breath until his fury subsided; when it finally abated, he drew his head back, looking into her eyes with a golden hunger.

"Miss Stanhope, Titania, you cannot tell me my reputation has so ruined me in your eyes you cannot abide my presence. Please, tell me there is another reason so I can hope to find at least one honest woman in the world." His ferocious tone changed midway to an anxious query.

She could not say a word, could not lie to him as she knew she must, so she did the only thing that felt true: she reached up for his neck with the one hand he hadn't captured while holding her mouth up to be kissed. Edwin took her invitation as greedily as a drowning man takes air, his kiss as ardent and caring as the previous one had been charged with anger.

She opened her lips to allow his tongue entrance. He licked her lips lightly, then delved into her warm mouth, plundering its recesses until Titania thought she might faint from the sheer pleasure. One hand moved to support her back, while his other released her wrist in search of much more dangerous territory. He slid his hand up her waist to the underside of her breast, which he grasped with his palm as his fingers hunted for her nipple. It was easy to find, the peak strained against the thin fabric of her gown, and he drew lazy circles around it with his finger until he finally rubbed his finger across its surface, drawing a smothered moan from Titania.

She reached up to hold on tighter to his shoulders, their massive bulk strong against her hands and she kissed him deeper, using her tongue on him as he had on her. She was astonished to find herself losing control, succumbing to this man's caresses like the most wanton of women.

Her thoughts stopped their brief wandering as he maneuvered her against the wall of the small room. As he started to pull up her skirt, her breath coming in shorter and shorter bursts, a small noise startled them—it sounded like glass shattering in the other room—and they drew apart, staring at each other as their breathing grew more quiet. Titania held her fingers up to her mouth. They were swollen and sore.

"You understand now, my lord, why I think it best we not meet under these circumstances." She grabbed her skirts and fled the room, knowing if she said any more, she would be begging him to finish what he had started.

Edwin stared, forcing himself not to chase after her. Confound it! This kind of situation was exactly what he had promised himself would never happen again. He tried to keep his mind occupied by thinking steadfastly of his favorite battle tactics.

His traitorous mind insisted, however, on drifting back to his broken-nosed Titania, a woman whom he had been struck by—literally and figuratively—as soon as she had barreled into his chest. By the time he actually knew her name, he was enthralled. Tonight's events were sure indication he was not in control of his destiny and emotions nearly as much as he thought.

Edwin attempted to straighten his cravat, smiling as he recalled how it had gotten mussed. His heart did a flip as he saw Titania gesticulating wildly to Lord George. Apparently, she was trying to extricate her escort from a pastry so she could depart, most likely before seeing him again.

Edwin did not attempt to speak with her again; right now, she was as skittish as he, and he needed to think. If he could only keep his mind on the parts above the neck that fascinated him, it would not be quite as hard to maintain some sort of nonchalance. As it was, his heart was in danger of being captivated. Again. Would the result be less disastrous than the first time?

Chapter Nine

"Can you hurry, please?" Titania urged her companions. She spotted Lord Gratwick and gave Miss Tynte a little push. She wasn't in the mood for his version of oily charm. She grabbed Lord George's arm, pulling it to haul him along as she walked quickly to the door of the town house. When they had finally all been bundled into the carriage, she sank back on the squabs in relief. Her mouth felt bruised where Edwin had kissed her, and her breasts were still tingling from having been caressed so thoroughly.

How could one kiss, and yes, some corporeal explorations, make one's wits so befuddled? She recalled a conversation she had had with her mother about love and marriage. It was not long before her mother died, and she had been insistent that Titania marry for love, as she did.

"But," Titania probed, "wasn't it hard?"

"Yes, of course it was, my dear," her mother replied. "But when I met your father, none of it—disgrace, disapproval—mattered. What mattered was that I had found my love, a man whom I could be with until the end of my life. Which," she finished with her usual talent for dry understatement, "looks as if is coming pretty soon."

Titania's reverie was broken by Lord George's bluster.

"The Earl of Oakley is not the most, shall we say, au courant in fashion, is he, Miss Tynte?" Lord George inquired, his jowls quivering in disapproval. "So careless in his clothing, I swear his cravat was wilted!"

Titania smothered a smile as she realized she had played a part in earning Lord George's disapproval.

"And those boots!" he exclaimed.

At least I don't have those on my conscience, Titania thought.

Lord George continued, his mouth pursed in disapproval. "They were scuffed as if he had been tromping around in the mud! Really, I know he has just come from America, but he is a gentleman's son, after all, and as a future marquess, he is obliged to make proper appearances!"

Miss Tynte gave a soothing smile. "Lord George, not everyone is as—how do the youngbloods say it?—bang-up to the mark as you. You have an unerring, and some would say remarkable, eye for color." Titania tried hard not to giggle, and caught her friend's eye in a conspiratorial glance. She knew she would laugh if she tried to speak, so she kept silent, as did Miss Tynte. Lord George did not seem to notice, chatting nonstop until he waved good-bye from his carriage window.

"Oh my goodness, that was close," Miss Tynte gasped when they were back home. "When you looked at me—"

"—I thought I was going to burst out laughing right there. Elizabeth, how could you? 'Some would say a remarkable eye for color.' The poor man."

They chuckled together, then Miss Tynte cleared her throat.

"What happened tonight, Titania?"

"Wh-what do you mean?" Titania tried to look as innocent as she had been five hours earlier. Miss Tynte regarded her with a look Titania had feared ever since she had earned it by attempting to conjugate Latin in the pluperfect without paying attention to her verbs. Or something like that.

Anyway, suffice to say, it did not appear that Miss Tynte was fooled.

"Titania," she continued, "were you doing something improper?"

Well, Titania thought to herself, if by improper you mean allowing a man to kiss me passionately, stroke my breasts and attempt to lift my skirts up, than yes, I guess you could say I was doing something improper.

"What do you mean by improper?"

"You cannot pull the wool over my eyes, young lady. First you were on the sofa with Mr. Fell, then when I next looked for you, you had disappeared. Then when you did reappear, you were somewhat flushed and made us leave rather precipitously. What were you doing with Mr. Fell?" Miss Tynte demanded.

Huzzah! She didn't have to lie! She pulled the shreds of her tattered dignity around her like a cloak. "Nothing. Mr. Fell and I continued our discussion on the sofa, then I discovered I was in need of some privacy. I am shocked that you thought something had happened between us. If I had known London Society would have corrupted you to the extent of thinking a lady would disappear with a gentleman, I never would have asked you to accompany me."

Miss Tynte pursed her lips. "I knew it was a mistake to let you read Caesar's battle tactics. Well, you did ask me, and I'm here, so don't think I'm not watching you." Titania decided on a counterattack.

"And what about you? What are you doing with that flush on your cheek and that spring in your step? You didn't have that at Ravensthorpe!" she declared self-righteously. Miss Tynte rose out of her chair, shaking her skirts out.

"I am going to bed, Titania. It is clear I need my strength to fight the battle on all fronts. Good night." She patted Titania's cheek and walked out of the room, leaving a faint scent of roses.

"You are an absolute disgrace!" Henri shouted when he saw Edwin at the end of the evening. "You are absolutely unable to keep your boots out of the streets, your coat from getting completely wrinkled and you look just like what you are: a man who has come from the American backwater, with no sense of how someone in your position *should* look." He scowled at Edwin, planting his hands on his hips.

"So quit. You could always go back to what you were doing before we met—I bet those men you cheated are much less angry now." Edwin gave Henri a disingenuous smile, then turned away from him and began to loosen his neckwear.

Henri made an impatient clucking noise, then swatted Edwin's hands away. "And your cravat looks as if a flock of chickens has been pecking away at it in search of food." He skillfully removed Edwin's cravat, then began to shrug him out of his coat.

Edwin allowed Henri to continue, stretching his neck as he felt its freedom. He held his arms over his head, letting Henri remove his shirt. When that, too, was removed, Edwin absentmindedly ran his hand down his chest. He paused, remembering Titania's small, but strong, hands on his shoulders. He drew a deep breath, then exhaled, thinking furiously on something—anything—but her hands and where they had been. It would hardly do to embarrass himself in front of his manservant, who was also his best friend. He sat down suddenly, just as Henri was gesturing towards his feet.

"Henri, you have been pestering me to start wearing clothing proper to my position. It did not matter before, but now I think it is a good idea."

"Yes, my lord." Henri was grinning so wide Edwin was worried his face was going to split. "Provided, of course, you listen to me in regard to the treatment of your neckwear." Edwin nodded in resignation as Henri handed him his robe.

Henri turned the covers down on Edwin's bed, then practically pranced towards the door. "Tomorrow to Bond Street to see Weston, and Hoby. Oh, Edwin, you have made me so happy!" He gave one last delighted smirk, then bowed out of the room, Edwin chuckling at his glee.

Edwin removed his robe, laying it on the chair. He stalked naked to the bed and slipped under the cool sheets, which were soothing on his heated body. Folding his hands under his head, he gazed up at the ceiling. Titania. Even her name was luscious. She was lovely and intelligent and sensitive and quick and all he had never believed he could find.

He wanted to spend time loving her properly in a bed, and not in a side-cupboard; of course, he thought with a wicked smirk, if a side-cupboard was what she wanted he would certainly acquiesce. It took all his patience not to go hammer at her door now, wearing nothing but his heart, and demand her hand.

Perhaps, though, it would be more proper to wait until Henri had worked his magic. Titania, he had heard, was well dowered and he did not want anyone to presume he was an impoverished fortune hunter.

His impoverished lady woke up the next morning feeling as if she had just discovered Croesus' riches. She practically vaulted out of bed, chirping merrily for Sarah as she foraged through the wardrobe for something to wear down to breakfast. Sarah came in, holding a pot of tea.

"What are you bein' so dern cheerful for, then?" she asked. She watched as Titania hauled out her old riding habit, which Sarah had tried to make sure remained safely back at Ravensthorpe. She marched over, slopping tea onto the floor as she went, grabbing the habit from Titania's hand.

"Miss! You cannot venture forth in public in that old thing! Besides being hopelessly out of fashion, it is altogether too tight! You are much—" She paused, searching for the right word.

"Sturdier?" Titania supplied helpfully, gesturing towards her ample bosom.

Sarah sighed, putting the tea down on the table. "Yes, miss, sturdier if that is 'ow you term it. In any case," she continued brusquely, "you cannot wear that in public, and that is final."

With that, she folded her arms and glared. Titania, knowing when she was beaten, walked back over to the wardrobe and extricated another piece of clothing.

"Does this pass inspection, then?" Titania held out her new habit, a dark chocolate brown that fit almost as tightly as her maligned black one.

Sarah gave a reluctant nod. "It will contain you, at least, even if it shows just as much as that other one."

"It looks good, then?" Titania asked, peering at herself in the glass. Sarah's response was a low grumble, which Titania interpreted as a "yes." Satisfied, she picked up her jacket and ran downstairs.

"Oops, sorry, Stillings." Titania barely avoided a collision with her butler as she entered the breakfast room. She scooted around him, grabbing a piece of warm bread as she sat down at the table. Stillings gave her the same look he had always bestowed when she was dashing about the house as a young lady should not, and gestured towards the letters at the edge of her plate.

"Miss, it appears that there is some correspondence that deserves your immediate attention," he said in his most butlerlike tone.

"Yes, Stillings, I see," she said meekly, quickly stuffing the last crumb in her mouth. She picked up the first letter and felt a frisson of fear down her spine. She had seen too many of them not to recognize a bill.

It was indeed a bill, and very large at that. It appeared that in addition to stealing the tenants' rents and pocketing the money intended for improvements to the estate, the ridiculously greedy overseer had also bought many items on the Stanhope credit. As Titania stared at the paper in her hand, she glanced over at the remaining pile and realized there were many more such letters there. She began to sort through them with a trembling hand.

Bills for jewelry, wine and clothing. She quickly opened each one, consigning the bills to their own, malignant pile. Totaling them all up, she slumped in her chair. The remaining pieces of her mother's jewelry would not even begin to cover the debts. There was also the matter of maintaining the London house and appearances. And paying the taxes. And her aunt. The list went on and on.

If any potential suitor—*wealthy* potential suitor, Titania quickly amended—realized that allying himself with her would also bring a swarm of debts around his head he would run as quickly as possible towards the next available debutante—probably blond, tiny and young. She sighed, all notions of riding, or anything fun, for that matter, chased from her head.

Just as she was about to throw her head on the table and have a good sob, Stillings returned.

"Well, Stillings, what good news are you bearing now?" Her butler ignored her sarcastic tone.

"Miss, Lady Wexford is here to see you. She says she knows it is a trifle early, but she was hoping you were ready for your ride. She is waiting in the drawing room." He gave her a tiny bow, then left quickly, probably anticipating her throwing something at his head.

Titania rose slowly, gulping down the cup of tea that

Stillings had placed in front of her. It was, she thought even more grumpily, prepared exactly as she liked: plenty of milk with just enough sugar to take the edge off. She couldn't even justify lashing out about that. She left the bills where they were, and went to greet her friend.

If she were lucky, Claire would have purchased a new riding habit or something and wouldn't insist on discussing Lord Gratwick. Or any other peer of the realm.

Once safely perched on her horse—a very staid old mare, this time—Titania felt almost . . . happy. She sniffed the fresh spring air, loving the way the scent of the new grass mingled with the leather of the saddle. "Do you smell that?" she asked, turning towards Claire.

Claire looked confused. "Smell what—the horse?"

Titania giggled. "No, silly, the grass, and the air, and everything. It smells lovely." She felt a great warmth inside her that had nothing to do with duty, or obligation or sacrifice. She wanted to shout her happiness to the world, but that would require explaining it to herself.

Claire gave a hesitant sniff. "Mmm. At least it smells better than London usually does. And speaking of smelly London"—she gave Titania a naughty smile—"are you going to the Landon masquerade?"

"Yes, the Duke was a friend of my father's, before they both got respectable. Not that my father *stayed* respectable. Who are you going as?"

"A mermaid, or a fairy, or something like that. Lord Chatham says costumes should be an outward manifestation of the soul. Isn't that delicious?" Claire sighed. "And you?"

Titania wished she could go as a critic and disabuse Lord Chatham of his talent for poetry. She turned to Claire.

"Mrs. Hastings, the Ravensthorpe housekeeper, sent some of my mother's old court gowns, probably thinking I would need them for my presentation at court. So I thought I would go as the Duchess of Devonshire, she was always one of mother's favorite people. They wore the most outlandish clothing back then, I only hope I can navigate those wide skirts."

As well as navigate the path of a singular lady. Why did wearing a disguise suddenly seem so appealing?

Dispatch from the Battlefront, March 1813

Is it some sort of Descartesian geometrical absolute that insists that the less eligible a gentleman is, the more likely he is to be all that a young lady would want?

Why is it that financial security is also almost always affiliated with only a vague awareness that there are things in the world other than port, prime goers and fetching waistcoats? Meanwhile, the men who simply will not do are those with wit, humor, understanding and looks. It is enough to make a young lady question the order of the universe.

Or perhaps not.

Perhaps if those paragons had money as well, their consequence would get so puffed up they could not do anything save gaze lovingly in the mirror as they muttered bon mots. No, it is good for all that the world is as it is, it is just awkward for a young lady who is hoping for security and a decent conversation over the morning rolls and marmalade.

A Singular Lady

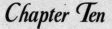

Chapter Ten

"Blast!" Titania's mood plummeted even further when she returned home from her ride. "Are there more?"

She shuffled again through the pile of bills, which seemed larger than when she had left. She was relieved to see the additional envelopes contained just letters. Titania's expert eye could discern a bill from across the room.

She ripped open the first envelope, a single sheet of paper falling into her lap. Picking it up, she scanned its message quickly, then frowned in confusion.

Look for the knight tomorrow night. He will fulfill your every wish.

That was all it said.

It was frustratingly cryptic. Who could have sent it to her?

Her first thought, of course, was that it was Edwin, who had come as close as any man had to fulfilling her wishes (known or not) the night before. But wouldn't he be much more likely to wrap her in a passionate embrace without warning rather than send her this mysterious, enigmatic note? It also obviously wasn't Mr. Fell, who was more poetic in his language. Was it Lord George? No, she smiled as she examined the note more closely; there were no crumbs or stains upon it. Without ever observing it first-hand, she knew that Lord George would require sustenance to pen a note to a young lady, and this bore no signs of such treatment.

Could it be Lord Gratwick? She tapped the note against her teeth, pondering just what it meant. After a few moments of thought, however, she realized it was a futile exercise. There would be time enough to discover the note's sender tomorrow night.

She opened the second letter, squinting a little at the tiny, crabbed handwriting.

Dear Niece,

You and your baron brother have less than six months' time to pay Ravensthorpe's taxes. You already owe my sister money for sponsoring your presentation. How many more debts will you run up before you fail?

My offer stands until August 1: If your brother agrees to cede Ravensthorpe to me, you will not have to be thrown onto the streets to fend for yourself. Your mother's jewelry will only buy so much time. Be careful you do not gamble away your future.

Mr. Hawthorne knows how to contact my solicitor if you wish to agree to my terms.

Otherwise, I look forward to taking what is rightfully mine.

Sincerely,
Uncle Norbert Stanhope

Titania leaned back against the chair, her optimism crushed under the weight of her uncle's letter. She wanted so badly just to give up, to fold her hand, but knew doing so would betray everything her parents had ever taught her. Even if one of her parents had also taught her how duplicitous he could be.

She straightened her shoulders and marched upstairs, determined to do the right thing.

Even if it was not the right thing for her.

"Welcome, Lord Gratwick. How lovely to see you." Titania hurried downstairs as she spoke, twitching the skirts of her blue gown into place. Titania had had just enough time to toss her papers into her desk, then hastily scrape her hair into some sort of order as she heard the downstairs door opening. She saw Miss Tynte already scurrying into the drawing room.

It was the fashionable hour for late callers, and Titania had already cajoled Cook into making gingerbread cakes, the odor of which was wafting through the house, making Titania's mouth water.

At least there was one bright spot to receiving visitors.

"Miss Stanhope," Lord Gratwick said, holding her hand a bit longer than Titania would have liked, "you look lovely today. Especially since you seemed so out of sorts last evening at Mrs. White's when I saw you."

"Ah, Stillings, there you are." Titania was grateful for the interruption since his comment left her at a loss as to how to respond.

"Miss Stanhope, Mr. Farrell is—" he managed to announce, before Alistair strode into the room as if he were being carried on a gust of wind.

"Miss Stanhope." As if his height and regal bearing were not enough, his coat, breeches and cravat were all in varying shades of lavender. The top of his cane was encrusted with a large, asymmetrical globe of gems: sapphires, emeralds, amethysts and peridots.

"Mr. Farrell, how delightful to see you today. I mean, quite delightful," she said again, looking him up and down. She met his eyes, which had a humorous gleam dancing in their brown depths.

"Your servant, Miss Stanhope," he said softly. "I see I find you in good health; you look lovely today."

"May I introduce Lord Gratwick, Mr. Farrell? Lord Gratwick has just returned from the battlefield also."

The two men nodded at each other, Alistair raising a black eyebrow as he surveyed the shorter man. "Where were you stationed, Gratwick?"

Lord Gratwick looked as uneasy as Titania had ever seen him. He smiled at Titania, then waved his hand in dismissal. "Here and there, Farrell. Miss Stanhope, do you attend the Landons' masquerade? And you, Mr. Farrell?"

Titania gestured for both of the men to sit and perched herself on the sofa. Lord Gratwick sat next to her, his leg only inches away from her own. She tried to hitch over surreptitiously, but caught an angry look from Lord Gratwick as he spotted what she was doing.

"Miss"—Stillings appeared at the door—"your refreshments." He entered the room, loaded down with tea and gingerbread and placed them on the table, his butler's implacability seeming to rattle when he glanced at Alistair's finery.

Titania smiled brightly at Lord Gratwick, whose face still wore a scowl, then leaned forward to serve the gingerbread.

Alistair dragged a delicate Egyptian-style chair towards the center of the room, then draped himself gracefully into it. Titania wondered if the chair could support his weight as well as his presence. "Yes, I will be there, but I cannot tell you who I'll be dressed as. The best attack is a surprise attack, would you not agree, Lord Gratwick?"

Lord Gratwick appeared to choke on his food. "Yes, indeed, Mr. Farrell."

Alistair beamed. "So glad you agree, my lord. Tell me, were you at Albuera?"

Before Lord Gratwick could reply, Stillings opened the door. Lord Gratwick looked grateful for the interruption.

"Mr. Fell, miss," Stillings announced. Julian glided into the room, his hair falling artfully across his brow. His clothing was just as startling as Alistair's, delicate hues of blue encasing his slender frame. The effect was ruined by his glower, however, when he saw Alistair's splendor. He ignored Lord Gratwick entirely until Titania made the introductions.

"Miss Stanhope, I am so pleased to find you here."

"Where else would Miss Stanhope be?" Alistair said with a grin. Julian looked nonplussed. "But speaking of being places," Alistair continued, "I must take my leave. Lord Gratwick, would you mind dropping me at White's?"

He winked slyly at Titania, who covered her mouth as she tried not to laugh. Lord Gratwick took his leave with a peevish air and Alistair followed in a sweep of purple.

Julian watched them go, then drew a chair close to Titania so Miss Tynte could not hear.

"Quick! Tell me what happened last night! I saw this . . . this behemoth practically haul you from your seat, then the next thing I knew you had disappeared. When I saw you again, you looked very mussed, and the behemoth had a very satisfied smirk on his face. Tell me, were you accosted by the gentleman in question? Should I plan on naming my seconds?" He drew himself up as large as he could, his resulting size still only half that of Lord Worthington.

"He did nothing that was not welcome. But," she said, launching the one topic—himself—that she knew would keep him from asking too many prying questions, "have you been writing poetry long?"

Julian raised his eyes skyward. "As long as the trees have had roots, as long as the clouds have had rain, as long as—"

"The Earl of Oakley," Stillings intoned. Edwin entered, his eyes searching for Titania.

"The behemoth," Julian whispered.

"Lord Worthington, what a pleasure to see you." Titania rose, walking to take Edwin's hand. "You met Mr. Julian Fell last evening." Met him last evening when your hands were not up my skirt.

"Well, Miss Stanhope," Julian said briskly, rising from his chair, "I must be off. I will see you at the masquerade—I will be the Cupid with the wings and the arrows." Titania laughed, then held her hand out to his. "I look forward to it. Thank you for coming."

"Oh, and Miss Stanhope," he said as he walked out the door, "please remember to bring your behemoth tomorrow. Although I believe the point of such a party is to disguise yourself, and you are clearly not able to do so—I believe I can read your mind even now." With that parting shot, Julian slid out the door, his chuckle rumbling down the hall.

Titania did not dare to even look at Miss Tynte, whom she was sure was glaring at her. She darted a quick glance from under her lashes, and was not very happy to find she was right. Miss Tynte was giving her an icy look that used to stop her bad behavior immediately, at least until she had started behaving so *impulsively*.

"Please sit, Lord Worthington." He did. But no one spoke.

Titania cleared her throat a few times, but wasn't sure just what to say: "how do you get your chest so broad?" "when can we finish what we started?" and "why does it feel like *that* when you touch me *there*?" didn't seem like good conversation starters. At least not with Miss Tynte in the room.

The ensuing silence was agonizing. Edwin stared hungrily at Titania, Miss Tynte stabbed at her embroidery as if it were, Titania imagined, a picture of her on the frame, and she herself did not know where to look.

"Cousin," Titania said finally, her voice a little squeak, "what are you working on now?"

Miss Tynte gave her a sharp look, then turned her eyes back down. "It is a sampler I am doing for my niece. It details Dante's 'Seven Circles of Hell.' "

"Which one is this, then?" Edwin asked softly. Titania stifled a giggle, while Miss Tynte gave him one of her governess-y glares. Titania tried again.

"My lord," she chirped, "is it not a lovely day? I do not think I have seen a more lovely day in all my years, which, I have been informed, are many. I believe the trees are extra green today, and as for the sky, it is as blue as, well, as something that is remarkably blue. If I were a poet, I would have to compose a sonnet about today. It is that grand."

"Your poetry could not possibly be any worse than Mr. Fell's," he said with a grin. "And, yes, the day is lovely." Miss Tynte, who had been following their conversation with all the avidity and head-turning of a spectator at a tennis match, got distracted by a raveled thread, and looked down as she began to tug.

Edwin leaned in closer so his mouth—his warm, soft, passionate mouth—was just inches away from Titania's ear. His breath made the hairs on her arm stand up, and she couldn't even describe what it was doing to the rest of her body. Or she could, but it would take a vocabulary she could not use without turning a profound shade of red.

"Miss Stanhope, I will not apologize for what happened last evening. I cannot regret it, even for a moment. In fact," he paused, "I want to do it again and again and again until we're both breathless." Titania darted a quick look at Miss Tynte; thankfully, the yellow thread was still tangled.

"My lord," Titania said slowly, speaking as softly as he was, "we must understand each other. I believe . . ." she said with a hesitant tone, "I believe we are in a similar position. There are reasons why we should not be *friends*."

Edwin frowned, and Titania watched as his gorgeous lips pulled down at the corners. "What reasons? Is it because of my past? Titania," he said, his voice a low thrum of passion, "I wish I could change the past, but I cannot." Titania cleared her throat, her whole body humming with tension. She cleared it again, then spoke slowly.

"My lord, it is not your past. How could *I* judge *you*? I did not come to London with a spotless reputation. My father made certain of that. Neither of us can . . . *afford*," she stressed the word, "to do anything to upset Society. Although there are certain rumors regarding my own state of affairs, that is," she said, blushing as she realized how what she had said might be construed, "my own financial state is not what it might seem. Like you, my future lies in my own hands, and it is up to me to decide it. Developing a *friendship* must be handled discreetly."

Edwin shifted slightly, a confused look in his eye. "Disc—" he started to ask, but Miss Tynte raised her head, a satisfied look on her face.

"That troublesome thread! I showed it. Now to start on the sixth circle. I think a bright blue would be nice, do you agree, Titania?"

"Mm, yes, Cousin, that looks lovely. My lord," Titania said as she moved her chair a few inches away from Edwin's, "do you attend the Landons' masquerade?" Edwin's look of confusion was replaced with a devilish smirk, that elusive dimple appearing as he spoke.

"Yes, I will be attending, although I have not yet decided as whom. Which obscure goddess will you be garbed as? Miss Tynte, do you not think that Miss Titania should be Sekhmet, the Egyptian goddess of war?" He gazed at Titania and she felt a warmth steal over her as she saw the admiration in his eyes. "Or maybe you should be Joan of Arc or Queen Elizabeth; I believe either would measure up to your resolute nature."

Oh, if he only knew how irresolute she was. At one time, all she wanted was to have her Season, meet some interesting people and see a world beyond Northamptonshire. Now she was pondering doing something so contrary to her nature, to her Society, it shocked her.

She surfaced from her fantasy to see two pairs of eyes— one green, one brown—staring at her, waiting for her to respond. "More cake?" she asked, holding the plate out to

Edwin. He stretched his fingers out and barely brushed against hers. She felt as if she were on fire.

"Yes, thank you, Miss Stanhope. I find I am famished for something, and my appetite has barely been whetted. I cannot wait for dessert," he finished with a smirk.

"Titania!" Miss Tynte thundered. Lord Worthington had just left, leaving a dreamy-eyed Titania in his wake. "You know as well as I do that that man—no matter how charming, intelligent, handsome and enamored of you he might be—is not a candidate for marriage. And since his green eyes and strapping build will not pay Thibault's school fees, I advise you to forget about him." Titania sat down with a sudden thump, nervously pulling strands of hair out of her coiffure.

"My dear," Miss Tynte continued, her voice breaking, "you know I would like nothing more than to have you marry someone who is truly your equal, and Lord Worthington certainly appears to be that. But unfortunately our circumstances—*your* circumstances—insist that you put your head ahead of your heart. Unless you wish to tell Thibault everything, and turn off the servants, you cannot encourage his attentions. I am truly sorry, dear," she finished, patting Titania's sleeve softly.

Titania looked down at the worn, wrinkled hand on her sleeve. The blue veins were darker than the shade of Titania's gown, the thin fingers still bearing the calluses of pens wielded long ago. Miss Tynte was wise, as always. How could Titania even think of jeopardizing her family's future, much less her own, by indulging her own longings?

It was a subdued Titania who later found herself still pondering her newfound emotions as she tried to write in her room.

This is what it felt like, love, that emotion that propelled her mother into her father's arms, that caused great countries to fall, to make Titania Stanhope change from a decisive, capable woman to a vacillating, blushing girl.

She shook her head, drew out her vellum and pen, and tried to concentrate. She could not control her heart, but she had to keep enough control of her head to be able to have a valid choice at the end of the Season.

Unless the woman who was heir to her father's estate suddenly appeared and handed over all of her father's money, she was going to have to find a tenable solution. As she mulled it over, she knew that marrying a wealthy man just for the sake of his funds was looking less and less tenable. So she bent to her task, rolled up her sleeves, and scribbled frantically away in the hours before dinner.

Chapter Eleven

Edwin hummed a little tune as he descended the stairs from Titania's house. For the first time in years he was happy, and as soon as he and Titania were safely betrothed, he would be content at last. Contentment was an emotion he thought never to experience again.

As he bounded into his carriage and settled into the soft, plush padding, his mind wandered to when Titania would be his wife. She could assist him with his writing, and aid him in setting the estate to rights. When he woke up in the morning, her hair would be lying poker-straight on the pillow. When he needed the right word for an article, he could discuss it with her.

As he strode up the stairs to his house, and saw Henri's beaming face (almost completely obscured by the mountainous pile of boxes from Bond Street), he smiled, feeling like "home" was only a broken nose away.

Henri immediately began to jabber at him, but Edwin waved him away, treading softly upstairs to his room. Although he honestly would have liked nothing better than to sit and grin stupidly at Henri as he chattered about his various purchases, he had promised to write an editorial on the British attitude of the war they were waging against America. His firsthand opinions and access to people in powerful positions would put his work into the spotlight as it had never been.

He sighed, knowing until he made his deadline he should

not even be thinking about his personal affairs. He pulled out a fresh piece of paper, undaunted by its blankness, and immediately started to write, his small, jagged handwriting quickly filling the page.

After only a few hours, Edwin had assembled a rough draft of the article and, after carefully placing it in his escritoire, called for Henri so he could dress for dinner.

"What dazzling splendor will I be sporting tonight, my friend?" he asked, waving a hand in the air.

"Well," said Henri, obviously pleased to finally be able to discuss the topic with his employer, "I was not able to obtain any new clothing for you without your presence, but I did purchase some new gloves, a walking stick, a stickpin and some new cravats. I have given the old ones," he sniffed, "to the cook for cleaning her pots."

"Henri, I will not look like an idiot wearing all these fripperies, will I? I want to look a man of fashion, but I certainly have no aspirations to becoming a dandy." Would Titania think he looked like an idiot? Maybe if she hated what he was wearing, she would rip his clothes off that much faster.

Henri chuckled slightly at Edwin's naïveté, shaking his head. "Edwin, my friend, there is no fear of that. I have merely outfitted you with the appropriate accessories a gentleman requires. You will be unexceptional, a gentleman to the core, with cravats that fit and boots that sparkle. I would not lead you astray, my lord. I know what I am about." Edwin shrugged, striding toward Henri with his arms spread wide.

Gorgeously attired, Edwin left his house about an hour later. He was wearing his favorite pair of boots, which had been polished to a high shine. His coat fit snugly, encasing his broad shoulders in a dark brown superfine. His cravat—impeccably arranged, no creases—was simply adorned with a topaz stickpin, its square-cut design catching the light and reflecting soft amber twinkles. His breeches were, as fashion dictated, skintight, but fashion did not suffer as it usually did when overfed lords stuffed their sausage legs into the latest creation.

He was looking forward to his evening; he had a dinner engagement with Alistair at their club, and afterwards he might head over to Jeffery's, where the most die-hard gamblers flocked.

"Alistair, exactly how and when did you become such a dandy?" Alistair's waistcoat was a crimson red, his fobs (which were numerous) were various shades of pink, orange and red, and his coat was a cherry velvet that must have required more than one individual to assist him into it, it was such a formfitting garment. Although Alistair was not as broad as Edwin, his presence lent him an elegance that almost—but not quite—removed the ridiculous aspect of his outlandish costume, and his challenging stare dared anyone to make a comment or criticism.

"My lord," Alistair replied in a mockingly servile tone, "*you* are in rare form this evening. Dare I hope that your current incarnation is one you will retain? I could not have remained your friend if you insisted on wearing those horrendous clothes that were no doubt suitable for the Americas, but here are positively démodé."

Edwin laughed, taking no offense at his friend's acerbity.

"Alistair, I knew I need have no fear that you would not say what you were thinking. You have not changed that much, even though your outward appearance is quite different."

Over dinner, Edwin and Alistair discussed Edwin's impressions of England after such a long absence, Alistair's work, the war on both fronts, the shipping business and myriad other topics. Although Edwin was by far the more learned of the two men, Alistair's dry wit and quick intellect more than compensated for his less scholarly mind. The two were chuckling over some youthful indiscretion involving a dog, an instructor's wig and half a dozen turnips when the conversation turned serious again.

"Worthy, my friend, I saw someone whom we both admire today," Alistair announced, resting his head against the back of his chair. "I paid a call on Miss Stanhope. She is a lovely woman, both her mind—which I believe is much harder working than my own—and her face, which is a continual delight. And her delicious sense of style. I swear, she might almost rival me in beauty."

Edwin's mouth tightened as Alistair listed Titania's attributes. He knew others admired her—the constant throng of men who filled her dance card was a pretty clear indicator—but that his oldest friend was now lauding his chosen lady was too much. He replied in a curt, almost brusque, tone.

"Alistair, you tread on dangerous territory here. Obviously, I cannot forbid you to continue to pursue a friendship with the young lady in question, but I would caution you against forming a deeper attachment. That honor is mine, if she will have me."

Alistair rolled his head forward, clutching his wineglass a little closer to his chest. "I did not realize the lady had already ensnared you. I thought you had sworn off women—at least respectable ones—after the experience with the Lady Who Must Not Be Named?" He took a long swig of wine, draining the glass, and then looked inquiringly at Edwin, who was casting his friend a predatory glance.

"What I said before and what I say now are two distinct matters. Leticia hurt me, but she did not break me. I intend to ask the lady to marry me as soon as a few details have been sorted out."

Alistair, by now having poured himself another glass of wine, drained that as well and set it down on the table in a particularly deliberate motion. It was clear that although both men were slightly inebriated, Alistair was in worse shape than Edwin, having drunk at least half again as much as his friend and with many fewer pounds to his frame. His chocolate brown eyes were now bloodshot; his usually perfectly styled hair was rumpled as he had raked his hand through it several times in the course of the evening. He spoke after draining his glass again.

"You cannot expect to throw down a challenge like that and have me walk away. When have I ever backed down from anything? The only times I even considered it," he said, his face getting drawn and somber, "was in battle, watching my friends die and I could do nothing for them. But enough about that," he continued, gesturing to the waiter for yet another bottle of wine, "let us drink to the lady. That, at least, you will allow me, I am certain."

Edwin smiled, raising his glass to the thoroughly foxed man sitting opposite him. "To love, broken noses, friendship and the banishment of bad memories." His elegant toast was somewhat diminished by his simultaneously falling off his chair, landing with an audible "plop" as his large frame hit the polished floor. Alistair blinked widely at him for a moment, then slid off his own chair, still clasping his wineglass delicately between his fingers.

"To love and friendship, then," he toasted, gesturing towards Edwin.

When the two had become so thoroughly tipsy that one of them no longer cared what his cravat looked like, and the other did not mind wearing one, they staggered home to collapse into their respective beds, each thinking on a certain young lady with as much brains as beauty.

Dispatch from the Battlefront, April 1813

Masquerades, disguises, secret identities: all these things may, oddly enough, reveal a person's true nature. Is it any wonder the ton *revels in such playacting? It is only then that they may show themselves as they truly are.*

Take a lady, for example, specifically a singular lady; yes, she appears to be a lady, but is it truly a lady's nature to hunt down a husband with all the battle genius of a modern-day Hannibal?

She is armed with only a few weapons: skill on the piano-forte, a trim ankle, an intriguing profile. She has no army, no artillery, and no horses, save the dainty little mare that takes her riding on Rotten Row. But she is no lady, for she is determined to succeed and will take no prisoners. She is audacious, forthright, strong and determined. If the defini-tion of a lady is that she is all that is polite, subservient and gentle, then may I be so bold as to submit that there are truly no ladies.

Unless we change the definition of a lady by winning the battle, the fair sex will be required to hide their true natures in perpetuity.

Wish me luck. I am off to the wars.

A Singular Lady

Chapter Twelve

"I look ridiculous!"

Titania stood in front of the mirror, Sarah behind her trying to lace her up. Ladies in the eighteenth century—at least the specific one who had owned her gown—had a much smaller bosom and a larger waist than she. She looked as if she had been squeezed, bottom up, from a sausage casing. It was not the most elegant outfit, but Titania realized that having her bosom so thoroughly exposed and almost right under her chin was not necessarily an impediment to filling her dance card.

Having stuffed herself into her dress enough so that she would not cause a scandal on the streets, she and Sarah began to work on her hair, which would be powdered and assembled in an intricate arrangement with flowers, looped pearl strands, feathers and maybe, Titania thought with a rueful grin, there'd even be room to exhibit some of the more pressing bills she had been sent lately.

As Sarah cursed and combed, Titania's mind was preoccupied with the mysterious knight. Who could possibly be so bold as to assert he would "fulfill her every wish?"

Whoever it was, she decided, was just going to have to flush her out like a quail from a hedge. She was in no mood for games; she had enough to gamble on even without this late entrant to the table.

"You are as done as I can make you, miss," Sarah harrumphed.

Titania gathered up her gloves, fan and reticule and marched downstairs, attempting to keep the panniers of her gown from scraping the walls of the narrow corridor. Thibault gasped as she made her way gingerly down the staircase.

"Titania!" he squealed, forgetting to maintain his blasé affect in the shock of his sister's appearance. "You look . . . marvelous!"

"Do you mean marvelous in a good way, or marvelous in a 'you are an oddity' kind of way?"

"Difficult to say," he drawled, seeming once again to remember he was—in his mind, at least—an elegant young man of fashion. "You look so un-you, it is remarkable. And if I were a better kind of brother, I would insist that you wear something to cover your top, since you are practically obscene. But I am not, and you would not anyway, so, yes, you look marvelous in a wonderfully anachronistic way."

Titania raised her eyebrows at Thibault. "Anachronistic? And who, pray tell, has been teaching you words that do not include references to sighing, ferocious animals or atrocious waistcoats?"

Thibault scowled as his sister stared pointedly at his waistcoat, a brand-new monstrosity that seemed to have every shape represented: circles, squares, triangles, rectangles, and, Titania was almost certain, a parallelogram lurking right near Thibault's collarbone.

"My dearest sister," Thibault said, drawing himself up to his full height (only four inches taller than Titania, but he never let her forget them), "you seem to be under the misapprehension that you are more of a word on fashion than I. May I inform you," he said in an icy tone, "that no less a personage than the Prince Regent has been noticed casting his quizzing glass to this very waistcoat?"

"Yes, I imagine he would," Titania replied dryly. "Who are you going as? Not as you are, it is a masquerade, not a circus performance." He started to stick his tongue out at her, then apparently thought better of it.

"It's a surprise, Ti, and you will not guess what we are going to be! All of us—the twins, Percy, even Cedric—are going, and we are certain to have the best costume. And there is a prize for the best one. We have got to win!"

Titania leaned over and ruffled his hair, something she

could not resist doing when he was acting like the boy she adored, not the incipient fop she tolerated. He bounded up the stairs, two at a time, shouting as he ran, "You will not see me, Titania, but I will certainly see you! How could I miss *those*?"

Luckily for Titania's modesty, his last words were drowned out in the slamming of his bedroom door. She turned to Miss Tynte, who had quietly descended the stairs herself while the siblings were baiting each other, and who was now regarding Titania as if she were one of the exotic species at the zoo.

"My dear, have you forgotten something? Perhaps the top of your bodice?"

"This was perfectly acceptable in my grandmother's time." Titania looked doubtfully down at herself, wondering if it was too late to run upstairs and put on a nun's habit.

"So were men wearing red-glass heels and more cosmetics than someone on the stage," Miss Tynte replied with an acerbic tone. She glanced at the hall clock, then shook her head. "It is late, Titania. Let all of us—you, me, your bosom—get to the party."

Titania hiked her gown up to cover herself a little, but it did not help much. There they were, resplendent in all their soft, white glory. She shrugged, and the gown slid back down. She met Miss Tynte's eyes, and they both began chuckling.

"This is truly absurd. If my friends here and I do not get noticed by some eligible bachelor, I will have to hide my head in shame."

"It will not be your head that should be ashamed if that happens, Titania. Should you call for the carriage?" she asked with a pointed look.

"Mm, yes, I should. Stillings?" The butler came up at a brisk pace, then halted abruptly. He started to quiver all over, Titania presumed, with disapproval.

"Yes, miss?" Stillings' eyes were fixed about a foot above Titania's head. Apparently he did not want even to look at her.

"Stillings, please ask Wilton to bring the carriage around."

"You are going out . . . like *that*?" he blurted out, his

face almost a caricature of shock. Titania cleared her throat, casting an amused glance at Miss Tynte.

"Yes, Stillings. Is something wrong?" She blinked as innocently as she could. Stillings squinted for a moment, took another look at the ceiling, and exhaled.

"No, miss. I will go call the carriage."

Titania and Miss Tynte collapsed in giggles as soon as he left the room.

The rumble of the wheels was the only sound inside carriage until Titania spoke.

"They do not love that do not show their love."

"Hm, what?" Miss Tynte blinked as she refocused her eyes.

"Shakespeare."

"I know who wrote it, Titania, I taught it to you. Why are you quoting it?" Titania leaned forward, reaching for Miss Tynte's hand.

"*Show* their love. What do you think he meant by *show* your love?"

Miss Tynte arched an eyebrow. "Probably not what you were thinking when you put that gown on."

"No, really. I was not thinking about my appearance. Do you think it could mean that love demands a show, even if it might be dangerous?" Her friend regarded her warily.

"Dangerous how?"

"Dangerous as in . . . danger. Like risk. Do you think love is risky?"

"Anything that carries such a possibility of failure is risky, Titania. But I think Shakespeare meant that love demands acknowledgment. That you have to state it, somehow, for it to be valid. What brings this on, anyway?"

"Oh, Thibault was asking me for help with his work."

"He was, was he?" Miss Tynte's voice held a distinctly skeptical tone. "Which of his courses is this for?"

"Oh, look, we are here! Look at all the bright lights. This house is stupendous!" Titania stared out the window, truly impressed with the ducal residence, but also just as pleased not to have to answer Miss Tynte's questions.

There were plenty of other guests arriving, so it was some time later that the two ladies actually descended the carriage steps. The butler cast one scandalized glance at her chest, then dragged his eyes up to her face. "Your name, my lady?" he exhaled breathlessly.

Trying hard to ignore the glimmerings of saliva glistening on his lower lip, Titania replied, "The Duchess of Devonshire, please."

"The Duchess of Devonshire," the butler declaimed, his butlerly demeanor now firmly back in place. Titania descended the small set of stairs placed at the door into the ballroom, a fabulously large room decorated in shades of black and gold. Her hosts were the only people present not in costume, so it was easy for Titania to spot the duke and his duchess, an oasis of two normally dressed folk amongst the sea of harlequins, queens, pirates and mermaids. There were quite a lot of mermaids, actually, Titania noticed, and most of them had eschewed wearing much on their upper bodies as well, leaving her a bit more relieved as to her own appearance. Thanking her ancestors for having the sense to wear flat shoes (even if her panniers might mow down unsuspecting guests), she glided over the highly polished floor to greet the duke.

"Your Grace," Titania curtsied, "I am Miss Titania Stanhope, Baron Ravensthorpe's daughter. I have not yet had the opportunity to thank you in person for the kindness you showed to my brother and me when my father died. Thank you, sir," she finished, looking up into the older man's eyes. A pair of lively gray eyes met hers, laugh lines creasing as he smiled warmly back at her.

"My pleasure, Miss Stanhope. Your father was a good friend. I had heard you were recently arrived in town for the Season. I have been escorting my daughters to Almack's faithfully every Wednesday. Why have I not seen you there yet?"

"Your Grace," Titania replied in an awkward tone, "I have not sought out vouchers for that establishment, although I know it is expected for any young lady making her debut; but my parents' history, and my father's later . . . excesses virtually require that the patronesses exclude me, and I would not want to embarrass them or myself in requesting entrance."

The duke frowned, his bushy eyebrows drawing together over the bridge of his nose. "Perhaps, my dear, one of my wife's friends might be able to assist you. You should not be tainted by your father's wicked reputation, no matter how well deserved," he finished with a laugh. "The sins of the fathers should not always be visited on the children, now, should they? I will see what I can do." He touched her briefly on the arm, and moved away with an elegant grace that spoke of his ease amongst Society.

To obtain entrance to Almack's would bring her to the notice of all sorts of eligible, wealthy bachelors. After all, the place was reputed to be so dull that no one but a man in desperate need of a wife would bother even going there. She heaved a great sigh.

"Duchess, I swear boredom has never looked so enticing." A man garbed in a knight's costume lowered his eyes conspicuously to Titania's chest.

She looked up—and up—as he was an exceedingly tall knight, her breath catching as she recognized the watery blue eyes glittering covetously at her. Titania had known her knight was not Lord Worthington, but she had just as surely known that the last person she wanted it to be was Lord Gratwick.

Before he could utter another word she scurried away without replying, panniers swinging wildly. She felt him watching her, even without looking back, and imagined the satisfied smirk on his face. Miss Tynte grabbed her arm as she sped by.

"Duchess, where are you going so quickly? Lord George Ward, or should I say Blackbeard the Pirate, was hoping you would honor him with a dance. He has been searching for you all evening," she said pointedly, gripping Titania's upper arm with an intensity that would allow for no escape. Titania curtsied, unable to do anything else with her friend's hand still maintaining absolute possession of her arm.

"Thank you, yes. I would care to dance." Miss Tynte relinquished her hold and Lord George held his arm out to her. She placed her fingers lightly on the sleeve of his coat.

"I must commend you, Miss Stanhope," he gushed. "You look so . . . so . . ."

On display? Titania thought. She could not seem to look him in the eye, since both his orbs were firmly fastened on her orbs. And he was not looking at her eyes.

"Enchanting!" he declared with a triumphant tone. It

was clear he had been sending his few brain cells into a tizzy looking for a word that was not nearly as lascivious as what he was thinking.

"Thank you, my lord, and may I say you are a very convincing pirate." Lord George gave a bow in reply, a very elegant gesture halted midway as his gold earring got hooked, somehow, into the lace of her bodice. Thankfully, it was the upper part of the shoulder and not lower down.

"Oof, Miss Stanhope, I cannot imag—" His words were muffled by her upper arm, which had reflexively grasped him as he began to stagger a little. She felt his damp forehead graze her sternum and his odor—a mixture of sweat, sugar and wine—assailed her nostrils.

"Lord George, could you, that is, can you possibly . . . ?" Titania felt her face heating up with color, and she twitched her hair forward to cover her face. She had to lean forward, just over his neck, and she saw it begin to glow a bright cherry red.

He was frantically trying to remove the earring from something, either himself or her gown. She tried to breathe deeply, but that in itself caused a problem; he was so close to her bosom every one of her breaths was answered by a little pant from him.

"Uh, how is it going?" she asked, feeling his fingers on the strap of her gown. If she got out of this without losing her top or her dignity she would consider herself very lucky.

"Fine, that is, I seem to have encountered a problem." He turned his head as much as he was able to look at her. "Miss Stanhope, I am dreadfully sorry. I cannot think— wait a minute, I think I have got it." He buried his nose into her clavicle, gave a little jerk, and held on to her as they both stumbled.

"Well. At least your earring is not stuck." They had both fallen on the floor in a heap, his head in her lap, her skirt poofed out around her like a mushroom. She scrambled out from underneath him and tried to smooth her skirts.

He raised his head, staring straight at her breasts. "Uh, uh," he stammered, "I am sorry, Miss Stanhope. I do not know what happened. My earring, your gown, it is all a muddle."

"Please, my lord, do not concern yourself. I am fine. Do

you think you might help me get up? I would like to return to my cousin, please.''

He nodded, slowly lifting himself off the floor. He turned to her, still not looking at her face and held his hand out so she could rise. Once they were both upright, and relatively steady on their feet, he held his arm out in the most chivalric gesture possible, as if he had not just been within betrothal distance of her.

His mother stood with Miss Tynte amongst the rest of the chaperones. Her narrow eyes narrowed even more when she spied her son's vibrantly hued face. "George, my dear, could you get us all some ratafia? I believe we could use some refreshment.''

"Hopefully,'' his mother murmured to Miss Tynte, apparently thinking she would not be able to be heard by Titania, "he will be able to lose that flush between the refreshment table and back here again. I do wish he had inherited a little bit more of my sense and a little bit less of his father's gustatory passion. Although, it's not food that's got him so agitated tonight." The two ladies chuckled. Miss Tynte cleared her throat.

"Perhaps you can get him married off to a woman who will understand him and protect him from a world that is just a little bit smarter than he is.'' She looked over at Titania, who was trying hard to look really, really dumb.

She knew Miss Tynte wanted her to settle for Lord George. Claire was equally pushing about Lord Gratwick, and Lord Worthington—the man who made her breath come faster and her bosom heave, even as it threatened to spill over its slight constraints—clearly had honorable intentions, but he was the last man she could consider.

If anything, he should be on the hunt for a wealthy wife. That he would even make his intentions so plain to her the previous afternoon must mean he did not care that they were both destitute.

Even if he were willing to live on love, she could not. Could she convince him a short burst of shared passion would be all she could offer—and would it be enough?

"My dear lady,'' a voice interrupted, "would you grace me with a dance? My armor clanks somewhat alarmingly when I move, but it is no less loud than the beating of my heart when you are near.''

Titania raised one eyebrow as she absorbed Lord Gratwick's comment; even when he was being overly unctuous, he had not been this excessive in his flattery. She bowed her head slightly and gently laid her fingers on his sleeve. She wanted to discover if, indeed, he knew her secrets.

"Ah, the delight of dancing with such a beauty, the most lovely lady in the room."

"Thank you, Lord Gr—that is, Sir Knight. You flatter me."

"No, I only speak the truth. Who else"—he waved a negligent hand—"could compare? Your face, your form—stunning!"

"Mm, yes, thank you."

"And even your nose has a certain charm."

"Surely not, my lord."

"Ah, but to me, Miss Stanhope, it does." Gratwick cleared his throat portentously. "I wish to speak to you of a matter of mutual concern. Can I persuade you to meet me in, say, two dances?"

Oh, dear. Was it a proposal or something more sinister—if that were even possible.

"Yes, my lord, I would be happy to. Let me see," she said, consulting her dance card, which she knew full well had barely been written on, "I am free for the quadrille, which is in three dances. Meet me by the refreshment table, we can adjourn to those chairs over there," she said, nodding towards some chairs half-hidden by an enormous potted plant.

Lord Gratwick frowned, saying, "That is not the place for a private conversation, and I have something I particularly wish to convey to you. But it would not do to sully your reputation; rumor has it that the ladies of Almack's might actually unbend enough to give you a voucher, despite your family history?"

Titania stiffened. "My lord, you are a friend of my friend, but that does not give you leave to make unsubstantiated references to my family. And—" she continued, her eyes widening in surprise.

"It was only half an hour ago that the duke promised to look into the matter?" Gratwick finished. "And only, let's see, fifteen minutes since he spoke to one of those dragons, I am not sure which one. I have my sources. And I have knowledge regarding you, as well. We will meet there," he said, pointing to the corner of the room, "and if the arena is not suitable for what I have to impart, we will simply find another spot. After all, finding things—eighteenth century costumes, long-lost relatives, husbands—is a very singular thing to do, is it not?" And with that, he walked off, leaving Titania rooted to her spot as she reviewed what he had just said.

Singular. He had to know. More importantly, however, what did he want from her to keep quiet about it? Titania knew the column was not so shocking in itself; after all, her primary intent was to make her readers laugh as they enjoyed her marriage quest.

No, the problem, as she knew, was that she was actually a member of the *ton*, and her quest was a deadly reality. How would any prospective suitor feel if it were known she would say "yes" to a proposal just because of the state of his bankbook? Not to mention that ladies simply did not do anything so forward as to pen a column for a newspaper that anybody could read.

She sidled next to Miss Tynte, hoping her emotions did not show in her face. She settled in next to her chaperone and discreetly consulted her dance card to see if she was spoken for the next dance. No, she was not; she relaxed a little, looking around her as she tried to gather her torn shreds of dignity around herself.

"Duchess! So lovely to see you!" A large, thin man dressed as a king came strolling up to her, his voice booming from high above her head. Titania had no trouble recognizing Alistair, even behind his mask; his gait, height and gray-streaked hair gave him away, not to mention his outlandish costume. He wore a large, golden crown amply studded with jewels of all colors. His large, pointed shoes were made of purple velvet, with contrasting stripes of fabric running down his foot. His stockings were a particularly vibrant shade of pink, whereas his vest and coat were in slightly different shades of orange.

He reminded Titania of a beautiful sunset. "Miss Stanhope," he swooped her a deep bow as he drew closer, "would you do me the honor and bestow a dance on your king, King Oberon?"

Titania laughed out loud as she realized who Alistair was dressed as: Oberon, king and partner to Titania in Shakespeare's *A Midsummer Night's Dream*.

"Yes, of course, how could I refuse my own king?" Titania was flattered that he felt so strongly as to make such a cake of himself at the masquerade, but perhaps it was not as difficult as she would think; he did seem to thrive on being outlandish.

She let Alistair guide her onto the dance floor, energetically guiding her through the steps. He was really an excellent dancer, and there was something so charming about him; it was good he did not have enough wealth to afford her, since she did not want to saddle herself with a more brightly colored version of her father anyway.

Intuitively, she recognized the drive toward destruction, the disregard for convention and the inner anguish that seemed to be the motivation for his behavior. Her father had that, too, and she would be paying for his transgressions for the rest of her life.

"What is it that spurs you to such outrageous action, Mr. Farrell?" she asked, tilting her head up to look at his eyes through his mask. "You look like a popinjay, but your demeanor is far more sober. If I had less of a questioning mind, I would think you were nothing but a languid dandy, the epitome of what my brother is trying to be. He's been reading too much Byron, you know," she confided.

Alistair seemed a bit thrown at her question—the first time Titania had seen him at a loss for words—but recovered quickly, only clutching her hand a bit more tightly as an indication that what she had said had actually affected him. "My dear lady," he chortled, "please do not take my sartorial splendor as anything other than an homage to the great tailors of London. They are my guides, since what can an ex-soldier possibly know about style?"

Since it was clear he had no intention of answering her question seriously, she gave a mental shrug and decided to enjoy the experience of a graceful partner in silence. At the dance's end, Alistair led her back to Miss Tyntc, saying slyly as he left, "My lady, you make an excellent consort for this broken king. Do save me the next Scottish reel since I do not believe I can withstand lengthy conversation."

With that, he whirled around in a flurry of color, accosting a startled footman and grabbing two glasses of champagne, downing them one after the other.

Titania shook her head at his careless consumption, then

gazed out at the crowd, hoping to see Lord Worthington. Was he never coming? Perhaps he was here, but in such a disguise she could not recognize him? No, she knew she would feel his presence if he were here, and she was definitely not feeling anything but naked right now. Just as she was beginning to wonder if she had gotten dressed—or undressed—for naught, she spied a tall, barely dressed man being announced at the portal.

It was him, and he was nearly as naked as she. She stood on her toes to get a better look, causing more than a few gentlemen to get a bit dizzy with trying to follow her assets with their eyes. The movement caught Lord Worthington's attention, and he smiled at her, smiling even deeper as his eyes raked her up and down. As he moved determinedly towards her, a footman intercepted him, handing him a note. Perhaps Lord Gratwick was sending him notes, too?

Titania's giggle was stifled as she saw Edwin's face pale. His mouth barked out a question and his whole demeanor changed in an instant. The footman nodded in assent and moved to one of the side doors, Edwin following as closely behind him as possible. What could possibly be wrong?

"No, blast you, I will not wear that ridiculous hat!" Edwin yelped, throwing the offending item on the floor.

Henri sighed dramatically, picked it up and advanced determinedly towards his friend. "Edwin, you boor, must I remind you that you are attending a masquerade ball and therefore you must be in costume? And since you have chosen to attend as this misbegotten man-fairy, you must look the part! Now, will you wear this hat, or will you be attending the party only as a half-naked man? For sure, your fellow countrymen will be able to discern the disgraceful North American savage in you!"

Edwin grunted at Henri in submission, and allowed him to place the hat—a crown, really, made of twisting leaves and the occasional flower—onto his head. His ardor had convinced his brain to attend the masquerade dressed as *A Midsummer Night's Dream*'s Puck, Shakespeare's "shrewd and knavish sprite," the mischievous goblin who cast a love spell on Queen Titania. When he had first envisioned it, it had seemed clever; now, with a shirt open to the waist exposing his chest, his legs encased in green stockings with only a few twining vines of ivy to make him relatively decent for mixed company, it seemed awfully stupid.

Would Society's duennas be shocked at seeing a half, or perhaps more truthfully, three-quarters-naked man at one of their functions, even if it was in the spirit of a masquerade? Could he possibly manage to wear a plant on his head while simultaneously dancing and keeping his identity secret until the unmasking? It was really too late to be asking himself these rather pointed questions, he thought, glancing at the clock that appeared to be glaring back at him.

He sighed again, allowed Henri to drape the ivy more discreetly around his slim hips, and headed for his carriage, thanking the weather gods that it was not too cold for him to venture outdoors barely clothed. The carriage ride to the Langdons' was long enough for Edwin to regain his natural composure; after all, he had been in a boxing ring in much less, although there were never ladies present.

Edwin ascended the wide, curved stairs to the front door, then ascended another, even more curved staircase to the main ballroom, where he glimpsed blazing candles, flirting misses, raking gentlemen, scandal-brewing matrons—in short, Society at its finest. He took a deep breath before telling the butler his name.

"Puck!" the butler announced in stentorian tones. He inhaled again, noticing several young ladies' eyes widening, and strode into the room, determined to find Titania as soon as possible so he could get on with this courtship stuff.

Just as he spotted her, a footman appeared on his right-hand side. He held out a silver plate with a note on it, gesturing towards Edwin. "A note for you, sir," he intoned somewhat unnecessarily. Edwin frowned, wondering who found it so crucial to summon him that they had to send a note, then shrugged as he slid his finger into the envelope and drew the plain cream-colored paper from its cover. It was brief, direct, and shook Edwin to the core:

Edwin:
  Please meet me in the duke's library immediately. The footman will show you the way.

                                                    Worthington

His father. After so long and at such an inopportune time. A meeting with his father, however, was the one thing that could tear him away from his bluestocking. He turned to the waiting footman, then gestured to the closest doors.

"The library. I assume you can show me the way?" The footman bowed, then turned on his heel and walked to the exit, Edwin following in his wake. The two men walked silently down a long, narrow hallway, passing the gaming room, where it sounded as if some of the husbands were busy losing their wives' dowries, an antechamber where curious servants were all in varying degrees of servitude, and a small room where the duke's children and their friends were having their own party, since they were not allowed to be at the adults'.

Just as Edwin was beginning to wonder if the library was even on this continent, they arrived in front of an outsized oak door. The footman rapped on it with his knuckles, and without waiting, opened it, bowing for Edwin to step inside. It was a large room with floor-to-ceiling bookshelves and rows and rows of books. A large globe stood in the corner, a huge, clearly masculine desk dominated another corner and big wingback chairs were scattered around, making the entire room look like a gentleman's club. Two men were already inside: Edwin's father and another man, whom Edwin presumed was the duke.

He paused at the doorway, aware suddenly of the ludicrous sight he must present: a half-naked Prodigal Son scurrying to meet his father's peremptory summons. He squared his shoulders, drew a deep breath, and advanced into the room, removing his mask as he approached the two men.

The other man walked towards him, holding his hand out in greeting. "I am Langdon, you must be Worthy. Well," he said after shaking Edwin's hands, "I believe you two are acquainted? I will leave you to it, then, and Worthington, please give me the specifics as soon as you can."

The duke left, leaving Edwin and his father to regard each other in silence. After a moment, his father spoke in a soft, hesitant voice unlike what Edwin had ever heard from him before.

"My son, I asked you here for two reasons. The first is to ask if you can forgive me. I know you can never forget.

I have spent every day of the past five years regretting my actions, but also being too stubborn to admit it. Circumstances have changed, and I am just glad that it is not too late. It is not too late, is it, Edwin?" he queried.

"No, Father, it is not too late." Edwin moved towards the older man, enveloping him in a deep embrace.

After several heartbeats, Edwin stepped away, regarding his father with curious eyes. The wings of gray that had graced his father's temples had overtaken the dark brown, and his face was lined and worn. He had always been tall, but before, his height had been balanced by his width, a barrel-chested man with long, strong legs. Now he was substantially thinner, his clothes even hanging slightly away from his frame.

"You mentioned two things. What is the second?"

His father turned away from him briefly, resting a finger on the globe and spinning it with an abstracted air. "You would not know that I have been working with the War Office advising on strategy, current campaigns, negotiations—although I am not particularly skilled at those, am I?" he said with a rueful glance at his son. "Basically, anything that comes up in the course of this terrible war. The War Office is scrambling to anticipate all potential maneuvers, and we need some expertise in the field. That is where we need your help."

"But I, as you know better than anyone, never served in the army. My time spent in the Americas has meant I did not keep up as much as I would have if I had been here."

"No, we do not wish you to go on a campaign. Having just found you, I cannot even bear the thought of you leaving again. We need some strategic insight on what battle tactics the Corsican might have planned. You already do such analysis for your scholarly journals. We are merely asking you to apply your knowledge to *this* war."

"Is maintaining your position in the government what inspired you to find me? Because if this is just your pride speaking again, I would prefer not to have had this conversation."

"You are my only son, Edwin, and my heir."

"Yes, and I will be the next marquess, no matter what you or I think of the matter."

His father chuckled dryly at his angry tone. "Worthy, I

have missed you, and your temper, no matter how much you always tried to hide it. No, this is not about my position, or the potential embarrassment of having an estranged son walking around London rather than Halifax. I sent letters asking you to return but just—well, just never sent them." Lord Worthington walked slowly around the room, then turned to look at Edwin.

"The government needs your expertise, and I need my son." Edwin's heart softened, but rather than open his heart to let the words fall, he turned his attention towards what his father had asked him. It was easier to do things, he had found, than to say them.

"For this project, you mean I will just do analysis? I am not cut out to be a spy, you know, Father. I can seldom keep my emotions in check, as you well know."

The two men chuckled together, almost comfortable with their altered relationship. They had never shared this kind of rapport before. His father had always been so unapproachable, and Edwin had such a shy and scholarly nature, at least until his passions were inflamed, that he had never dared to overstep his bounds.

"There will be no spying, I assure you. So, I can tell the duke you will assist us?"

"Yes, I will help however I can, Father."

"Good, good." His father rubbed his hands together and began to pace quickly around the room.

"I must go, but perhaps you would come to the house—our house—tomorrow, my boy? I have someone I want you to meet." He cleared his throat. "You will also want to refamiliarize yourself with our holdings and, of course, reacquaint yourself with the staff."

"Yes, tomorrow would be fine. Can you not stay?"

"No, mmm, must get home, Let—must get home. Well, I will see you tomorrow. Come in the morning, as soon as you have recovered from your evening, and Edwin?"

"Yes, Father?"

"Do try to find some clothing by tomorrow. I would not want you to shock the servants," he smiled, giving a pointed nod towards Edwin's exposed chest as he walked out of the room.

Edwin's head was spinning. That he and his father had

reconciled so quickly was astonishing. He recognized he no longer felt resentment towards him.

It was as if a burden he had not known he was carrying had been lifted, and the pent-up emotion cast over him like a wave, causing him to blink his eyes. He moved to the window, looking out of it without seeing anything. He would have to go back to the ballroom eventually, if only to share his news with Titania.

His eyes were bright with tears as he looked out on the street below, which was still filled with carriages discharging Society's most famous and infamous denizens.

"Lord Worthington?" He heard the soft voice, and turned to see the woman uppermost in his thoughts standing at the threshold. She looked at him for a moment, then moved towards him, concern on her face as she saw his tears.

He walked swiftly to meet her, and before she could say a word, gathered her in his arms and lowered his face down to hers, capturing her mouth in a kiss that spoke of his emotional intensity as no words possibly could.

He explored her mouth with his tongue, and she responded with alacrity, showing him all she had learned from their previous encounters. She touched his teeth gently with her tongue, running it along his lips and nibbling gently on them, then more roughly as he groaned in response. The only sound in the room was their breath.

He drew his head back for a moment to stare deep into her eyes, holding her face between his hands, then reached his hands behind her back to lock the heavy wooden door behind them.

"My father just left. I was hoping you would come, I could not return to the ballroom just yet."

He gazed at her for a moment more as she looked at him in quiet sympathy, then swooped down again for another, even more passionate kiss.

This time, he partially lifted the restraints he had held on himself the previous times he had kissed her. He placed his strong, work-roughened hand on her neck, pulling her close so she could feel him along the length of her body. He put the other hand at her waist, slowly trailing his fingers down her hip and up her abdomen in lazy circles as he thrust his tongue into her mouth.

She found her body responding to the cadence of his
fingers, and she was swaying in a slow circle, gradually moving her leg so it was between his. She wanted only to reach
the conclusion of what they had started.

What that conclusion was, and what it would mean—or
not mean—for the two of them in the long run she reso-
lutely pushed to another place in her head.

What Edwin was doing with his tongue, his teeth, and
oh-my-goodness his hands was far too intoxicating to give
her any time for a sobering thought. She took her own
hand and placed it hesitantly on his chest between the open
folds of his shirt. His chest was even more magnificent than
she had remembered, and being able to see it as well as
feel it, even just once, was an experience she would gladly
trade any of her cherished books—even Ovid—for. His
chest felt smooth and hard under her hand, and she grew
more bold as she caressed him, running her hand along the
wide golden expanse, feeling the cut and curve of his muscles. He gasped as her fingers stilled by his nipple, lazily
circling it as he had done to hers the last time they had
kissed. She spoke to him in a deliberately wicked tone.

"All's fair in love and war." She took her hand away for
a moment, causing Edwin to sigh in disappointment, but
his sigh changed to an approving rumble as she licked her
fingers and placed the now moistened fingerpads back onto
his nipple. He sighed in luxurious contentment and started
to move her back towards the enormous desk in the corner.

Her panniers proved some impediment to their progress,
so she reached behind her and untied the fastening with
impatient hands, allowing the garments to fall to the floor.
His eyes widened in amazement as he drank in the sight
of her, her lower garments flung to the floor, leaving only
a scanty petticoat, and her upper garments hanging on by
a thread or two. Her ivory-white lush breasts were rising
and falling in a mesmeric rhythm and for a moment, all
Edwin could do was follow their tempo with his eyes. He
trailed his eyes down to her hips, which flared out confi-
dently from her tiny waist, her womanly curves as perfect
as he had imagined.

He might possibly die if he could not fully possess her
now, even though it meant finding a special license tomorrow, a conundrum he was sure he could solve, once his

brain—which had turned to mush—had returned to working normally.

He pulled her back to his chest, tearing at his shirt with irritation, anxious to feel his bare skin on hers. When his shirt was removed to his satisfaction—and hers, too, apparently—he slid both his hands behind her and lifted her onto the hard, wooden desk, mercifully cleared of papers.

She was suddenly aware of just how powerful he was, his hands holding her tightly as he ravaged her mouth with his lips and tongue.

He chuckled softly against her lips, then slid one hand up her waist to capture her breast, sliding it out of its flimsy covering easily. He cupped it in his hand, then began to brush her nipple lightly with his finger, feeling it start to harden under his attention. He took his other hand and extricated the other breast from its covering so she was bare to the waist.

Still kissing her, he began to caress both her breasts, moving his warm, slow hands so they almost completely covered her full curves, her nipples erect as they reacted to the attention being lavished on them. He pulled his mouth away from hers, and before the soft "oh!" of disappointment could come from her lips he bent his head down to her chest and took her nipple into his mouth, sucking and licking it as if it were the most delicious treat he'd ever tasted.

Titania couldn't believe how the simple placement of his mouth on her breast could cause such a sensation of feeling all over her body, a languorous warmth stealing over her, her entire body begging to be touched and licked as her breasts were. She could only hold on to his short, golden-brown hair as he continued to suckle her breasts, taking one, then the other, as much into his mouth as he could, tracing his tongue on the sensitive underside where it began its curve out from her body, licking her lightly, delicately, then sucking on her with an intensity that made her gasp.

She released her death grip on his hair, sliding her hands back onto his shoulders, feeling the bone and muscles underneath the warm, golden skin. She feasted her eyes on his body, drinking in the sight of the muscles shifting as he held her tighter, his large hands grasping her as if he would never let her go. She slid her hands down as far as she could reach, past the shoulder blades to the middle of his back, stroking her hands on his skin in frustration that she could not touch more of him.

Just as she was certain she couldn't take anymore, he was suddenly still, his eyes closed as he caught her wrist with her hand.

"Titania, you understand what we are doing, if you wish to stop this, now is the time?" he asked, his voice a low murmur. "Because I will not be able to stop in a moment, and we will have to have the banns read right away, which is sure to cause all kinds of scandalous talk, since I will not be able to keep my hands off you once I've tasted you."

Titania drew back. "Banns read," she repeated dully. "I cannot marry you, Edwin. You cannot afford me. I was hoping, that is, I assumed that we, that neither of us, was free to do what we truly wanted for the rest of our lives, that is, that perhaps just for now we could enjoy ourselves without thinking too much of the future."

Edwin's face froze for a moment, and his next words were like ice water thrown on Titania's warm heart. "You wish to make love to me but you will not marry me? You thought this"—he gestured between them—"was what, exactly? What kind of man do you take me for? I have been used by a woman once before. I will not be used again. Is it possible you are as ugly in your heart as Leticia was?"

Titania shook as he spoke. He wanted to marry her, even though she knew he was destitute, had seen the shabby clothing he wore, the dilapidated carriage and old nags he drove, even heard how he was on the hunt for a woman who would restore the luster of his title.

She had just delivered him a facer from which he might never recover—at least not enough to forgive her.

She turned away from him, unconsciously adjusting her garments so she wasn't as naked on the outside as she felt on the inside. Having made herself somewhat presentable, she turned again to face him, her hand balled into a fist at her side, her other hand holding her throat as if she were struggling for air.

"Edwin, I am sorry to have so disappointed you. I thought you understood me when we spoke at my house the other day; it appears you did not. I must beg your forgiveness, my lord. If you will excuse me . . ."

"Excuse you!" Edwin thundered, moving towards her as menacingly as he had lovingly just a few minutes ago. "Excuse you for assuming I would fall in with your plans for me, as if I were a stallion to service you? And did you even think about the consequences, Miss Stanhope? What if there was a child, would you allow some other man, some dupe, to believe that he had sired it? What of me?"

By this time, he was standing as close to Titania as before, his eyes glittering emerald sparks. She wanted to take a step back, but her pride—her stupid pride, she could admit to herself—would not allow her to back down.

No, she hadn't considered the consequences. Nor had she thought much beyond what had been about to happen in this room. Did that make her irresponsible? Yes, it did.

She was acting just as hedonistically as her father had, determined to gain her own pleasure at the expense of others. She was using Edwin as if he were no better than . . . than, she couldn't even say it to herself. Her insides crumpled.

It was one thing to sell yourself off to the highest bidder who would presumably know the rules of the game, but to involve an honorable man in a dishonorable action was a much different thing entirely. It was a good thing that whoever would have the honor of marrying her had no use for her heart, because it was lying at the feet of the ferociously angry man now glowering at her.

"You are right, my lord," she said softly, her voice so low he had to bend closer to hear her. "I have led you on. I never had any intention of marrying you. You see, I must marry someone who is wealthy. My livelihood depends on it."

"Your livelihood?" he said with a scornful grimace. He backed away from her as if repelled. "What could possibly be worth throwing away a passion like this for? You demean yourself and me, Miss Stanhope. I hope your books and jewels and whatever else you spend your husband's money on keeps you warm at night, since there is no way, *no way*," he repeated, moving so close to her that his breath tickled her eyebrows, "you will find anyone who would love you as I do. Neither as deeply," he said, putting his mouth next to her ear, "nor as well," he finished, lightly tracing his tongue down her neck.

"And, if you will excuse me, I have to return to the masquerade, where people in disguise are less devious than you." He quickly brushed by her, turned the key in the lock, and was gone. Titania stared at the closed door, her breath coming in such short gasps she felt she might suffocate.

She plopped down on the carpet and held her head in her hands, trying hard not to lose control. Her efforts were in vain, however, and she surrendered to her anguish, crying in great, gulping gasps as she lay on the carpet.

After a few minutes of relentless sobbing, she attempted to sit up and put herself to rights. Her clothing was still disheveled from Edwin's attentions, and she was mortified to think someone might have walked into the library when she was wailing on the carpet.

It was a good thing, she thought with a slight return to her normal frame of mind, that there had not been some sort of library room emergency, like if someone suddenly needed to ascertain whether Brussels was closer to Athens or Constantinople. Thank goodness the party guests were far too engrossed in discovering the locations of the eligible (and ineligible) members of the opposite sex.

She busied her hands—and her mind—with the re-arrangement of her clothes. Her breath caught in her throat as she thought just how close she had come to giving herself completely to Edwin.

If he had not mentioned marriage. If she had not been honest with him. She would never come that close to such passion again. A man like Edwin came along once in a lifetime, and he had just walked out the door.

Chapter Thirteen

"Titania, where have you been?" Miss Tynte gave her a keen-eyed look, her features softening as she met Titania's eyes.

"Out ruining my life." She plopped down on the chair next to her friend and sat her face in her hands.

"Miss Stanhope, perhaps you forgot our engagement?" Lord Gratwick had sidled up on her other side, and his smooth tones were an unpleasant interruption.

She inhaled and stood up, pasting a cheery smile on her face. "Why, no, my lord, of course not. I am sorry to have kept you waiting." It was hard, but not impossible, to maintain an air of sanguinity when your heart lay broken in some duke's library.

"Miss Stanhope, it appears you do not value your secrets as much as I had thought . . . Perhaps when it is time for the unmasking we should unmask the Singular Lady as well?" He tapped his finger against his lips. "I wonder what the other guests would think of a lady in Society who is making such fun of their diversions. I wonder if your suitors would be pleased at being compared to various forms of animal life? And so, Miss Stanhope, if you have no objection—" He moved forward as if to address the crowd. Titania shot her arm out to hold him back. He turned to her with a smug smile on his face.

"No. I will not deny exposure would be exceedingly unpleasant. But what, my lord, do you want from me?"

"Merely, Miss Stanhope," he replied, placing his other hand on top of hers as it still held his arm, "to be allowed to take you for a drive tomorrow afternoon. You would not think I would be so ungentlemanly as to reveal all, do you? It will be our secret, that is, unless you find yourself otherwise engaged tomorrow afternoon. Until then, Miss Stanhope." With that, he walked away, armor clunking as loudly as Titania's heart.

The rest of the evening was a blur. Titania knew she had danced, laughed and flirted with a number of kings, gods, sorcerers and monsters; unmasked with the guests and listened to the "oohs" and "aahs" as everyone sorted out whom everyone else was; drank at least one more glass of champagne, leaving her light-headed but no more light-hearted; and watched in amazement tinged with envy as Miss Tynte danced with all the joy that had fled Titania's heart.

Would the morning bring anything beyond a new day?

The morning brought no relief. Titania lay in her bed, unable to move. If this is inertia, she thought, is there such a thing as ertia? And where would she get some? She could not seem to lift herself out of her warm, cozy bed.

She lay still for a few minutes, hearing the normal household rumble below—Stillings pontificating, Cook grumping, the housemaids giggling—when she heard a knock at the door. That was odd; it is scarce eleven o'clock, and no fashionable person is about now. Oh, dear, she thought, hurriedly throwing clothes on, perhaps the bill collectors have come to collect. She would not want anyone to start making a scene, possibly ruining her plans.

A politely surprised Stillings was opening the front door to Julian and his mother as Titania scurried downstairs, thrusting her hair behind her ears.

"Good morning Mrs. White, Mr. Fell. What brings you here so early? Not that I am not pleased to see you, of course," she added hastily. "Would you like to join me in the sitting room? Stillings, tea please."

Julian stood in the foyer and dragged a chair from against the wall nearer to a table holding a vase of flowers. He swept the vase off the table, handed it to Stillings, and pointed to the chair. "Mother, you sit here, please. I brought you a book, too."

Mrs. White bestowed a loving smile on her son. "Miss Stanhope, this is what comes of allowing your son to dismiss his tutor at an early age. I will sit right here, Julian, and pretend I am a proper chaperone."

Julian waved Titania into the sitting room. "I will keep the door open, Mother," he called as they sat down. "I would not want to offend your sensibilities." A muffled chuckle was his only response. He turned to Titania, a concerned look on his face.

"My friend, you are in trouble—I know you are—and you cannot deny it. Well?"

His dark brown eyes filled with concern as they gazed at her. She began to feel some of her rigid control fall away. She shook her head, drawing her chair a little closer to his.

"It is a complete muddle. I believe I will have to tell you everything, although I wish I did not have to involve you in any deception. I am a Singular Lady."

Julian looked puzzled. "Yes, that you are, but what does that have to do with anything? If you were not singular, I would not be out on the streets at this awful hour."

Titania poked him in the arm. "No, you looby," she laughed, "I mean I write that column as a Singular Lady, the one detailing a certain young maiden's quest for a husband."

"Ah, so you're a writer, too? I should've guessed. How clever of you!"

"Yes, thank you, but that is not the point. The point is that Lord Gratwick has discovered my identity. I cannot imagine what he will want for his silence—he has demanded he take me for a drive this afternoon."

"But why?" Julian questioned. "Why do you need to find a wealthy husband?"

"I know rumors have it I have a more than adequate dowry, but the truth is actually quite different. My father, well, as you know, my father was not the most . . . responsible person. When he died, he left everything—or so we thought—to Thibault and me, but when I arrived in town, his lawyer told me another, later will had been found, leaving everything but what is entailed to someone whom I do not even know. It was one of his . . . female acquaintances."

"Infamous," Julian muttered. "How can he have been so reprehensible? A lady should not have to worry about where her next bonnet is coming from."

"It's more than my bonnet, it is my family's very livelihood. You see, my father was none too responsible before he died, either, so the estate is in serious need of repair, and all the funds we had were supposed to help in that effort. And my uncle . . . Well, without those funds, the land, the people working the land, our servants, all suffer. Marrying wealth is my only chance at putting the land and the people back to rights. At least, I thought it was my only chance, but then I had the idea to write the column. My editor says there is a chance the columns will be collected and published, but I will not know that until the end of the Season. I can pay my current bills with what he is paying me for the column, and by selling some of my mother's jewelry, but that money alone will not last forever."

Julian sat back, silent for a moment. "You mentioned your uncle. Can he help?"

Titania tried to stem the flow of tears. "No. He's actually making it worse. I do not know if he can, but he seems quite certain he can take Ravensthorpe from Thibault if we are not able to pay the taxes. He offered to let us live with him if we hand it over, but I cannot do that. Ravensthorpe is all Thibault has."

"What about Lord Worthington?" Julian replied. "It is no secret—to me, at least—that you have an inclination towards him. Must he marry for money as well?"

Titania swallowed hard. "It seems the earl does not plan on marrying for money, but as for marrying me . . . well, I am afraid I have made a terrible mess of things. It is true that he has a . . . fondness for me, but now he knows I cannot marry him, and when I told him my situation last night . . . well, I am afraid he hates me."

"If you could just find this mystery woman," Julian said, "you would be able to explain your situation to her."

"And she would take one look at my sad face and decide to return the money? That kind of thing happens only in fairy tales."

"You could go through your father's papers, maybe there is a clue there, or one of us can go find one of your father's companions and ask her."

"Ask a lightskirt about which one of her cohorts might have known my father? That hardly seems like a realistic plan."

Julian frowned, stroking his chin. "You're probably right; there could be dozens of them."

"My father would be honored you think so highly of him," Titania said dryly. "But, honestly, I think the number of, of women who would speak to us would be none. Thank you for trying, though."

With a friend like this, Titania thought, it was impossible for one's heart to be completely at the bottom of one's shoes. Perhaps it was lodged now around her knees, which was not so bad considering how far it had plummeted last night.

"Perhaps the best course of action would be for you to keep your eyes and ears open. And your mouth shut." She walked Julian and his mother out to the door, feeling as if a tiny bit of her burden had been lifted from her shoulders.

Titania climbed up the stairs with a weary step, intent on writing to escape her thoughts. Pen and paper was an inadequate substitution for Edwin's arms, but it was all she had left.

"Damn all women!" Edwin swore, opening his eyes.

"Damn *her*," he clarified, pulling his dressing gown on as he got out of bed. He stalked over to the washbasin, throwing cold water onto his face. It did nothing to ease the burning of his heart.

Five years ago, he had been entranced by Leticia's face and adulation; with Titania, it was much more. And she was no better than Leticia. Women really were the devil. The sooner he forgot about her, the better. Now if only he could convince his aching, forlorn heart of that fact he would be all right.

Edwin groaned and sat back down on the edge of the bed. He held his head in his hands, shaking it softly from side to side.

"My lord?" Henri came in at a tentative pace. He paused

at the doorway for a moment, then headed determinedly towards the mess of clothing Edwin had tossed on the chair last night.

"Henri!" Edwin barked, glaring at his friend. "Stop fussing. I need to make a call today, a very important call."

"The lady?" Henri's smile was impertinent for a servant, but exactly suited for a close friend.

Edwin scowled. "And I do not want to wear any of those frippery things you insist are in fashion. Something plain, please."

"Not the lady, then," Henri said with a frown. He walked to the wardrobe, drawing out the most somber of Edwin's new coats and held it out to his master for approval.

"Yes, that will do," Edwin admitted with a grudging nod. Edwin picked the soap brush up from his washbasin and began to lather his face. He placed the brush down and lifted the razor, eyeing himself in the mirror with a grimace. The razor scraped against his prickly stubble, the rough sound the only noise in the room.

"Henri, were you not supposed to remind me never to get married?"

"Yes, but there is no stopping you once you have an idea in your head. Was it clear thinking that compelled you to leave your betrothed at the altar? No. Did it make sense to arrive in Canada with your fists clenched, trying to take everyone's head off who looked at you sideways? No. And was it wise to—"

"To rescue a down-on-his-luck émigré from the wrath of the men he had just fleeced? No." Edwin removed the soapy cloth from Henri's hand.

"And the lady?"

Edwin felt his body stiffen. "Never mind the lady. Help me get dressed." Henri dressed him in silence, leaving Edwin to his own thoughts.

Would he ever recover? For just a moment, he considered going to her, his pride swept aside, revealing to her that he was indeed as plump in the pocket as any of the other bachelors eyeing her person in the Marriage Mart. And then what? Marry her, knowing that she was able to commit her heart only after she had committed her head? Spend the rest of his life with a woman whom he was not certain loved him or his fortune more?

Plunging headlong into his studies had helped when Leticia had proven herself false; perhaps working with his father would be just as effective now.

"Edwin," his father said at the door, "I was not certain you would come." Lord Worthington put his arm around Edwin's shoulders, leading him into the large, open foyer. He gestured impatiently to the butler hovering at the side of the room.

"Mutter!" he barked. "Take my son's books." He paused before hoisting open the heavy oak-paneled door to the study. He stepped over the threshold and spoke to someone within.

"My dear, you will not believe who is home again. Edwin, I know this will be somewhat of a shock to you, to both of you, but I wish to present my wife, Lady Worthington. Of course you know each other."

Facing him, smiling in a superior cat-ate-the-cream kind of way, was Leticia. Leticia, still blond and beautiful, her diamond-hard eyes glinting in the morning sun as it came through the windows. Edwin could not speak for a moment, could not even move.

That his father had been duped as the son had was not even a question; whether he knew what his wife was really like remained to be seen. Edwin touched his fingers to Leticia's briefly.

"A pleasure, my lady."

"I had hoped," his father continued, "you would have heard of our marriage. We were the season's scandal for almost a month, a lifetime in Society's view, but apparently," he finished, looking at his son's drawn face, "you had not. It happened not so long after you left."

"About four months after," Leticia interjected. "Your father just swept me away, my lord, since I need not tell you I was suffering a bit at the time."

His father gave a quick grimace. "It *was* sudden. I suppose I did sweep the lady away. We were living abroad for some time. We only returned when the duke asked for my help. We have not been in town long; we certainly have not attended any functions. Nor will we, since there is so much work to be done."

Edwin heard a slight growl emanating from his ex-fiancée, now his . . . stepmother, and realized his father's comment was aimed more towards his wife than his son. Edwin looked at Leticia a little more closely, noticing the fine lines spidering over her forehead. She was starting to show signs of aging, which must frighten her, as vain of her looks as she was. She appeared like a fragile piece of pottery that if handled too forcefully would fall into pieces.

"We could not entertain with the house in such a state anyway," Leticia said with a look of disdain on her face. Her eyes widened as she saw Edwin's father's look of disapproval and she moved back a few steps. Edwin almost felt sorry for her.

"My lady, this house has secrets even my father does not know. Remember, Father"—Edwin turned to the older man—"how I used to go missing for hours? You could not find me until I wanted to be found." He gestured towards the fireplace. "If you work one of those bricks, you can open the door to a secret passageway. I bet there are still a few candles in there from when I used to hole up to read."

His father chuckled. "I always wondered how you managed to make your escape. You will have to show us. And now, my dear," he said, looking at Leticia, "you will excuse us? Edwin and I have a lot to catch up on. I believe you were going to consult with Cook on the evening's menu?" He paused, raising his eyebrows as he spoke.

"Yes, my lord, I was going to do that. Excuse me." She scurried out the door, shutting it softly behind her. His father eyed the closed door for a moment longer, then turned towards Edwin.

"She is young, although not as young as when you knew her. She was so broken after you . . . you left, and I was in pain, too. But that was a long time ago, and people change. I would prefer not to speak on it again."

His father drew him towards the desk perched in the corner, its top strewn with so many papers and books it was impossible to see the wood underneath. They began to work, slowly, hesitantly, until their shared enthusiasm and knowledge made them as giddy as schoolboys, gesticulating wildly towards maps, quoting long-dead and long-forgotten generals as if they were the latest players at the Drury Lane Theatre.

If it were not for that agonizing gash in his heart, Edwin

thought as he glanced at his father, he would actually be happy.

"Edwin, are you listening to me?" His father was eyeing him with an amused glint in his eye. "You always were prone to daydreams, but it would be useful if you could concentrate on this for just a moment."

"Certainly, and . . . Father?"

"Yes, Edwin?"

"It is good to be home."

"It is good to have you home. I missed you, Edwin. Now, where were we?"

If nothing else, Edwin thought as he bent his head towards the papers on the desk, at least he was happy his father was returned to him. Or, more accurately, that he was returned to his father.

An hour or so later, Edwin was startled by a faint rumble. It had been completely quiet while he worked, the way he preferred it, and he had almost forgotten his surroundings. He looked over at his father, whose soft snores had interrupted his concentration. Edwin stretched, feeling his muscles protest at having sat in the same position for so long. It was time to leave.

He murmured a low "good-bye" to his father, who muttered something in his sleep, and slipped out the door, beckoning to the footman waiting in the hallway. "Please convey my compliments to Lady Worthington and tell my father—"

"Tell your father what, my lord," Leticia said as she descended the grand staircase. Edwin turned to her, consciously striving to keep a light tone in his voice.

"My lady, I was just making my departure. I have brutally attacked my father with maps and strategies and other scholarly insights, and he is resting after the assault. Tell him I will return tomorrow, if you please."

Leticia looked at him blankly, plainly not understanding just what her stepson was saying. Edwin recalled her air of dim-wittedness had always made him feel superior, and he realized it was not just one of her affectations.

"My lady, I return tomorrow. Good day."

Edwin took the hat and coat the butler handed him and walked through the door without once looking back.

Chapter Fourteen

"A gentleman to see you, miss." The maid gave a breathy squeak as she spoke, surprising Titania into dropping her pen as she tried to disguise her papers. Was Edwin here? Was it possible he had come to persuade her to change her mind?

The maid's next words were like water on her imagination's overstoked fire. "It's Lord Gratwick, he says you have an engagement to go riding?"

It was an unnaturally subdued Titania who collected her bonnet and gloves and descended the stairs, hoping against hope that some disaster would transpire so she could avoid this extremely unpleasant ordeal: a rampaging chicken, perhaps, or a scuffle between Thibault and his most noisome waistcoat or Miss Tynte's swain serenading her through the sitting room window.

Nothing occurred to save her.

She stayed silent as Gratwick assisted her into his phaeton. Titania had a few moments to enjoy the drive—she did love being outside, no matter the company, and she had not yet tired of seeing the same London parks every time she left her house with a horse—but Gratwick's very existence pulled her from her enjoyment.

He drove the team to a somewhat secluded spot in the park, although a few carriages were still in view, slowing the horses to a walk as he leaned back against the seat.

"My dear Titania."

She startled at his presumption. "I have not given you leave to use my first name, my lord," she said in her most Managing voice.

"Have you not, my dear? I thought with all we had shared it would perhaps be understood. If not, then I will have to keep calling you Miss Stanhope . . . that is, until you agree to an elevation in title and become Lady Gratwick?" He turned his head and looked directly into her eyes. He wore what he probably assumed was a winning smile and what Titania thought looked just like that mean snake in Paradise. She was certainly not even close to being tempted by *his* apple.

She launched into the speech every young lady learned in the schoolroom. "My lord, I am aware of the honor you do me, but I cannot accept your proposal."

First of all, she thought, the idea of spending more than the duration of this ride in his presence was enough to make her ill; second, she was not so desperate as to sell herself for a pile of collectible books and some indeterminate amount of money; and third, she did not want to marry anyone but Edwin. And he despises me, so that is probably not an option.

Gratwick's voice came cutting through the jumbled haze in her mind like a vicious dog through a pack of peahens. "Ah, the suitable maidenly reply, Miss Stanhope. I hope I might flatter myself you do not really mean what you say, and rest assured, I will keep your secret safe while you consider the idea. If you decline . . ." His eyes revealed his implied threat.

"Why would you want to marry me, my lord, if you must blackmail me into it?" Titania spoke in as cool a tone as she could muster, although she quivered inside. The revelation of her identity would not be the worst scandal ever to hit the *ton*, but it would ruin her chances of marrying well and securing her family's future.

Much as she hated to do so, she had to keep Gratwick thinking she might say yes. "And my final decision, my lord, is due exactly when? I like to meet my deadlines, as I am sure you are well aware."

He chuckled. "A week should suffice. Any longer than that and it will be too late in the Season to announce the happy news. You have a week to become accustomed to the idea of being Lady Gratwick, and I believe, as you weigh its merits, you will find it will not be all that bad. I am intelligent, reasoned, and will not mind if you continue to write, provided we keep it our little secret. As for our congress, I have every confidence we will manage." He stared deliberately at her mouth, darting his tongue to lick his lips.

She felt nauseated by the sight.

She would not marry someone she actively loathed. She could not let him see the extent of her dislike, however, at least not until the time he had deigned to give her was up.

She smiled in mute acquiescence to his time limits, and changed the subject to the array of books she had discovered in his uncle's library; at least if she was going to spend time with this too-knowing blackmailer, she was going to discuss something of interest to her, and she knew that for all his faults at least he was not stupid.

Finally, after what seemed like hours, he returned her home. She hopped down from his carriage before he could assist her.

"Thank you, Lord Gratwick." Thank you for possibly the worst few hours of her life. She'd be damned if she would allow him to condemn her to live the rest of her years in such agony.

"Thank you for driving out with me today, Miss Stanhope, and I look forward to you making me the happiest of men in a week." She was unable to repress a shudder, which he noticed, at his confident tone. He gave a little nasty chuckle as he urged his horses forward.

Working with his father was a blessed interval, Edwin thought as he tramped down the street, since it made him forget—or at least not remember—Titania for a few hours. Now, however, the pain was back, as searing as before. He decided to visit Gentleman Jackson's boxing saloon; he was in just the sort of mood to beat the stuffing out of some unfortunate lord, and he wanted to do it in a place where others would make sure he did not lose control.

Edwin found his punching bag in the person of a brawny lord who was apparently accustomed to being the strongest man in the saloon. Edwin quickly made the arrogant oak aware that his power was no match against a man who had slightly less strength, but more than made up for it with incredible speed and finesse. Edwin dropped him with a blow to the stomach.

That did not do very much to ease his agony, he thought as he stood over his foe. The pain was still there, almost as palpable as that of the man who lay groaning at his feet.

"Lord Worthington! Perhaps you would like a real match?"

Edwin turned, absentmindedly wiping the sweat from his neck with his hand, and saw Lord Gratwick leaning nonchalantly on the back of a chair, an obnoxiously superior look on his face. Edwin felt his chest tighten.

"Whom, Gratwick, would you suggest? Certainly not yourself; no offense, my lord, but I believe I could snap you like a twig. I cannot oblige you. I do not prey on the weak, you see."

"Oh, but there are contests, my lord, and there are *contests*. Anyone will tell you I have bested many of the men who visit here regularly, but that is not my point. Perhaps, my lord, I was speaking just now of the contest to win a certain lady's hand. I would oblige you by acting the twig, but I have just returned from a driving engagement with a lady, and," he said, gesturing towards his clothing, "I am not suitably attired, and I must make an appearance at my mother's house quite soon. I wish to make her aware of some upcoming alterations to my life, the addition of another dependent. But I will not bandy the lady's name about here, perhaps you know to whom I am referring?"

Edwin spun around slowly, hating to see the look of triumphant malice in Gratwick's face. Was it possible Titania had actually accepted this loathsome worm's offer over his? And even if she did not, was it at all fair that he got to see her today, while Edwin was forced to take out his frustrations at *not* seeing her? He knew that to say anything would be to provoke an argument, so he walked silently towards the changing area, Gratwick's final words ringing in his ears.

Edwin could barely see for the rage that enfolded his brain, and it took a great force of will not to tear off after Gratwick. But, he mused as the fire in his heart burned down a little, it was good practice for the force of will he was going to have to exert for the rest of his life: "No,

Lady Gratwick, I did not expect you would be here. And how is your delightful husband? And your seven children? Yes, well, I must be going back to my estate, the livestock are missing me. It has been my experience that animal husbandry is so much more rewarding than the human kind. Pleased to see you again, please convey my dislike to your husband."

Titania heaved a huge sigh as she entered the house, pulling off her bonnet and pelisse and handing them to Stillings.

"Miss, might I suggest some tea in the sitting room? I have taken the liberty of asking Cook for some gingerbread, as well."

"Thank you, Stillings. It is very nice to be so well taken care of." Titania shuffled slowly into the room, dropping herself down on the sofa.

She had never been so muddleheaded before, not even when her father had died. She held her head in her hands, speaking aloud, thankful no one was around to hear.

"Titania, you are a fool. How wrong you were." Now that she truly understood what was at stake, how could she possibly do what she planned? At least it had inspired her column, which was the only ray of hope she had. She clung to it with impractical hope.

What if her columns actually were successful enough to be printed, as her editor was implying? She knew there was not much money in writing books, but it might be enough for Ravensthorpe for just a little while.

What if she confided in Thibault and the two of them worked together to retrench the estate? Could they make it work? And could she tell Edwin she'd made a terrible mistake and would be glad to be his wife, even if it meant both of them writing to eke out a living? Would that be so awful?

It would be a gamble. She raised her head, speaking softly to herself. "I am my father's daughter, and I am willing to take the risk. I love Edwin. I cannot envisage a life without him, his wrinkled cravats or his knock-kneed nags."

"Are you giggling, Titania?" Miss Tynte said in surprise as she entered the sitting room. "Stillings told me you were as sad as when you discovered Cambridge did not admit females. And yet, here you are with a silly grin on your face and I do believe you are actually laughing! Tell me you are not losing your mind, are you, my dear?"

Titania laughed even harder at seeing her old friend's bemused face. "Certainly I am not losing my mind, and even if I were, do you think I would recognize that? After all, if I am going mad, I am not of sound enough mind to figure that out, now am I?"

"You are up to something, then, and you must tell me what it is. Just this morning you were moping and sighing as if the world were coming to an end, and now you are behaving like a giddy girl. I know that look, young lady, even though I have not seen it for many years . . . you have not switched the sugar and the salt again, have you?"

Titania rolled her eyes. "I suppose I had better confess, you will discover it eventually."

She pulled her old friend near to the sofa, and told her everything: about the column, her editor's kind words and the potential for some financial remuneration, her uncle's threats, Gratwick's blackmail, her own misery at playing out the hand she had dealt herself, and the last encounter she had had with Lord Worthington, leaving out, for discretion's sake, the near miss she and her virtue barely avoided.

Miss Tynte seemed to guess what had not been spoken, however, sitting back in the seat cushions as she narrowed her eyes in concentration. She glanced over at Titania a few times, but did not speak for several minutes. It seemed like a lifetime.

"I did not fully understand the depths of torment you have been suffering, my dear," Miss Tynte said in a low, sympathetic voice. "It is natural for you to guard your feelings a bit more than your parents, who were, well, a bit over the top with their emotions." She reached out and took Titania's hand, continuing to hold it as she talked.

"There is nothing more shameful than being like your parents, especially at a certain age, is there not? But I am so accustomed to your taking care of everyone, from Sarah's aches and pains, to Thibault's latest caper to Cook's chickens, that I do not always remember that underneath your very competent demeanor, your Managing Ways, is a young woman. My love," she said, turning to Titania with a determined look on her face, "if this scholarly pugilist is your destiny, you must follow it, even if it means we cannot help those people whom we all think of as 'family.' I will not allow you to sacrifice yourself so, now that I know how much your heart is engaged."

Titania threw her arms around her old friend, her wise teacher, in a fervent clasp that told more of Titania's feelings than her normally carefully chosen words could.

Drawing back, she looked down at her hands, rubbing one finger on her palm in an absentminded rhythm. "I must find Edwin, explain the situation, apologize for being so stupid, and find out if he can forgive me. It is all so easy," she said with a rueful smile.

"And if he will not forgive me," she continued, "I will never forgive myself."

Dispatch from the Battlefront, April 1813

A girl's first Season is a delightful time, filled with parties, new gowns, new friends, the latest scandal and the most eligible bachelors.

It is also a time when a girl can become a woman.

Not in that way, you lurid people, but in a way far more difficult to accomplish: realizing that life is not about eating your cake, and having it, too.

My heart is not engaged. My head will not take no for an answer.

The inevitable conflict is the stuff of poetry, epic romances, and this humble column.

Even I do not know the ending, and yet the end is fast approaching. Until then, I remain,

A Singular Lady

Chapter Fifteen

"The damask rose? Or the violet?" Titania asked, as much to herself as to Sarah and the undermaid who was assisting in the all-important task of getting Miss Stanhope prepared for the evening, a party that seemed to be the most important event of the Season.

"The damask is lovely on you, miss," Sarah said, "but I think the violet makes your eyes sparkle, and of course you can wear your mother's amethysts, too."

Titania smiled, remembering seeing her mother stop by her room before she went out when Titania was just a young girl.

"Yes," Titania said, "I do believe you are right, Sarah. The violet is the best choice."

Titania had not yet worn this particular gown, finding it so delicately lovely she was afraid of ruining it by spilling something or tripping. But if she never wore it, what was the point of having purchased it? And what better time to wear it than tonight, when her very life hung in the balance? She needed to play her hand with as many advantages as she could muster, and this violet gown represented a veritable pair of aces. She eased into it, taking a long look in the glass as Sarah adjusted the hem.

The gown was molded to her figure, enhancing her bust and slim waist, revealing the subtle flare of her hips as it cascaded down to her feet. Just under her bust, a darker-hued purple ribbon encased her ribs and the straps that held the gown up were made of the same material. Hopefully the gown would provide her with the confidence she knew she would need to speak to Edwin.

The soiree was already an overstuffed, hot, uncomfortable affair when Titania and Miss Tynte arrived.

Titania looked for Edwin immediately, knowing she would be in agony until she spoke to him. Not spotting him, she found a footman bearing champagne and discreetly sipped it until it was gone, then found herself another glass.

And then she saw him: Edwin, sumptuously attired in a black evening coat, a black waistcoat picked out with gold embroidery and a black cravat. The black and gold drew attention to his sun-darkened skin, the tawny lights in his hair, and the emerald green of his eyes. He was a breathtaking sight, and Titania could almost hear all the susceptible females in the room heave a collective sigh. He seemed unaware of the effect he was having, heading directly for the gaming room.

"Quite a display, is he not?" Alistair said in her ear, startling her so much she spilled some of her champagne. He gestured quickly to obtain her another glass—her third, she counted in surprise—and continued, "It seems the boy has taken my advice and gotten himself some decent clothing. You would think he would have done so upon arrival. He would have saved himself a lot of idle speculation."

"Idle speculation? What do you mean?"

"Oh, only that my friend is not nearly as impoverished as he appears," Alistair replied. "The estate he inherited, although apparently in need of some attention, will yield a healthy per annum, and he had already gained a small fortune while in exile. So although he wished to give the appearance of a pauper, for reasons known only to himself, he is actually quite flush in the pocket."

Titania felt in her pocket for the small of piece of wood she still carried. She dug the sharp end into her palm until she felt the urge to scream subside.

Edwin was as wealthy as any of her other suitors. She would never be able to convince him she loved him before discovering the truth about his fortune. The perfect man, in intellect, looks and yes, fortune, despised her.

"Are you all right, Miss Stanhope? Perhaps you need to take a turn on the balcony to get some fresh air?" Alistair escorted her quickly to the balcony entrance and led her outside, taking care to refresh both of their glasses.

"Here," he said, returning her glass to her limp hand, "drink this. You will feel better." She drank it down unprotestingly, noticing that the world seemed a little fuzzier and she was having slight difficulty figuring out where she was.

"Are you all right, Miss Stanhope?" he repeated. "You are so pale. Should I summon your cousin?"

Titania held up her hand to stop him. "No, no. A slight dizziness, that is all. Please, do not trouble Miss Tynte. She would worry, and it is nothing. If I could just ask you to sit with me for a moment, I will be fine."

"Of course," Alistair replied, seating himself next to her on the stone bench. It was a warm night, and a light breeze brought some temporary relief, although Titania barely noticed since her insides were completely frozen.

"Miss Stanhope," Alistair said, looking more serious than Titania had ever seen him, "I realize now is perhaps not the most appropriate time, but I've lost my nerve so many times that I just must talk to you now."

"What . . . what is it, Mr. Farrell?"

Please do not propose right now. Please let it be anything else but that.

"Miss Stanhope, I know you believe me to be nothing but an empty-headed fop, and perhaps I am, but I am also someone who believes that a man can change if he has the right person to help him. I want you to be that person, Miss Stanhope. I want you to marry me. Will you do me the honor?"

She had no honor. Not anymore.

"Mr. Farrell, I am aware of the great honor you do me, but . . ."

"But you will not," he finished. "I suppose it was too much to hope that you would wish to be married to someone as brainless as I am." His glum expression wrung Titania's already sore heart.

"Mr. Farrell, do not think my refusal has anything to do with any presumed lack found in you. My . . . my affections are already engaged. But you *are* my friend. And, Mr. Farrell," she said in a low aside, "you might want to make sure your bride is someone who will not be overwhelmed by your sartorial splendor."

"Oh, but Miss Stanhope," Alistair said with a quick return to his normal, urbane mien, "no lady could possibly compare. I pledge that whoever finally accepts this elegantly attired ex-soldier will be a drab wren so as not to compete with her devastatingly gorgeous husband."

Titania chuckled, as she was meant to, giving Alistair a friendly smile. She felt her insides warm as well. She laid an impulsive hand on his arm, turning to look directly into his dark brown eyes.

"You must know I respect, admire and trust you. You can depend on me if you need help."

"Any help except agreeing to be my bride, correct?" Alistair said with a sly grin. She laughed again, removing her hand from his arm to cover her mouth.

"Yes, anything but that. Is it a bargain, then?"

"Indeed it is, Miss Stanhope, indeed it is."

And without warning, with barely a second to register what was happening, he swept her up into a huge embrace, nearly enveloping her with his long arms. She stayed there for a moment, shocked, while he breathed deeply into her hair.

"Excuse me," a clipped voice said. Drawing back, Titania saw that Edwin was on the balcony, regarding the two of them—his best friend and the woman he'd been indecently caressing not twenty-four hours before—with undisguised disdain.

"It appears I am interrupting. I had hoped Miss Stanhope would oblige me with a few moments of her time, but I believe that will now be unnecessary.

"Excuse me," he repeated, striding quickly back into the ballroom. Titania felt as if she had been punched in the stomach.

Alistair continued looking at Edwin's retreating form, then gave a heavy sigh and twisted his neck to regard Titania with a piercing gaze.

"Miss Stanhope, you are terribly pale again. Judging by your face, it appears you have just informed me of the object of your affections. As if I did not already know. If you want me to speak with him, to explain the situation . . ."

"No!" Titania burst out. "No, thank you," she said in a milder tone. "I will do whatever explaining is to be done."

He must think she was the loosest woman of his acquaintance, going from man to man in some sort of mad rush. And how wrong was he? In the course of one day, she had received proposals from no fewer than three men, and turned them all down.

She rose stiffly, feeling as if she were one hundred and twenty-three instead of just twenty-three. "Thank you, Mr. Farrell. I believe I would like to be alone for a little while, if you do not mind."

Alistair bowed. "Of course. Please, Miss Stanhope, if I may repeat what you just said—please, call on me if you need any help." Titania gave him a slight nod of her head, then took several weary steps back into the ballroom. As she passed through the doorway, she squared her shoulders and threw her head back. A good bluff, her father used to say, is better than a good hand.

The problem was, she realized a few hours later, was that you needed someone to play with, and her chosen partner was proving maddeningly elusive.

Titania watched in frustration as Edwin danced and flirted with any number of ladies, all of whom were either married or otherwise unattainable. He danced a languorous waltz with Lady Carteret, a woman whose passions were only slightly less discreet than her cleavage, a quadrille with Mrs. Jennings, a widow who had just come out of mourning with an ample fortune and no desire ever to let it out of her control again, and the young Miss Jane Ellingsworth, who was in the unfortunate position of being the younger sister of a girl who could not enter a conversation with anyone without disagreeing with them.

"Titania, my love, you should stop staring." Miss Tynte's voice interrupted just as Titania was willing herself not to march over and remove Edwin from the woman who seemed to be gripping him as tightly as Lord George did a sugary tidbit. She tilted her head to stare at the ceiling, thus avoiding Miss Tynte's eyes.

"No, I was just admiring the chandeliers. Have you ever seen such a lovely fixture?"

Her friend's tone was as dry as Plutarch. "No, I have not. I do admire a good *fixture*."

"Well, I see my next partner arriving. Mr. Ramer, I believe this is your dance?" Titania smiled brightly at Miss

Tynte as her partner whisked her away with a brisk twirl. Unfortunately, everyone seemed to be discussing the last person she wanted to talk about.

"The Earl of Oakley, he is a bit of a dark horse," Mr. Ramer said with an admiring nod. "First he returns to town, no one knows he's got anything—fact is, most everyone thinks he's still the dog in the manger—then he shows up dressed like a prize rooster on the strut! Turns out he's got gobs of money."

"Tell me, Mr. Ramer," Titania asked, "does your family estate feature a wide assortment of livestock?"

"Yes, Miss Stanhope, it does; why do you ask?

"No reason, Mr. Ramer. No reason."

"Thank you for the delightful dance, my lord. I do not think the marquess minded that much when you stepped on his toes."

"Thank you for the exciting dance, Lord Yorksley. I have never performed the cotillion quite that way before."

"And thank you, my lord, for asking me. It was wonderful."

At last it was over. The evening wore the unmistakable signs of age: portly lords, their corsets creaking, were gathering their winnings from the gaming room while their ladies fanned themselves with some poor unfortunate's notes of hand. More unfortunates were obsessively going over each hand with one another, certain they could discover the one play that turned their luck bad. Young misses were yawning in fatigue, their white gowns almost as tired, showing the marks of having been whirled around the room at least a dozen times, scraping by the refreshment table, the potted plants, and some slightly inebriated fellow's wineglass; Miss Tynte was conducting a tête-à-tête with the same shortish fellow she had danced with the other evening.

Miss Tynte looks so happy, Titania thought as the two ladies waited for their carriage to arrive. It would be selfish of her to burden Miss Tynte with her troubles right now.

I wonder if even now he is with that widow. I hate her. I hate him. Well, I wish I did. I will work on that tomorrow.

Miss Tynte paused on the steps, looking with a guilty start into her reticule. "Oh, my dear," she exclaimed, "I must have left my handkerchief inside. I know I had it when I was waiting for you while you danced with Lord George, perhaps it is still near that chair. Let me just go and check. You go ahead into the carriage. I will follow presently."

She scurried inside, and Titania caught just a glimpse of Mr. Short Man (she really should get his name) before turning to enter the carriage. It was dark, and she fumbled for a moment before sitting on something hard and unyielding, not at all the comfortable cushions she was accustomed to.

Chapter Sixteen

Edwin was drunk. Not so drunk he could not maneuver through the ballroom without mishap, not so drunk that he felt sick and dizzy, not so drunk that he could not watch Titania so discreetly that he did not think even she noticed.

No, he was just drunk enough to muddle his thinking.

Tonight, he had wanted to show the world in general, and Titania in specific, that his heart could be left for dead one night and he would be none the worse for wear the second night. He deliberately allowed Henri to dress him in his most extravagant outfit. He did not have to hide his wealth any longer; now that he had returned, and more importantly, reconciled with his father, it was only a matter of time before he would assume some of his father's responsibilities.

As soon as that became common knowledge, the exact information regarding his own personal fortune would become an open secret. The irony of the fact that he was on the path to becoming a lauded member of Society just when he wished Society would pack up its trunks and go away did not escape him.

Titania could trade her affection for whatever it was she felt she was in such desperate need of, and he would sit on his estate, counting his money and his sheep. He stood up, wobbling a little, and thought he should probably go before he fell down.

"Damn you," he groused to the chair as it almost overturned when he hooked his toe in a rung. The door to the garden was directly opposite him, and he wandered through it in search of his new carriage, purchased just that afternoon to match the splendor of his attire.

Where was it exactly? And what did it look like?

The only thing he recalled was that the horses he had bought to pull it were as black as Titania's hair—or her heart, he thought, feeling his insides twist.

He ambled slowly to the back of the house, where the guests' vehicles awaited their owners' calls, and found his without rousing his coachman. If he could just sleep a little bit he might feel better.

He woke with a start when a soft, warm and decidedly feminine form landed right on his lap.

"Oof!"

A hand snaked around her waist, and a low, throaty chuckle rang in her ear. Titania could not move for a moment, imprisoned as much by her own emotions as by Edwin's hand.

"What are you doing here? Release me!" she squeaked. She could smell the spirits on his breath and about his person, a rich aroma that reminded her of sitting in her father's library while he reminisced and drank and she compiled the household ledgers.

His next actions removed images of her childhood from her head entirely. Tightening his grip, he lightly licked her ear, moving slowly from the sensitive top to the even more sensitive lower part. She did not know ears could be quite so exciting. Her skin got prickly all over, and despite her best intentions, she felt herself relaxing, savoring the feel of his warm, large hands around her, the soft puff of his breath in her hair. When he spoke, his mouth was so close to her neck she felt the rumble of his words.

"I was attempting to get out of the ballroom, away from your maddening presence, but now it seems that my mistake is to be our gain. We did not finish what we started the other night, greedy one—and unfortunately, I do mean that literally," he murmured. "I wish I were not such a gentleman. You *do* know what you will be missing, do you not?" he said, moving his hand upward to lightly graze her breast.

The gentle touch unnerved her, and she gasped, instinctively arching into his hand.

"Oh, Titania," he sighed, pressing a kiss onto her bared shoulder. "I wish you were not like every other woman I have met. But even knowing what you are, I cannot banish your image from my eyes, nor forget how you feel under my hands," he finished, sweeping his hands down her rib cage to rest on her waist.

"What . . . what are you doing?" she asked inanely.

He laughed. "I am taking you up on the offer you made the other night. I want you, Titania, and I know you want me. I wish we could do this the proper way, but you have made it clear that you will not consider love for love's sake."

"Yes, I made a terrible mistake last night, and I was hoping to be able to explain it all to you tonight . . ."

"Just after you discovered my wealth? What kind of fool do you take me for? I kept the truth of my fortune quiet to avoid just the sort of trap you are setting for all those unsuspecting lordlings. And I was proven right, was I not, when you thought to entangle me in an unsavory arrangement because I could not afford you? Well, I can afford you, but I think the price is too high. This, on the other hand," he said, nuzzling her neck as he placed his hand on her breast and began to rub gently, "this is something we can make a fair trade for.

"I want something you have," he said, running his hand lightly across her lips, "while you want something I have," he finished, pulling her other hand onto his leg.

"But, my lord," she said, a lot more breathlessly than she would have liked, "it is not at all seemly for us to be here. Miss Tynte will be returning in a moment, while . . ."

Abruptly, he rapped on the roof, alerting the driver to move on. The coach lurched a moment, then began a slow walk down the carriage-crowded driveway. The movement caused Edwin's hands to tighten unconsciously, and Titania was tantalizingly aware of the power resting under her body.

"But my cousin, that is, Miss Tynte, we cannot just leave her," she sputtered, trying to focus her mind on anything but what Edwin's hands were doing to her.

"My love," Edwin said with a soft, seductive murmur,

"your chaperone's whereabouts are the least of your problems. She will arrive safely home—she is a capable, trustworthy woman. Unlike the lady in this carriage."

"How," Titania asked frantically, desperate to distract him, not to mention his hands, "could you possibly have mistaken my carriage for yours?"

"Appearances are deceiving, are they not? And having decided to unmask myself, as it were, I just today purchased a new carriage and allowed those tired nags to go crop grass somewhere. And having had a little bit of an intoxicating beverage tonight . . ."

Titania pulled away from him, a sharp tone in her voice. "You mean that widow who was hanging all over you like she was huddling for warmth? Perhaps she was, since her gown certainly did not sufficiently cover her."

"You noticed? Yes, she was a bit opulent in her display, but I admire someone who is as they advertise."

"Unlike you, my lord."

"A hit, Titania, or as you would say, a facer. Yes, I did hide some of what I am, but everything else was true. I happen to have come into some money recently. That does not change the unalterable essence of me, Titania, and that is what I wanted people to know, not that I had so many heads of sheep or so much acreage."

He was right, of course. She sat in defeat in the dark until his hands began to move again, caressing her body in an intimately possessive way, increasing the gentle rhythm until she could no longer think who was right, just that this moment was right, even if it meant that she was wrong—and wronged—for the remainder of her life.

She twisted around on his lap to face him, needing to kiss him. She placed her mouth on his, all gentleness gone as she drew his tongue into her mouth.

She pulled away from him to kiss his neck, licking the rapidly beating pulse. She stroked and caressed his chest, feeling the muscles underneath her hands tighten in response.

The motion of the coach, coupled with the motion from his hands, made her feel as if she were on the brink of a precipice. Just as she had gotten accustomed to the almost excruciating pleasure, the coach hit a bump, and she was jolted into a feeling she had never experienced before.

It was heaven. It would be hell when she realized she would never experience it again.

She felt Edwin smile into her mouth as she began to regain conscious thought. She moved her hand and Edwin groaned, then caught her wrist and stilled it, staring into her eyes.

"You know where this is leading, my love," he declared in a shaky rasp. "I would have you on your back in this coach in a moment, if I thought there was a chance for us."

Stunned, Titania watched in silence as he rapped on the roof again for the coach to stop, then swung himself agilely down the stairs, wrapping his cloak around him in a tight embrace.

An embrace to which she had no right.

Facing her, he bowed, saying with a tight smile, "I am on my way, my dear, to find someone who will be truc to me, if only for an evening. And no," he clarified, "it is not another woman, but Madame Alcohol. I want to get so drunk I can forget your face and your body and how you make me feel. I do not think such oblivion exists, but I am willing to discover that truth for myself. Wish me luck."

He signaled for the driver to move on, and walked down the street, his slight rolling gait the only indication he was less than completely sober. Titania sank back onto the cushions, still feeling the warmth of his hands on her body as his biting words chased themselves through her head like a pack of wild dogs.

"Titania!" Miss Tynte pronounced, as stridently as when she used to recall Titania from her daydreams, "where have you been? I waited for you, but Mr. . . . that is, my friend suggested you had taken the carriage yourself. How could you think to leave on your own? Why did you do so reckless a thing? And let me guess; did you happen to get escorted home by an impecunious earl? I told you to follow your heart, not lead yourself to ruin."

Her glare softened as she saw Titania's face. "Oh, my dear," she said, echoing the same endearment Edwin had used, "my dear, I am so sorry. What happened?"

Miss Tynte took Titania's elbow and steered her towards the study, where a warm fire was crackling in the fireplace.

"I wonder if I will ever feel warm again," Titania said

as she collapsed onto the sofa. She rubbed her hands on her arms as she stared into the flames.

"It's all gone wrong. I love him. He cares for me, too, I even think he loves me. He offered marriage the other evening and I turned him down. I told him it was because he was too poor. As you know, I was trying to find him tonight to tell him what a terrible mistake I had made. And then I discovered he *is* wealthy. Now he is convinced I only changed my mind because I am a fortune hunter. He is right. I am nothing but an avaricious debutante out to capture the best prize."

She jumped up, unable to sit as the storm in her heart raged on. "I have ruined the only chance for true happiness I will ever have. Yes, I am being dramatic," she conceded, wiping her hand across her brow, "but if I am going to have to act a part—the loving wife—for the remainder of my life, I might as well grow accustomed to living a lie."

Titania plopped down again on her seat, feeling all her passions and emotions wrung out of her like a wet rag. Miss Tynte's eyes filled with tears.

"My dear," she inquired with a hesitant voice, "have you tried to explain to the earl why you appear as mercenary as he believes? Perhaps he would understand. After all, I saw you two together in this very room, and at that time I wondered that he did not simply pick you up and throw you over his shoulders."

Titania scowled, shaking her head "no." "Five years ago, he jilted his fiancée because he discovered she was more interested in his money than she was in him. And since he and his father are known to be estranged, Society assumed he was in no better circumstances than when he left."

"Ah. So you cannot explain anything to him, can you?"

"I could, but even if he were to understand, can you imagine how it would feel, the first time we have a disagreement, or something, for either of us to wonder what my motives were in marrying him? I cannot carry that around with me for the rest of my life, and I would not wish it on him."

"But, forgive my plain speaking, but is that not exactly what you are planning to do with some other man? Marry him, that is, for his money? I am not chastising you. I am merely pointing out that it seems rather . . ."

"Hypocritical? Yes, but I do not love those other men, and I do not think they will be in any way in love with me. Whomever offers for me will do so because he thinks I will make a good wife, or be a good hostess, or not eat all the desserts, or any of a number of reasons, but none of them will be in love with me. Oh, it all seemed so easy when I first thought of it; I never imagined I would feel this completely miserable. If only I could find Father's um, that woman."

"What woman?" Thibault queried, poking his head around the door. "Titania, I know I am not the smart Stanhope, but can I just point out that there are thousands of women here in London? I bet if you put your mind to it, you can even figure out the exact geometric equation of how many more women are here than are in Northamptonshire."

Looking quickly at each other, Miss Tynte and Titania started babbling, then stopped as Thibault raised a hand as he advanced into the room.

"One at a time, if you please," he said in a stern, most un-Thibault-like voice. "You first, Titania."

"You see, there is a woman who, uh, has something that belongs to me, to us, actually, and I was hoping to get it back. I did not want to distress you . . ."

"Or you did not want to involve me, but continue."

"Yes, well, Miss Tynte and I have been attempting to find her, and we cannot, and I was just saying I wish we could."

"What is it you believe she has?"

"Oh," Titania replied with a light wave of her hand, "just a piece of jewelry of Mama's. You know how Father was . . ."

"Yes, I do. Ti, there is no use getting in a dither about finding one of Father's many lady friends. Have you spoken to Mr. Hawthorne? It strikes me he would know as much as anybody about who Father was friends with here in town, even if it was a friend of whom we, and especially you, should not be aware."

"No, I have not. I would not bother him with such a thing. He would be dreadfully embarrassed, don't you think? I beg you will forget it, Thibault, as you say, it really is not important, it is just that the piece—it was a ring—

would have looked absolutely lovely with this gown I have just bought." She trotted out a fairly vacant smile for his perusal, hating the fact that she was forced to lie yet again. It was becoming a very bad habit.

"Hm," Thibault said, shooting his very guilty sister what appeared to be a suspicious look. "So remembering you do not have this ring is what made your eyes get all red-rimmed and your face all gloomy?"

"I suppose I am just a bit tired. Although why," she said, her voice getting less hesitant, "you should be so ungentle-manly as to point out just how awful a woman looks, even if that woman is your sister, is beyond me. You will not succeed with the gentler sex, dear brother, if you do not keep your criticisms to yourself.

"It is hopeless," Titania pronounced after Thibault had finally gone. "There is no use in speaking of it, so we will not. Let us not discuss it anymore. All it does is make my eyes red, and that will certainly make my suitors all run away. And, if you will excuse me, I am going to go up and cry in my room."

With a smile she hoped was brave and not pathetic, Tita-nia rose from her chair and staggered up the stairs.

"Titania!" The roar came from the floor below, the dim bellow making Titania open her eyes and look around in confusion. The call came again, louder as Thibault as-cended the stairs to her room.

"Titania!" he yelled again, now almost to her door. What could be so important he could not wait the four feet until he came into her bedroom, as he certainly seemed intent on doing?

She barely had time to blink both eyes open—she had spent most of the night crying, and had gone to sleep only two hours before—when Thibault burst into the room, a look of anger on his face so fierce that Titania shrunk back unconsciously into the pillows.

"Titania, I have just had a very enlightening conversation with Mr. Hawthorne. Titania, could you not trust me enough to tell me about what Father did? I was at Mr. Hawthorne's office this morning, thinking to help you in finding Mama's ring—which obviously does not exist—and he told me about the new will. What were you thinking, not to tell me? I am not so irresponsible and immature not to be able to handle something affecting our future so profoundly. And when I was there," he continued, drawing nearer to the bed and shaking a chastising finger at her, "Mr. Hawthorne asked me how your Season was going, and were there any likely candidates for your hand? I swear, I almost leapt across his desk and throttled him. He did not need to spell it out to make me figure out what you had decided to do. How dare you settle on such a fate for yourself? You had no right, Titania, *no right* to exclude me."

He was shaking by now, and Titania moved closer to him, placing a gentle hand on his shoulder. She had never seen him so upset. But Thibault was her little brother, and what's more, had inherited more of her father's characteristics than she had. Perhaps she had underestimated him, as she had overestimated herself.

"I am so sorry. You are right. I should have told you. At the time, it seemed so easy: continue as planned, have my Season, find someone to marry who could save us. I did not think I would end up in such a mess."

"What kind of mess? Do you mean Lord Worthington? I have seen the way the two of you look at each other. What is the problem?"

"Oh, far too many to list. Basically, I did many foolish things, and now I am looking forward to a life of being your grumpy old spinster sister. I cannot go through with it, Thibault. I cannot, even if it means we lose everything and the servants have to be let go, and Ravensthorpe is never what it has the potential to be."

"Damn Father!"

"And while we are at it, damn his brother, too."

Thibault gave her a puzzled look. Quickly, before she could cry again, she explained just what their uncle had threatened. Thibault's face grew drawn and grim.

"I will go speak with Mr. Hawthorne again, Titania, I believe I left his office rather abruptly. I probably owe him an apology, as well. I will post a query in the *Town Talk* for Father's woman. It seems as good a place as any to start."

"Place a query? 'Wanted: former mistress of ne'er do well baron?' And what will we do when we find her, or she finds us? We cannot simply ask for the money back. We have to think of something else." Thibault's face settled into a pugnacious frown.

"I am going to place the ad, and maybe we will have the satisfaction of knowing who the woman is, and she will know just what her lover did to his family." He dashed out her bedroom door, his last words trailing over his shoulder as he bounded down the stairs.

"Thibault, no!" Titania struggled up out of bed, scrabbling in the bedclothes for her wrap so she could follow him. This impulsive reaction was exactly why she had not told him in the first place, although if she had presented it to him calmly, he might not now be tearing off on a fool's errand.

Titania heard the door slam and collapsed back into the pillows. She hoped he would word the advertisement properly, and then chuckled at her own propriety. There was Thibault, going off to place an ad in the very paper where she was documenting her mercenary search for a husband.

Maybe it would be just as well if everyone in the *ton* recognized their family situation; at least then she would not have to act a charade, nor be frightened by threats such as those waved around by Lord Gratwick.

At least now she had someone with whom to share this onerous burden. No matter how impetuous his actions, Thibault would enter into this problem with as much enthusiasm as he had applied to his poor schoolmaster's hair pomade. Titania just hoped the result would not be quite as sticky.

"More, damn you!" Edwin had had just about enough, but not of alcohol. He could not seem to get enough of that, and he was tired of people trying to tell him he had had enough. He decided to punch the next person who tried to do so. Edwin had deliberately wandered into a less than savory neighborhood in search of oblivion, and had found himself in a tavern whose clientele ranged from seedy to seediest.

Oblivion would not come. Complete drunkenness seemed near impossible since it appeared he had found the only responsible barkeep in all of London. The man refused

to sell him any more, even though Edwin was waving all
sorts of coinage in his face.

"My lord," the man said with a prim look, "it seems
you are already quite inebriated, and I do not encourage
drunkenness in my establishment."

"But this is a tavern!" Edwin said with an exasperated
yelp. "Where else would one find drunkenness? You are
as nonsensical as a . . . as a woman," he finished with a
snarl, drinking the coffee the man had placed in front of
him instead.

Hours later, Alistair found him still hunkered down at
the bar, many cups of coffee down his throat.

"Edwin, I have been looking for you. There has been a
terrible accident. You are needed right away."

Whatever slight haze still remained in Edwin's brain was
whisked away by Alistair's words and his solemn face.

"What happened?"

"Your father. You must come at once. The doctor is
there."

Edwin deposited a stack of coins on the counter, then
swept up his cloak and followed Alistair quickly out the
door.

Titania was just mulling over ideas for her next column,
waiting for Thibault to return, when there was a knock at
the door, and enthusiastic voices carried their way upstairs
to her bedroom. She quickly dropped her pen, and ran to
the top of the staircase. Who could possibly be employing
a joyful tone when her world had completely collapsed?
Mocking her own solipsism, she descended the stairs and
saw Julian and his mother, both of whom looked ecstatic.

"How lovely to see you both," Titania declared, quickly
drawing them into the study before they burst. Clearly they
had some Important News.

"Miss Stanhope!" Julian exclaimed, his normally perfect
hair as rumpled as if he had slept on it, then rolled around
on it in the morning just for good measure.

"Let me handle this, Julian," his mother interrupted. She
had two bright spots of color on her cheeks, and she appeared to have trouble getting enough breath.

"Miss Stanhope, I understand from my son that your

father, Lord Ravensthorpe, left you in somewhat straitened circumstances?"

Titania glowered at Julian, who looked embarrassed.

Mrs. White flapped her hand in front of Titania's face. "Never mind being angry with my son, he has never been able to keep himself from telling me all sorts of things . . . I remember the time he developed an unseemly crush on the woman who painted my miniature, and he kept running in with all kinds of inane . . . but never mind that, just let me say you will be glad that he is as much of a gossip as he is. Miss Stanhope, I am the Woman!"

"What woman?" Titania asked, confused. No wonder Julian's poetry was so awful if this was the grounding in sense and logic he had received.

"The woman your father left his money to. I did not realize he had been so foolish as to leave his family nothing, and shortly after your father's death I myself got married to Mr. White, a lovely man with loads and loads of lovely money, which he left to me when he died—somewhat unexpectedly, you see—on our honeymoon. Such a dear," she said with a soft sigh, dabbing at her eyes.

"Mother," Julian interjected with an impatient glance, "I am sure Titania would mourn your late husband's loss as much as you if she had even met him, but you have not even gotten to the crux of the story. Get to the part where you did not get a chance to meet with the bankers and the money just kept growing and growing—"

"Yes, well, Mr. White was such a dreadfully wealthy man I never knew quite how much he had left me, and he had so many different financial interests that it was difficult to keep them all straight, so I just trusted my man of business to handle it—such a nice man, always clearing his throat and explaining things to me as if I were a ninny—and so I did not know your father's money had been added to that sum. It seems I was out of the country when the will was read."

Titania felt her mouth gape open in surprise. Her father had left his money to his mistress, and his mistress was—Julian's mother? Did that make Julian her—?

"No, dear," Mrs. White said, intuiting her thought processes. "Julian is not your brother; he is indeed Mr. Fell's. I met your father sometime after Mr. Fell died, while Mr.

White was courting me. I will not embarrass you with the details of my relationship with your father, but at some point, I do believe I was finding it difficult to manage Julian's school fees, and he must have changed his will right around that time. If your father had only listened a little more closely, however, he would have realized I was having problems with the fees because of the conversion rates. You see, Julian was in school in Greece, and there was a terrible muddle with the exchange."

"Wait," Titania said, shaking her head in disbelief, "not to put too fine a point on it, but my father changed his will because you were confused about converting pounds into whatever kind of currency they use in Greece?"

Mrs. White wrinkled her brow in concern. "Mm, yes. I am so very sorry to be the cause of such a predicament. When Julian told me about it, I remembered all about what my man, that is, Mr. Tetchley, had told me about your father leaving me some monies, but I had no idea it was everything, and that everything was so much. As soon as Julian told me, I sent for Mr. Tetchley immediately. And of course it need not be said—or perhaps it does—I will be returning all of that money to you as soon as Tetchley can dislodge it from the Funds. I am more than wealthy from Mr. White's estate, there is absolutely no need for me to keep possession of your money as well, and from what Julian tells me, you and your brother are in dire need of it. I do so like that earl, he is such a fine measure of a man, even if he is far too serious. Now, dear, are you in need of any funds immediately, just to help until Mr. Tetchley can sort it out?" she asked, pulling a fat wad of bills from her reticule.

Titania watched, dumbfounded, as Mrs. White counted out a couple hundred pounds and placed them into her unresisting hand.

"Thank you." She stared down in her hand, trying to gather herself to say something—anything—that would make sense. Mrs. White patted the hand holding the money, then spoke again.

"I believe Miss Stanhope might need to be alone for a bit, Julian. Miss Stanhope, will we see you at the Pomeroys' ball tonight? It is scandalous that such fusty bores would invite someone like me, but I met Lady Pomeroy at the dressmaker's, and we had a lovely conversation. I do believe Lady Pomeroy is hoping my presence will liven things up a bit—now where could she have gotten an idea like that?" she said with a sly laugh. Mrs. White stood, gesturing towards Julian.

"Come along, dear, let us leave Miss Stanhope in peace. We have done enough to unsettle her for today." She led an unprotesting Julian to the door, stopping when Titania started with a jerk.

"Wait! Oh, Mrs. White, I have not thanked you enough for coming here today. It is a difficult thing you have done, not so much the money, but telling me who you are. I am glad my father had a . . . friend like you. And Julian," she said, pointing at him with her free hand, "I will forgive you for spilling my secrets."

She slid towards him, kissing him gently on the cheek before he could react. Then she turned to his mother and embraced her warmly.

"And just like that," Titania said as she closed the door, "your problems are solved. At least the financial ones."

The estates would remain intact and flourish and Thibault could begin to learn how to manage his land and monies without having to pension off the staff and marry for money himself. She could tell her uncle just where he and his threats could go. And she could tell Lord Gratwick the same thing.

Too much too late, she thought with a sad smile. Even with her own substantial dowry, how could she convince Edwin that she loved him for himself? She stood still for a moment, her eyebrows knitted together in a look of fierce concentration, then the shadows lifted and she giggled to herself.

She scooted out of the room and tripped upstairs, determined to see her plan through before her resolution had dimmed.

Dispatch from the Battlefront, May 1813

It is with great delight, dear readers, that I reveal that I am a liar. I lied when I wrote I would only choose a mate who could bring me financial prosperity; I am in need of much more than that, and there is not enough money in the Bank of England to balance the needs of my heart.

I have tried to approach the field of matrimony, battle plan in hand, but I did not account for the most important weapon: love. I have been slain by its arrow. My love is bestowed, not sold, and I am happy beyond measure to report that the object of my affections has no need to dip into his pockets to satisfy me.

A Singular Lady

Chapter Seventeen

There. That should do it. She folded her papers, tucked them into her reticule, and rang for Sarah. She would deliver it to Mr. Harris this very afternoon, even though her column was not due for another couple of days.

"Sarah, we are going out," she announced, drawing on a pair of gloves.

"Not with that 'air you are not," Sarah replied in a belligerent tone. "Miss, I do not know what you do to yourself between the time I dress your 'air in the morning, and when I next see 'ou, but whatever it is, stop it. It looks as if 'ou 'ave been trying to pull it up straight off your 'ead. 'ave you been thinking again?" she asked with an accusing glare. "Thinking causes nothing but trouble. You stick your 'ands in your 'air and cause all kinds of rumpus. Just sit down, do not think, and let me fix this rackety mess."

"It would take me longer to argue with you than for you to do what you want to, so just try to hurry, please," Titania said in a grumpy voice.

"You know I am right. That is why you are so cross, miss." Titania sat in silence as Sarah brought the tangled mess under control, bolting to her feet as soon as the last hairpin was laid to rest.

"Now may we be off? And what now?" Titania asked in dismay as the door below was heard to open. She could discern the low hum of male voices, and her heart leapt into her throat. Was it possible—? She could barely contain herself as she heard Stillings' slow tread on the stairs.

"The Earl of Oakley to see you, miss," Stillings intoned blandly, as if he—and the whole staff, for that matter—were not perfectly aware of how their mistress felt about this visitor. "I have put him in the study. Are you receiving?" Titania rushed past him without answering, running down the stairs, then slowed to a leisured pace as she approached the doors. She took a deep breath.

"My lord," she said in a demure tone, looking down as she entered the room. "I did not get a chance to speak with you to thank you for escorting me home the other night."

Titania was shocked to see his face was gray and drawn. He strode towards her, gathering her in his arms as he started to sob.

"What is it?" she asked, her voice muffled by being crushed against his huge chest.

"My father. He was attacked last night at his house, and now my stepmother is accusing me of having perpetrated it. My father and I saw each other, we were reconciled, something that made me almost as happy as—" He stopped speaking, instead withdrawing from the safe circle of her arms to prowl around the room.

"Attacked? But where? And how? Is he all right?" Titania sat down, her hands unconsciously clutching the skirt of her gown.

Edwin turned to face her, his expression one of unrelieved anguish. "He is thankfully alive, but unconscious. The doctors say there is nothing that can be done for him, at least not until he gains consciousness . . . *if* he does."

"And what is your stepmother accusing you of?"

"She . . . she says I broke into their house and attacked my father in his study. She did not actually see anything, of course, but she may have misinterpreted something I said when I was there. She . . . she has reasons to wish me ill."

"Surely you can prove you were somewhere else when your father was attacked?"

"Perhaps, but perhaps not. You see, he was attacked at about the same time that I was escorting you home, and as you know, I walked. I ended up at a tavern. I am afraid there are a few hours there that are a bit fuzzy for me."

Titania pushed his unresisting form onto the sofa. "Sit there. Let me— Stillings!" Stillings arrived so quickly Titania suspected he had been listening at the door.

"Stillings, we need tea and pen and paper, please." Stillings nodded, shooting an apprehensive look at Edwin.

Edwin sat, his head resting on his hands. Titania perched on the sofa next to him, taking one of his hands from his forehead and holding it in her lap.

"You know this will be cleared up. Someone will remember seeing one of you last night, even if you were seeing two of everyone. Your stepmother, why would she falsely accuse you?"

Edwin looked down at their entwined hands, silent for a moment as he ran his fingers over her palm. The contact made Titania remember their proximity last night, and she felt herself starting to blush.

"My stepmother is, *was*, my fiancée," Edwin explained in a low voice, still stroking her hand. "I did not know until the other day; it's hard to believe someone did not tell me, if only to see my reaction. She must still hate me a great deal."

They sat there, silently holding hands. Despite everything, Titania felt oddly at peace, as if the tumult in her heart had been stilled for just a moment.

"Well, then, Lord Worthington—"

"Edwin."

"Edwin, then. Can you tell me your movements, I mean," she said, feeling herself blush, "your activities, um, where you were last night?" She moved over to the desk where she could hide her face.

"Well, I attended the party. Walked through the garden. Escorted you home." She heard him stand and saw his feet plant themselves next to her desk. Titania was unable to resist looking up.

The expression on his face must have reflected her own, since he gave a lazy smile, then glanced over to the door. A careless Stillings must have closed it behind him. Edwin's eyes returned to hers, and his smile deepened. She rose slowly, feeling a tingling awareness start somewhere in her stomach and rise up through her chest.

Edwin took her hand, placing it on his chest. She could

hear the thump thump of his heartbeat, and it was as regularly insistent as her own breathing, which had quickened. He drew her over to the sofa, then sat, looking up at her with an expectant gaze.

She lowered herself slowly, her eyes only inches from his. Edwin saw the desire mingled with an emotion he was too battered to name, and knew that when he kissed her, he would be able to forget, just for a little while.

It was glorious. It was the best kiss yet. Titania boldly thrust her tongue into Edwin's mouth, grabbing ahold of his shoulders.

He had never felt so complete as he had at that moment, ravaging her mouth as his hands roamed over her body. Titania was just pulling up his shirt, impatient to get her hands on his chest, when they were jarred by the unmistakable sound of the door opening.

Quickly, Titania scooted back to her side of the sofa, frantically smoothing her hair back and trying to look as if they had been exchanging commonplaces about the weather or the latest party, not on the verge of exchanging her clothing for the feel of Edwin's naked body.

Miss Tynte narrowed her eyes as she entered the room. "Stillings told me you were receiving the earl, Titania. I hope the visit has been pleasurable?" she finished with an acerbic tone.

Titania could not help it; she began to laugh at the absurdity of it. "Yes, cousin, the earl's visit has been pleasurable in the extreme," she replied, throwing a wicked smile towards Edwin.

"Miss Tynte," Edwin said, blushing, only to be stopped when she held up a thin, wrinkled hand.

"No, my lord, do not explain. I understand perfectly well, and I also know I am a woefully inadequate chaperone." With that, she stalked as gracefully as she could to a nearby chair and sat down, a frosty smile plastered onto her face.

"Lord Worthington," Titania said with a prim nod, as if she had not been sticking her tongue in his mouth just five minutes before, "we should continue our list. Miss Tynte, Lord Worthington has had some terrible news regarding an attack on his father, and his stepmother—Lord Worthington's, that is—is accusing Lord Worthington of having perpetrated the attack. So we are making a list of the earl's activities last evening, his whereabouts, that is," she finished hastily, as Miss Tynte's eyebrows start to rise.

Edwin rose, clutching the piece of paper that was only slightly wrinkled from having been pressed between their two bodies. "Miss Stanhope, Miss Tynte, I appreciate your assistance, but I must try to find the perpetrator myself before Bow Street pays me a visit. Very few people were aware my father and I were on speaking terms again, and many would be only too happy to believe—and spread to anyone who will listen—my stepmother's lies. I cannot sit around and wait to be ostracized, or worse, again. Goodbye."

He strode out of the study, resolve informing every line of his body. It was in marked contrast to the way he had entered the room, and Titania knew she had helped, even if that help had mussed her hair and left both of them feeling unsatisfied. She recovered from her musings to encounter, once again, the look Miss Tynte seemed to wear most often when regarding her previously reliable charge.

"Titania. You cannot behave like that, not unless the earl is prepared to offer you marriage again, and I do not believe I saw him on his knees just now."

No, Titania thought, he is in no circumstances to propose marriage, only she did not think it was because he did not trust her. He came straight here, did he not, to tell her about his father? And it was in her arms he found comfort, as well. Things were just about as awful as they could be, but a small glimmer of hope for her future began to glow very slightly inside. She held on to that faint hope when she heard the gossips mentioning Edwin's name at a party that evening.

"You know, do you not, that he had sworn to see his father in his grave before he would see him married to his fiancée?"

"I heard he pushed Lady Worthington down to get to his father, so enraged was he. He was making his living as a member of the boxing profession when he was banished by his father."

"He left that poor man facedown in his library, his desk ransacked and all his books disheveled. What was he hoping to find?"

It was a weary Titania who returned to her house only a few hours after she had left. She had not seen Edwin that evening, but she had seen Lady Worthington, who was making an appearance at the Lashleys' party. Titania watched in disbelief as Lady Worthington sopped up everyone's sympathetic words. How could she come to a social gathering when her husband was lying unconscious?

Titania had to admit Lady Worthington was beautiful, and there was something very fragile in her demeanor. It was no wonder that Edwin leapt at the chance to be her hero, since Titania had experienced his heroic impulses firsthand.

Now her hero needed rescuing. Could she save him?

Despite his admittedly bad situation—long-estranged father in a life-threatening coma, stepmother flinging accusations madly about, his freedom in peril—Edwin felt oddly happy, places on his body still tingling from Titania's touch, other parts of his body clamoring for her attention.

After directing his carriage to return home without him, he walked down the street from Titania's house, beginning to turn his researcher's brain towards the problem of who could have attacked his father.

Alistair had told him that, in addition to the attack, his father's library—the one in which they had met earlier that day—had been ransacked, as if the attacker were searching for something.

Perhaps his father had surprised the burglar? Edwin knew the house well enough, however, to know that there were no valuables kept in that room, and in fact, the safe was on the upstairs floor in his father's private sitting room. Would a burglar have known that?

Surely anyone foolish enough to enter a peer's house would have done some investigative work first, would they not? But whomever it was did not know the lord was in residence, or at least thought he was out for the evening. He would have to discover if his father's plans had changed suddenly that evening.

He meandered as he thought until he saw he had wandered back to the boxing saloon. Not a bad idea; perhaps with a clear head and bruised knuckles he could concentrate better.

He stripped down to just his shirt and breeches, and headed for the boxing ring. And, like before, he heard his name called in a voice dripping with disdain.

"My lord," Lord Gratwick called, "have you not had enough of vicious attacks? Perhaps you are looking for a younger opponent?"

Edwin turned, deliberately trying to withhold any reaction from his face. He saw the tall, blond man at the edge of the ring, dressed to enter it.

"Perhaps," the man continued with an insolent smirk, "you would care to join me for a match? It would not be as engrossing as analyzing battle plans to ferret out the Frenchies, but it would give me great satisfaction to pummel you as you did your father."

Edwin stopped, struck by Gratwick's words. Anyone who went to the trouble of asking a few questions knew that Edwin was a scholar, but very few people knew his research had any impact on the current war. And yet Gratwick seemed conversant with the details. Maybe he, too, was involved with the government's war efforts? No, he had recently sold out, and he held no official office. Maybe he was working as some sort of spy? Well, if so, he was a damned bad one, since to comment as he did was tantamount to wearing a sign that said I'M A SPY around his neck.

No, Edwin thought, watching Gratwick still eyeing him with loathing, it had to be that he knew something he should not, and his hatred made him careless. Lord Gratwick would bear watching, but not in the ring. If what he suspected was true, he would be hard-pressed not to kill the worm.

Still without speaking a word, Edwin turned back to the dressing area, deciding that discretion was the better part of valor, especially where it concerned his fist meeting Gratwick's face. Gratwick's taunts followed him all the way down the hall to the room where he had left his clothes, and it took every fiber in his being not to respond, whether with words or his fists.

"Worthy!" a booming voice exclaimed as Edwin was reassembling his cravat. Funny, he mused, even as polite Society deemed him unfit for their polite company, he was finally able to tie a presentable cravat. He smoothed the fabric as he awaited his friend.

Alistair stomped down the hallway, brushing his sleeve with a scowl on his face. He brightened briefly as he saw Edwin's neckwear, then scowled again.

"Worthy, we have to talk. Your house?"

"Why is your stepmother spreading such vicious lies about you?" Alistair poured more sugar into his coffee, then tasted it and wrinkled his nose. He poured two more heartbeats worth of sugar and tasted again. He smiled. "Well?"

Edwin shook his head, as much at the ridiculous amount of sweetener his friend deemed necessary for his coffee as to answer the question.

"Leticia, obviously, has no liking for me, but I did not realize her antipathy would extend to lying about something as serious as this. I was over at my father's house the day he was attacked, but I left him dozing in his chair. I was a bit fuzzy the evening he was attacked, I cannot quite recall my movements of that evening, which certainly seems suspicious. But listen to this—I was at Jackson's Saloon today, and Gratwick—that toad-sucking worm—mentioned something he should not know about. I know it seems providential for him to say something to me that would implicate him—"

"Especially since there is no question as to your opinion of him," Alistair interjected.

"Yes," Edwin acknowledged with a rueful laugh. "He and I never took to each other, and then when I discovered he was a serious suitor for Titania, and what is more, he implied the betrothal was all but announced—I know I have a dislike for him, but that does not negate the fact he might have had something to do with this. What do you know of him?"

"Not much, really," Alistair replied. "He sold out recently, his uncle passed away leaving him in possession of a title, if not a fortune—eerily similar to you, my friend, but you *do* have a fortune, do you not?—and he has been playing up his days as a soldier in hopes of impressing the young ladies. Most young ladies, however, have not been impressed by him. He is not a stupid man, but there is something unpleasant about him."

"That is what I felt," Edwin said. "I wondered if I felt

that way just because he was so obvious in his attentions to the young lady in question."

"And you were not?"

"And it seemed to me," he continued mildly, ignoring Alistair's comment, "there was something desperate about him. Until we started speaking of it, I had forgotten, but Lady Wexford, that blond woman who is a friend of Miss Stanhope's, introduced Gratwick to Miss Stanhope. They seemed to be on close terms. I do not trust either one of them."

Alistair frowned in concentration. "If Gratwick and Lady Wexford had some sort of scheme, that still does not explain where your father would come into it. Those two were not acquainted with him, were they?"

"I do not know," Edwin replied. Rising hurriedly from his chair, he gestured impatiently for his friend to rise also. "We will not know anything until we find out more about Gratwick and Lady Wexford. I will inquire of Ti—that is, Miss Stanhope—about her friend. Perhaps you could pay a call on Gratwick; I do not trust myself near him." Unconsciously, he curled his hands into fists, pulling his shoulders up in an aggressive posture.

"I do not trust you near him, either, but I do agree he bears watching. Why do you get to inquire of the lovely Miss Stanhope, while I have to chase after the rooster-legged braggart?"

"Because she happens to be in love with me, and I with her."

"Oh. Well, that settles it then."

"Claire, how lovely of you to call," Titania said, her tone at odds with her words. She had been hoping Edwin would visit, and Claire's arrival was more than a sad disappointment.

"Yes, well, dear, you did promise to take a drive with me this afternoon," Claire said, fluttering her hands.

"I did?" Titania queried, searching her mind for the forgotten engagement.

"Yes, do you not remember? Really, Titania, town does age one, but I did not think you would be forgetting things so quickly. Hurry, have someone fetch your pelisse, we should be on our way."

"But I cannot," Titania replied. What if Edwin were to come and she was not home?

"You must! My friend, it is crucial that you come with me today. It is of the utmost importance to me. Please—" her friend finished quietly, stretching out her hands in supplication.

"Yes, of course, if it is so important." A crucial carriage ride? The only thing she could think was that there was some shopping emergency Claire could not handle alone.

"I need to be back soon, will this take long?"

Claire rolled her eyes, saying with an impatient air, "No, it will not take long. You will be back in plenty of time to catalogue your books or whatever you need to do. Now, hurry!" She practically shoved Titania down the steps and into the waiting carriage.

"Stillings," Titania yelled out the window as the carriage started to move, "I will be back in an hour."

"I have wanted you to see my phaeton for an age, my dear," Claire chattered as Titania brought her head back inside. "Wex bought me this on our fourth anniversary. What a dear man he is." She sighed contentedly, trailing her hand down the red satin wall covering as if she caressed a lover's face.

"Yes, it is lovely, but what is it that is so important, Claire?"

"You will see, my dear," Claire said with an arch look. Claire's eyes squinted as she looked towards the park, which was filled with ladies and gentlemen showing off their latest clothing, lovers and jewelry, a vibrantly hued collection of all sorts of the finest folks the *ton* had to offer.

Titania felt a faint sense of alarm as the carriage was submerged into the verdant dark of the large trees over-hanging the narrow drive. It was only when they were safely beyond the main fray that Claire sat back in her seat, smiling beatifically at Titania.

"I have such a surprise for you, my dear," she said, her tone even more arch than it was before. "I know you have been too shy, or too modest, to admit the possibility of this gentleman's proposal, but he has spoken to me, and I, as a happy prisoner in the jail of matrimony—does that not sound poetic?—want everyone to be so shackled. When Lord Gratwick arrives," she said, "you are not to be too nervous. He merely wishes to make you Lady Gratwick, with possession of all those musty books that are so fascinating to you."

Titania inhaled sharply, then clasped her hands together in her lap, noticing with an odd feeling of displacement that her knuckles were turning white.

"I presume," Titania said, willing her voice not to shake, "that Lord Gratwick did not tell you he has demanded that I marry him or . . . he will reveal a secret of mine? He is not someone to whom I wish to be married. If you would be so kind as to return me home, I will address the matter myself with Lord Gratwick."

"Oh, no, Titania," Claire said sharply, turning her head so fast her diamond earrings swung against her neck, their light revealing the line where Claire's face powder stopped. "You will marry Lord Gratwick. It is unfortunate we could not accomplish it the usual way. No, we will see the gentleman shortly, and then he will tell you of the plan. Simple, but effective."

"No!" Titania declared, "if you are truly my friend, you will return me home, and we can forget this."

"Too late," Claire trilled as a closed carriage lumbered towards them. Titania knew she was being imaginative, but the sight of the carriage, an innocuous shade of brown, made her feel as if a shadow had just crossed her path, and she shuddered involuntarily.

She saw Gratwick's blond head poking out from the window, his face alight with an avaricious gleam. The look changed to one of supreme satisfaction as he spied the two women, and he barked an order to his coachman, who pulled the carriage to an abrupt stop.

He slid gracefully to the ground, unfolding his long length like a serpent. Or so Titania imagined. His eyes seemed to blaze with approval as he walked towards their carriage.

"Well done, my lady," he said, giving Claire a mock salute. He held his arm for her as she descended the steps. He held his arm out for Titania, who hesitated at the top of the steps. He chuckled as he met her eyes, apparently enjoying her predicament.

"I had confided in our mutual friend, Miss Stanhope, of my passion for you, and she kindly offered to assist me in my suit. Please join me in the carriage and we can discuss our future."

Titania descended the phaeton, shaking not from fear but from anger.

"I will not go with you, my lord, and if Lady Wexford will not return me home, I will have to walk."

Titania turned on her heel and started to stride back towards the clearing where she had seen so many people, knowing once she reached the safety of the open park she would be beyond Gratwick's reach. It was clear he knew it, too, since he bounded to her side and grabbed her elbow with a surprisingly strong grip.

"You will come with me willingly, Miss Stanhope, or unwillingly. It does not matter to me. Do you imagine that any of those kind folk," he said, gesturing towards the clearing, "would believe that you, the daughter of a well-known libertine and the columnist who has been skewering their superficial lives in her own right, is being abducted by me, a well-regarded war veteran? You will come with me, we will discuss our future, and that will be the end of it."

Was it possible members of Society would be so callous as to ignore her pleas for assistance because they assumed she was as bad as her father was reputed to be? As she weighed her options, she remembered the comments people had already made about Edwin; members of the *ton*, who had been only too happy to allow an eligible, handsome bachelor into their midst were only too happy to believe he was capable of an attempt on his own father's life.

Gratwick was right. She would be ruined either way.

Her disconsolate feelings were compounded by the feel of Gratwick's strong hand on her arm; even if she were to break free, it was likely he would subdue her and she would not even get the chance to test the mettle of Society folk. Rather than waste her time fighting his clearly superior physical strength, she resolved to fight him with her superior strength: her intelligence. She turned back to the carriage, glared at Claire for a moment, then got into the carriage on her own, refusing the arm Gratwick held out for her.

"Lord Gratwick," she began as soon as he was settled in the opposite seat, "you cannot but be aware I am here reluctantly, and would not be here at all if my friend had not tricked me." Titania spent a moment wondering just how much money Claire had required to sell her out. "I thought we were going to discuss your interesting proposal in just a few days, I do not see the need for this force."

"Yes, Miss Stanhope, I had given you a week to make your decision, but recent developments have determined that I take a trip to the Continent immediately, and I wish my wife to accompany me."

"But I have not said I would marry you, sir," Titania said, spreading her hands out in supplication. "In fact, I thought I made it fairly clear I was not in favor of accepting your suit; I have since come to realize that I cannot accept your suit, and you may tell whomever you like of my identity."

My paltry misdoings are nothing compared to the accusations being thrown at Edwin, she thought; how long could Society slaver over her little scribblings when he was living a front-page life?

She continued in a calm tone. "Let me out, Lord Gratwick. I wish you well on your upcoming voyage." She reached her hand up to rap on the roof of the carriage so the coachman would stop. She felt a sense of panic as his hand darted out to grasp hers.

"No, I do not believe you understood me, Miss Stanhope. I have need of a wife, in particular, *you*, and I need to go on a trip just as urgently. You will marry me."

Although his implacable statement should have come as no surprise to Titania, given his recent behavior, she still felt a rising frisson of fear climb up her spine at his words.

"But my cousin, and my brother, and my friends . . . they will wonder where I am, and come looking for me."

"No fear on that score, my dear," Gratwick replied easily. "Lady Wexford is even now on her way to your house to inform your family of your impetuous elopement, and you can write them when we are safely wed. Your suitors will merely be disappointed I had the good fortune to win your hand. Your earl is even now in a great deal of trouble, so chances are he will not even notice you are gone. I do not see, my dear," he mused, examining his fingernails, "what you would see in a man like that. Attempting to murder his own father. Shameful."

He let go of her wrist, then settled back cozily against

the cushions as if getting comfortable for a long ride. Titania looked out the window, determined to discover a way to lose her companion before she lost her reputation, her freedom, or her life.

"Lord Gratwick," she said, trying to sound friendly, "circumstances would seem to allow for a lack of propriety . . . may I ask why you are so determined to marry me, of all the ladies this Season?"

Gratwick smiled in an almost genuine way. "You, my dear, have a fortune. I am in need of just such a fortune."

"My lord," she said with a hitch in her voice, "I do not wish to call myself a liar, but I have to confess that my fortune is not what it is reputed to be."

Thanks to Mrs. White, it was more than it was, but he did not have to know that. "My father left my brother and I nothing," which *was* true. "I had my servants spread those rumors so no one would know quite how desperate my situation was."

He laughed, a nasty chuckle that seemed to wiggle its way down her spine to her feet. "You are a treasure, and such an imagination! Lady Wexford herself told me you were well setup, and you would not lie to your old friend, would you?"

"My lord, I swear to you my father left me nothing. I arrived in town with no money, only some jewelry my mother left me. I am worthless to you."

"Oh, no, you are not, Titania," he said with a grim smile. "Your little story is quite charming, but I know you have enough money to set us up in a new life away from here."

"Why must you leave?" She knew he was a snake; she just wanted to find out what kind of snake.

"Your friend Mr. Farrell is much more insightful than he appears. He's been asking quite a few questions about my war record, and my employers in France are becoming quite agitated. They've demanded I return, and since I have recently obtained some crucial documents, they will have no choice but to reward me generously. Unfortunately, it appears I will no longer be welcome in London, so I require companionship and a sizable fortune. I like living well. As does your friend Claire. Very well." He grimaced, then shrugged as he folded his hands across his chest and appeared to sleep.

After a few hours of rolling through increasingly pastoral countryside, the coachman drew up to a small inn, a few chickens pecking about beleaguered in front of the modest two-story building. Gratwick roused himself long enough to inform her they were changing horses here, and would have time only for a light snack before they were on their way again.

Titania was grateful for the respite, no matter how brief, because it meant a chance to escape her current situation, which she now saw was fairly desperate. She was bitterly regretting not screaming her head off when she was in London, no matter if no one came to her rescue; she felt like an idiot for not having done something, anything, to call attention to her plight when there were actually people around.

She knew neither Miss Tynte nor Thibault would believe she was eloping with Gratwick, but she also doubted their ability to marshal her resources before she was married in deed, if not in fact. Her mind veered from that unpleasant image—one awful thing at a time, Titania, she reminded herself—and stepped out of the carriage determined to make a horrific racket. Now if only there was someone to hear her.

The innkeeper's wife, a fluttery woman trailing her apron strings, a few children, and some stray parsley, appeared, her vague mutterings indicating Titania should follow her so she could freshen herself up.

She would be able to think better if she were less grimy, so she allowed the woman to escort her to a small upstairs room. She removed her pelisse—now she knew why Claire was so insistent on sending for it—and attempted to remove some of the wrinkles in her gown with the lukewarm water in the basin near the bed. She splashed more water on her face and smoothed her hair.

She was able to see some of herself in the small, cracked mirror hanging over the basin, and if she alternated eyes, she could get a general sense of how she looked. It was not a pretty sight. Random bits of hair had fallen from her hairpins and were hanging down as straight as straw. Her face was even paler than usual, and her gown, which was not designed for sitting long hours in a carriage, was limp and stretched out. But what does all that matter, she thought, since it is hardly likely my appearance will be a deterrent to my abductor.

Absentmindedly, she started to run her hands through her hair. She was startled by a noise at the door, and saw a tiny housemaid venturing into the room.

"Your husband thought you might like a bite to eat up here, my lady," she said with a shy stammer, proffering something on a tray that actually looked fairly appetizing.

"Is Lord . . . that is, my husband . . . downstairs?" Titania inquired.

"Yes, he is in the public area. There are no other customers today, so you have the place to yourselves."

Lovely, Titania thought, there goes another idea. She had been hoping someone—anyone—would be sipping ale downstairs, and she could slip them a note, or a plea for help, or anything to extricate herself.

"I will go downstairs as well, then," she announced, grabbing her ill-used pelisse and heading for the door. "You may bring the tray to me down there; I wish to speak with my l—him."

She walked downstairs, thinking furiously of what she could do to distract Gratwick from proceeding as quickly as they had been thus far. Demand he recite the Roman emperors, in order, from Augustus to Nero? Faint? Develop spasms? She arrived at the public room before she could settle on any kind of satisfactory answer.

"Ah, there you are my dear," he said, an ale in his hands and a malicious sparkle in his eyes. "I am glad you are feeling well enough to join me. We will be on our way shortly, do not worry."

"It is our honeymoon," he said in a confiding tone to the innkeeper. Titania felt her anger rise as she saw the knowing smile on his mouth. The innkeeper winked back at him with a suggestion of a leer, the two of them crossing class boundaries to indulge in some classless male kinship.

Likely the innkeeper would think she was a frightened bride, or a histrionic pea-goose if she made a fuss. He returned bearing another big pitcher of ale, setting it down with a splash in front of Lord Gratwick.

If she could encourage Gratwick to get drunk, she might be able to figure something out. With that vague hope in mind, she pointed to the pitcher accusatorily. "My love, if you drink all that ale, you will be fit for nothing," she said, loud enough for the innkeeper to hear, but not so loudly as to let Gratwick know she was trying to bait him into drunkenness. She smiled warmly at him as she said it, summoning up her newfound lying skills. Perhaps her recent duplicity would help extricate her from this situation.

"My love," he replied with an oversweet smile, "I could drink twice this amount and still be fine. I was a soldier, after all."

Titania wondered how time spent dodging bullets and camping out of doors could help him develop a tolerance for alcohol. "Then perhaps I could join you. Sir," she called out, beckoning to the innkeeper, "my husband wishes to relive his army days by drinking some more of your fine ale. Could you bring us another pitcher, please?"

Gratwick gave her a look of admiration. "I appreciate your acceptance of the inevitable. Nothing is more boring than traveling with a woman who is constantly whining. Let us have a toast to the future," he finished as the innkeeper returned bearing another glass.

Titania had never drunk ale before, but after a few sips was well on her way to enjoying it. She took tiny sips, and watched in satisfaction as Gratwick drained his glass and poured himself another one. Unfortunately, an hour later, Gratwick was proving he could definitely hold his alcohol. Titania, on the other hand, felt a little woozy.

"We should depart, my dear," he said, wiping a froth of ale from his mouth. "We have to reach our destination by nightfall."

"My lord, I wish you would reconsider this plan," she said, a desperate tone creeping into her voice. "Perhaps we could travel back to London, and we could meet with my barrister, who could explain the situation. We could take time to get to know one another, and perhaps, then, we could consider a proper betrothal."

"No, Titania, that will not do. I am in need of you and your fortune immediately, and I despise traveling alone. Will it be so terrible being married to me? I promise, I am an entertaining companion. I will not beat you or bore you. What more could you ask for?"

To spend the rest of my life with the man I love, the man whose touch makes me quiver, the man who I bitterly regret refusing when he offered for me . . . that is what I could ask for. Oh, Titania, you have managed this all very badly, despite your Managing Ways, she thought and turned her head aside so Gratwick would not see the desperation on her face, quickly wiping away the tears that had sprung to her eyes.

"My lord, perhaps you will allow me to return upstairs to collect my belongings?"

"Certainly, my dear, and I will accompany you to make sure you have not forgotten anything. You are so forgetful, my dear," he said in a loving tone, his eyes belying his words.

There goes another opportunity, Titania thought. She was almost prepared to try to jump from the second floor window, but now all she had managed to do was to get him alone upstairs, and that was certainly not her intention. Drat. Perhaps something would come to her, she thought optimistically as the two of them ascended the small, narrow stairs. Her salvation was sitting innocuously in the corner, unaware of the great role it had to play in Titania's escape.

"I did not think my rescuer would be quite so slim," she chuckled to herself as she spied the poker lying next to the fireplace. If she could just get him to turn away for a moment, she could whack him enough to run down the stairs, and hopefully find someone who might be able to help her.

It is not a particularly well thought-out plan, but it is a plan, she thought prosaically.

"Your belongings, Titania," Lord Gratwick said, handing her reticule to her. "I will buy you whatever you require—with your money, of course—when we arrive in France."

Titania moved slowly towards the fireplace, holding her hands behind her back, her fingers wiggling slowly so as to find the poker without too much movement.

"As I have said repeatedly, Lord Gratwick, my fortune is not what you expect. I . . . I, oh damn!" she said, throwing her reticule at her feet as she grabbed for the poker. He looked at her interestedly for a moment, as if she were an amusing pet, then smiled as he reached down to retrieve her reticule.

"You really must learn to control your temper, my dear," he said, his suave tone never faltering.

Titania wielded the poker over his head, closing her eyes as she brought it down between his shoulder blades. He fell down in a heap, and for just a moment, Titania looked at him, shocked at what she had done. She had to get out of there, and quickly; he would not be unconscious for long.

Damn again, she thought, he has fallen directly on top of my reticule. She could not bear to reach under him to grab it, and what if he awakened while she was sneaking her hand under his chest? The reticule be damned, too.

She fastened her pelisse hurriedly as she walked out of the door, closing it gently behind her. Descending the stairs, she made straight for the public room, where the innkeeper was washing glasses.

"Sir," she said, exaggerating the shaky tone in her voice, "I find the ale is not sitting well with me at all, could you tell me where to find the—?" she trailed off, holding her hand to her mouth. The man practically leapt from behind the bar and herded her towards the front door.

Before she could make her escape, however, a familiar pair of broad shoulders crowded through the doorway, and she stopped where she stood, her hand falling away from her mouth to clutch at her stomach.

Chapter Eighteen

"Worthy!" Edwin raised his head from his desk. He squinted at his right sleeve, which was covered in ink blotches, great circles of blue staining the white linen.

"Worthy!" The voice was closer now. Alistair?

"Worthy, come down here." Edwin shook his head, ran his fingers through his hair and stood up, a bit unsteady. He fumbled in his drawer for a clean shirt, pulled the old one over his head and put the new one on. Never mind the cravat or the jacket; he was in enough disgrace not to have to worry about the niceties of fashion.

Now fully alert, he bounded down the stairs, spotting his friend at their foot.

"Alistair," Edwin said as came downstairs, "and . . . Lady Wexford?" He looked from one to the other.

He gestured towards the sitting room. "Please come in." Alistair started speaking even before they had reached the door.

"First off, the good news. Your father has regained consciousness, although he cannot speak yet." Edwin clasped Alistair's hand in relief. Alistair continued, giving a baleful stare at Lady Wexford.

"You were right. Right about Lady Wexford and Gratwick, and now Titania is in trouble. I've been watching Gratwick for some time now, yes," he said, nodding his head at Edwin's widened eyes. "His story doesn't quite check out, so I've been assigned to watch him. The point is, I saw Miss Stanhope leave her carriage and get into Lord Gratwick's. Alone. It looked as if he was forcing her. It wasn't possible for me to stop them in time, and then I just *happened* to run into Lady Wexford, who was nearby. She tells me there is some sort of elopement planned. You and I know better."

Claire moved forward, putting her hand gently on Edwin's sleeve. "Titania and Lord Gratwick, well, they have fallen in love. Please do not think ill of my friend." She moved a little closer to him, looking up at his face as if to dazzle him with her beauty. He stiffened, then moved away from her as he removed her hand from his arm.

"Henri!" Edwin bellowed. He turned to Lady Wexford. "I do not think ill of *her* at all, my lady," he muttered through clenched teeth, "but you, on the other hand, are a lying, manipulative b—"

"Worthy!" Alistair clamped his hand on his shoulder.

Edwin drew a few deep breaths. His hands were clenched into fists. He stood in front of Lady Wexford, as close as he could without actually touching her.

"Where has he taken her?"

"I . . . I believe it is to Dover, and then on to the Continent. He has business there." She lowered her head and stepped back a few tiny steps.

"Henri! Come here!" Edwin bellowed again, then turned back to Claire. "And what business do you have with him? How much did he promise you in exchange for procuring your friend for him?"

"My lord," she whimpered, "all I did was arrange the meeting."

Edwin turned from her in disgust, smacking his hand into his fist so hard it made a loud *thwack* that made everyone in the room jump.

"Alistair, I will go after her, you and Lady Wexford here will go to Miss Stanhope's house and tell her cousin and brother what has happened . . . Follow along when you can, and do not let this woman," he said, pointing a finger at Claire, "out of your sight. She and her friend have a lot of explaining to do."

Henri scurried into the room, his face red from the exertion. "Yes, my lord?"

Edwin grabbed his arm, pulling him out of the room as he spoke. "Get my horse ready, pack my saddlebag for a night or two out of town and get me as much cash as you can. I am off to war." With that, he bounded up the stairs, taking them two at a time, the thundering echo of his feet reverberating in the room below.

Alistair took Lady Wexford by the arm none too gently, pulling her to the door. "You and I, Lady Wexford, are going to pay a visit to Miss Stanhope's family. And if you do not tell them the truth, I will personally break every bone in your body. Is that understood?"

"Edwin, that is, Lord Worthington," Titania gasped. He did not speak in reply, merely reached for her and pulled her to him.

She sagged, suddenly exhausted, murmuring against his chest, "I cannot believe you are here. That you came after me. If you only knew how idiotic I felt for not alerting someone. Take me home, please?" she asked, lifting her face up to look into his eyes, which blazed green with deep emotion.

"Where is he?" he asked finally.

"Upstairs, waking up with quite a sore head, I hope. I knocked him out with the fire poker. I distracted him, then *wham*. I thought it was very clever. Not that I knew exactly what I was going to do when I did manage to leave here, but I thought I should do something."

"And you thought leaving this inn unescorted was a brilliant idea?" Edwin said in a clipped tone, holding her even tighter.

"Why, yes, I did," Titania replied, her tone growing markedly icier. "How could I know you would show up? I know I acted foolishly in agreeing to go with him in the first place——"

"Yes, you did," he interrupted.

"But," she persevered, "I believe I can take care of myself, and have I not proven it?"

"By knocking someone out with a poker and running into the night with nothing but your beauty and your wits to assist you?"

He thought she was a beauty. Love truly was blind.

"Look here, my lord, I did the best I could under the circumstances, and perhaps we should be on our way before Lord Gratwick awakens. I am not sure how hard I hit him."

Edwin growled, pushing her away as he walked farther into the room. "And now, having disabled your man, you expect me to slink out from here without confronting him?"

"It would be the sensible move, I think," Titania said pedantically.

"Miss Stanhope—Titania—if you believe I will walk out of here without trying to take action to revenge your honor, you are completely confused as to what kind of man I am."

"You do not have to beat Lord Gratwick in some sort of primitive display for me to understand what kind of man you are. Damn it," she said, forever throwing all notions of proper lady's language out of her mind, "I love you, now let us get out of here."

"I love you, too, and we will not leave just yet," he replied firmly. "You will stay downstairs while I find Gratwick, and when I am done with him, we will have our own discussion about your penchant for getting into trouble. Since we are to be married," he pronounced, "I would wish my betrothed to behave with a modicum of propriety, and you will wait here while I deal with Gratwick. Is that understood?"

Titania glared at him, almost as angry as she was happy. Married! He had forgiven her completely, at least.

Should she continue to argue, or just leap into his arms again? Titania was preparing to take the latter option when Gratwick appeared, rubbing the back of his head. He stopped short on seeing Edwin.

"I was hoping this was going to be a lively evening, and you have not disappointed me. Now, my lord, will you fight? I look forward to finally feeling your face underneath my boot as I grind it into the floor."

Gratwick removed his coat and his cravat, revealing a thin, sinewy frame with long, lean muscles. Titania was mildly impressed. He was not nearly as skinny as he looked.

He gestured to his shirt, then removed it as well, and sat on one of the chairs to remove his boots. Edwin was moving equally quickly, stripping off his jacket and shirt and shucking off his boots.

Both men, now shirtless and in only tight-fitting breeches and stockinged feet, stood watching each other warily. Titania looked from one to the other, wondering just why grown men had to behave like children whenever their honor was attacked. It certainly explained all those wars.

"This is ludicrous, my lords," Titania objected. Both men turned to look at her, their expressions equally disdainful.

"Titania, my love," Lord Gratwick said with an oily tone, "your overgrown lover and I have nothing in common except for the shared sentiment that you should now stay out of this. This is between us, and has been a long time coming."

As he spoke, he lunged at Edwin, throwing a surprisingly quick punch to Edwin's midsection. The blow connected, and Titania saw Edwin's stomach muscles contract in reaction, the individual muscles standing out in relief against his skin.

Resigned to her role as observer, Titania retreated to the side of the room, where a large group of the local farmers had magically appeared to watch the show. The room had been as desolate as her hopes of escape just a half hour ago; where had they been when she needed help? Perhaps it was some magical male thing, where they could sense when to stay away, like when a female needed some assistance, and when it was wise to reveal themselves, like when a fight was brewing.

Men, she thought in disgust, then sat down and leaned her face on her hands. As she heard the labored breath of the combatants and the roar of the audience, she lifted her head, unable to keep her eyes from the action.

Gratwick was surprisingly light on his feet, and his punches came swiftly and accurately. Edwin's larger frame and broad shoulders made him the stronger of the two men, but it also made him a bigger target for Gratwick's relentless blows. The two men traded punches, the room now silent except for the occasional grunt, and Titania saw—with salacious interest, she thought guiltily—Edwin was getting sweatier, the muscles of his upper body flexing with his movements. Gratwick, she noted meanly, just looked thinner and paler the more he exerted himself.

After perhaps ten minutes of sparring, Edwin threw a quick, sly look at Titania, planted his feet and threw his right hand hard into Gratwick's solar plexus. The blond man groaned, then fell down in a heap at Edwin's feet. He was finally down. After a moment of satisfied perusal of his opponent, Edwin sauntered over to Titania, reaching for her as she stood up from the chair.

"You are a horrid beast," she said, trying to keep the exultation from her voice.

"Yes, I am," he said, "but you still love me."

"Yes, I do," she said demurely, looking conveniently down as she eyed his sleek, glistening stomach a little more closely than she had been able to before.

He put his fingers gently on her chin, then lifted her face up to look into her eyes. He spoke softly so only she could hear.

"Titania, it does not matter to me anymore why you lied. I love you. I do not care about anything else. Knowing you as I have come to, I am certain your reasoning rivals Plato's, and I look forward to hearing the whole story. But only after . . ." he said as he gave a wicked smile, "we go upstairs so I can compromise you as thoroughly as possible so there is no chance of your marrying anyone else."

Titania blushed and nodded, walking ahead of him up the stairs. Frowning for a moment, Edwin returned to Gratwick, still lying on the floor, and nudged him with his toe. Gratwick's eyes opened briefly, then he closed them again with an audible groan.

"My lord, where are the papers?"

"What papers?" Gratwick opened one eye, the one that was slightly less puffy, and gave Edwin as much of a glare as it seemed he was capable.

"Do not be deliberately dense. I know you abducted Miss Stanhope, I presume you are not so stupid as to forget to obtain a special license. I find I am in need of it myself."

Gratwick groaned again, then gave in to the inevitable, gesturing towards his coat, which was hanging on a wooden chair to the side of the room.

"There. Inside the pocket. Now leave me alone." He rolled over onto his back and exhaled sharply.

Edwin strode quickly to the chair, pulling out a sheaf of papers from Gratwick's pockets. He whistled softly as he saw the familiar writing. Without looking at Gratwick again, he nodded to the innkeeper.

"A friend of mine will be arriving shortly, and will take custody of the worm on the floor. Do not, under any circumstances, allow him to escape. I will deal with him, and my friend, in the morning."

"Edwin?" Titania's head peered out from one of the rooms. He took the two long strides to reach her, then pushed a strand of hair behind her ear.

"It is over. Every returning war hero should return to a prize as delicious as you."

He strode into the room, a small, simple chamber dominated by a large bed. He reached for her again, but seemed to change his mind as he looked down at his sweat-soaked body.

He walked over to the basin and flung water impatiently on himself, the drops joining the drops of sweat on his chest and back. He grabbed a cloth and briskly toweled his hair.

Titania watched him, glad to be able to feast her eyes on his masculine beauty.

Lord, but he was gorgeous. His chest was broad and smooth, the pectoral muscles sharply defined, his hips lean.

She felt suddenly warm, even though a cool breeze was wafting through the open window. His eyes traveled from her face down her neck, lingered at her breasts, then continued their lazy progress down to her feet. Hastily, she kicked off her slippers, wriggling her toes on the bare floor. She reveled in his sudden intake of breath, then walked over to him, wrapping her arms around his waist. His back felt slippery and wet under her hands, and she trailed her fingers over its broad expanse, enjoying the way his muscles clenched as she lightly stroked him.

"Before I am rendered speechless," he said huskily, "I have to tell you I found papers in Gratwick's clothing implicating him in my father's attack. Titania, I will be cleared." She could feel his relief reverberate through his body, and she leaned against his chest, folded in his arms.

If she could just have this man here always, she would never wish to escape, she thought as his hands began to caress her back, his lips nuzzling her hair. If it were not for food, her family, her books, and a general need for companionship, her practical self interjected, she would be content to stay here forever.

"Come sit with me, my love," he said, drawing her over to the bed. She nodded, holding his hand as he led her, placing her hands demurely on her lap as he settled beside her. He picked up one of her hands and turned it over so the palm was facing up. Slowly, he lowered his head and placed a kiss directly in the center of her hand. She let out a small sigh.

"Tell me now if you are not comfortable with this. We can wait until we are properly married—as I believe I suggested when we were at the masquerade," he said with a wry grin. "I can take another room here if you are at all hesitant. It is not as if you would be able to change your mind about marrying me, I would just have to throw my money around to get your attention," he finished, smirking at her.

"As it happens, my lord, people may wonder if you are marrying me for my money, but that is a big mess of a story, and I would rather be doing other things. No, I do not want my own room, I want to stay here with you and be thoroughly compromised. Now, do I have to throw myself at you, or are you going to help?"

He answered by placing his large, firm hands around her waist and turning her towards him. He leaned towards her and captured her mouth lightly, just pressing his warm lips against hers for what seemed an eternity. She sighed contentedly, squirming a little closer into his chest as she raked her nails lightly over his nipples. He gasped at that, opening his lips and sucking her tongue into his mouth. She pushed on his chest hard enough to topple him over, taking advantage of his vulnerable position to climb on top of him.

"And now will you admit I am a better rider, my lord?"

"It depends on your horse, Miss Stanhope," he replied, his voice a strained rasp.

Giving him a bold look, she hopped off the bed and slithered out of her gown, standing only in a thin chemise. He could see her nipples, hard and rosy, and see the soft, abundant curve of her breasts.

She lifted her chemise impatiently, tossing it to the floor and returning to lie on top of him in the bed. Quickly, he shucked off the remainder of his clothing, and pulled her to him.

She nipped his neck with her teeth as her hands began to explore again. He groaned, then found her mouth, kissing her with an assured confidence. He stroked her breasts, smoothing his hands around their curves, touching underneath where her breast met her chest, and placing his palms flat on top of her nipples. He traced the circle delicately around the nipple, then removed his mouth from hers and licked gently, then harder, where his fingers had just been.

As he sucked and kissed her breasts, his hands moved possessively down her body, only stopping as he stroked the soft skin of her thighs. He moved one hand back up to the breast he was not sucking, and rubbed its nipple as if to make sure it did not feel neglected. With his other hand, he found her most sensitive area and began to rub it softly, gently, until she could only think about him and what he was doing. A low, burning sensation began to thrum inside of her, and she began to move against his hand, holding onto his shoulders with all her strength.

"I think you are ready, my love," he said softly, lifting her hips slightly off him. She felt an odd, not unpleasant sensation as he began to thrust inside her.

"Whatever you do," she muttered in his ear, "do *not* apologize for causing me any pain."

"I would not dare, Miss Stanhope," he replied as he pushed inside her, her hips completely pressed against his. She felt some discomfort, but it was overwhelmed by the sheer pleasure of having him inside her at last. She heard him take a deep breath as if to gain control, and start to move in a small, circular rhythm. She felt, well, nothing like she had ever felt before, and she could only hold on to him, squeezing her eyes shut as he moved against her.

After a minute—or an eternity—she felt an inexorable build, a slow momentum churning towards its inevitable conclusion. She felt him tense and gasp, and she collapsed against him, feeling the warmth of his hands on her suddenly cool body.

"You know, Titania, you are a quick learner," he said, smiling. His eyes were closed, his breathing was slowing, and she could tell it was only a matter of time before he fell asleep.

She kissed the corner of his mouth softly. "Learning something completely takes practice, study and practice. My governess taught me that."

"Wise governess," he said as he drifted off to sleep.

After watching him for a few minutes, Titania rose from the bed, feeling new muscles objecting as she reached for her chemise. Throwing it on almost as quickly as she had discarded it, she walked to the small desk, which she hoped would house writing implements and paper. She found them, pushed her hair impatiently behind her ears, and began to write.

Dispatch from the Battlefront, August 1813

Every good general knows when to accept defeat.

It was not possible to withstand the enemy, and we have been taken.

Who could have conceived the hunter would be hunted? There is no way to prepare for the attack of such a resolute and better-armed (and broader-shouldered) foe.

No matter how many pretty gowns are fitted to intrigue, no matter how many fans are waved in secret semaphore, no matter how many witty banters are enciphered, the heart can always betray the general's plan.

My conqueror is a gracious victor, however, and honors us both by his declaration of terms: we shall share the spoils of war—love, marriage, children. I have surrendered.

In defeat, I remain . . .

A Singular Lady